RED IS THE FASTEST COLOR

GUERNICA WORLD EDITIONS 75

RED IS THE FASTEST COLOR

DAVE CARTY

GUERNICA
World
EDITIONS

TORONTO–CHICAGO–BUFFALO–LANCASTER (U.K.)

2024

Guernica Editions Founder: Antonio D'Alfonso

Michael Mirolla, general editor
Margo LaPierre, editor
Cover design: Allen Jomoc, Jr.
Interior design: Jill Ronsley, suneditwrite.com

Guernica Editions Inc.
287 Templemead Drive, Hamilton (ON), Canada L8W 2W4
2250 Military Road, Tonawanda, N.Y. 14150-6000 U.S.A.
www.guernicaeditions.com

Distributors:
Independent Publishers Group (IPG)
600 North Pulaski Road, Chicago IL 60624
University of Toronto Press Distribution (UTP)
5201 Dufferin Street, Toronto (ON), Canada M3H 5T8

First edition.
Printed in Canada.
Legal Deposit—First Quarter
Library of Congress Catalog Card Number: 2023943438
Library and Archives Canada Cataloguing in Publication
Title: Red is the fastest color / Dave Carty.
Names: Carty, Dave, author.
Series: Guernica world editions (Series) ; 75.
Description: Series statement: Guernica world editions ; 75
Identifiers: Canadiana (print) 20230509355 | Canadiana (ebook)
20230509371 | ISBN 9781771838832
(softcover) | ISBN 9781771838849 (EPUB)
Classification: LCC PS3603.A77414 R33 2024 | DDC 813/.6—dc23

Summer was like your house: you knew
where each thing stood.
Now you must go out into your heart
as onto a vast plain. Now
the immense loneliness begins.

—Rainer Maria Rilke

Chapter 1

Beyond their quarter section of trees and cropped grass, beyond the skeletal cottonwoods along the Shields River, Monna saw the stark spires of the Crazy Mountains, the rampart that stop the valley from throwing its snowmelt at the prairies running east to North Dakota. She stared blankly out the window, one hand holding the phone, the fingers of the other on the sill, resting there. Frost had deposited a layer of sparkling rime along the base of the window, like the snow-filled panes on a Dickens Christmas card, the warped pine water-blackened after sixty winters of freeze and thaw. Beyond the window it was painfully clear, as if there were too much light, the overarching roof of blue sky absent a single cloud, in the way it always was when the temperature bottomed out. She felt the cold through the glass as though a portent.

"It's worse, then?" Jamison asked. Her brother's voice on the line sounded faint, as if the 1100 miles of frozen prairie between them were numbing his tongue.

"Some days it is. It comes and goes. It's hard sometimes. It hurts." Monna walked to the kitchen table and leaned against it.

Jamison said: "I saw on the news it's 23 below out there."

Monna's eyes rose to the ceiling. "I thought we were talking about my disease."

"Okay. Sorry."

Monna lowered the phone, then put it back to her ear. Her hand trembled, and she pressed the phone against her ear to stop the shaking. "All right, once again," she said. "That's in the *park*. It's always 23 below in the park, that's why it's always on the news.

When I got up this morning it was nine below here in Aden. That's
not exactly warm, but it's better than Yellowstone. Besides, I know
what Minneapolis is like in February. I remember."

"You're talking about the humidity thing. You're always talking
about that." Jamison chuckled.

Again, Monna stared out the window. Across and back from
the river was all she and Ben had put together: the small, drafty
frame home and detached, single-car garage that had come with
the land they'd bought when they were still young, the two-room
log studio he'd built for her to paint in, and the abandoned Quonset
hut–cum–wood shop Ben and a half-dozen friends had taken apart
and reassembled on the Van Hollen's land. Later, when Monna had
scraped together enough money from her art shows in Livingston
and Bozeman, Ben had built her the partially enclosed stable for
the horses she intended to board, a hedge, she told him, against
their sporadic incomes.

"Can we just be serious for a moment, Jamison? Ben won't ask
for help. He never will. But he can't keep things up around here and
take care of me at the same time, not when it gets really bad. And
we can't afford to hire anybody."

"Sorry. I mean, no, you've told me all this before. Could I think
about it? I've got some loose ends to tie up. I don't know. It might be
okay, but I'm not committing to anything. Never been to Montana
in the dead of winter. It would be like vacationing in Siberia."

"Not any worse than Minnesota. You could finish out the winter here and maybe even stay for the summer. Free, of course. It
would save you a ton. I'm not asking you to stay until, you know."

"I'm not sure I want to pack up and move to Montana just like
that. Would you?"

Monna turned and walked, wincing, to the front of the house.
She gazed out the broad, single-paned window that gave on the
gravel access road dropping down from the highway. A mile to
the south of their home was the little town of Aden; she'd set up
her easel countless times across from the Infirmary to paint the
limestone façade of the bar against the backdrop of the rolling,

sagebrush-covered hills that unfurled from the Bridger Mountains directly west. She sold paintings of the north Bridgers to the upscale clientele in Bozeman, an hour's drive south and west. Paintings of the Crazy Mountains, east and directly opposite the Bridger Range, the flinty plain between the two like the vast, scaly back of a dinosaur between up-thrusting spines, sold mostly to locals, those few with the cash to buy her art. She walked back across the living room, mindful of where she placed her unsteady feet. From that side of the house, the side farthest from the road, she heard the restless murmur of the Shield's River gurgling beneath ice. A dozen years earlier, after three quarters of a century of constant use, first by ranchers, one of whom had carved up his grandfather's homestead to sell the land to the Van Hollens, and then during the course of the Van Hollen's forty-year marriage, the bridge over the river had been undercut by an angry spring flood. They'd driven over it anyway—there was no other way to get to town—gripping the wheel in terror as the aging timbers popped and sagged from the torrent below. The pilons in the bridge had been hammered into the river bed by an unknown contractor more interested in utility than endurance, and now, at last, the raging water had exposed the bridge's aging bones. But the county had refused to let Ben rent a back hoe and do the repair work himself and instead had assessed them and the two other landowners on the road for the cost. That was before her Parkinson's.

"It's different for us," she said. "We've been here a long time. Why don't you just sublease your apartment to one of your students for a few months?" She tried to switch the phone from her right hand, which had begun to shake, to her left, but holding a phone with her non-dominant hand felt awkward, and she awkwardly shifted it back again. She saw Ben's Ford pull off the highway and drop into the snow-filled ruts on the access road. "Oh look," she said. "Ben just pulled up. Why don't you talk to him?"

"That isn't necessary."

"Would you just come out for a little while?" Monna said. "No wait, here's Ben. I'm going to give him the phone."

"Hello?" Ben said. Monna saw her husband frown, then idly scratch his face. Bits of chaff were stuck to the gray stubble on his chin.

"Ben!" Jamison said. "How are you, man? It's been a while."

"Yeah. I was up on a job in Bozeman. I put in a bid in Billings but it didn't include drive time and subsistence and I ain't gonna pay for that all by my lonesome. Not this winter, anyway. But we're doing all right. I'm busy as a one-armed paperhanger."

"Still doing the handyman thing?"

"Yeah. What else? I can't afford to quit."

"Well, at least you love what you do. That's something."

"I don't know about *that*," Ben said. "This week I got to rip out insulation. It itches like a mother. But that's the absolute worst for a Dutchman like me. Most of the time it's not too bad." A pause. "Monna says you're coming out for a visit."

"She said that? I was thinking she was *asking* me whether I *would*. There's a difference."

"Yeah. Well, it's like I keep telling her, it's nothing we can't handle. I mean, it's not like she started running laps or walking to town on her hands or something. She's painting a little; we still get out dancing some. Her footwork is all shot to hell but she still looks pretty good for an old gal." He laughed.

"Sounds to me like you have everything under control," Jamison said.

"Yeah, well, that depends on what you mean by 'control.' Didn't Clinton say that? But if you mean, we get up in the morning, and then we go to work, and then at night we go to bed, then we got it under control. Hold on, Monna's giving me a look."

"I think he said 'it.' It depends on what you mean by 'it,'" Jamison said. "That's what Clinton said." The connection buzzed.

"I know that. So she says you can stay in the studio. She says she'll move her paints and stuff into the house. She's not doing all that much painting anyway. I'm taking directions here."

"That's encouraging."

"That's why I make the big money," Ben said. Monna folded her arms, hiding her trembling hands. And grinned.

* * *

She didn't look all that bad. No hand tremors that he could see, no shuffle in her gait. The lines on her face had deepened and she'd stopped coloring her hair. What she'd told him over the phone had apparently been true: the symptoms came and went. She'd given him a weak hug, and in their embrace it was clear to him that the disease had stolen her strength, but she had never been a robust woman to begin with. He frowned and closed his eyes, and when he opened them again he was gazing at the Crazy Mountains, white and cold in the near distance. He stepped away from her and extended a hand to Ben.

Ben grinned up at him. "I know I always ask this, but tell me again. How tall are you?"

"Six six. That was last year's physical. I may be shrinking." He towered over his sister. He towered over Ben.

"Aren't we all," Monna said.

Ben smirked. "Still got the bald thing going on, huh Jamison?" He flipped up his ball cap and slowly ran his fingers through his bristling hair, bending forward a little so Jamison could get a better look. Ben's cropped, iron-gray hair was thick as the pelt of a beaver.

Jamison's fleece stocking cap was pulled low over his ears. He'd grown used to the teasing from his brother in law as well as his friends and even his parents when they'd been alive. He'd noticed the hair on his pillow his senior year in high school. By the time he got out of grad school it was mostly gone, the remaining fringe of blond hair, now white, that encircled his bald pate lending him an air of gravitas that he had distinctly mixed feelings about. He'd hidden his shiny head under ball caps for years but finally, at an indefinite juncture in his fifties, decided that he would decide he no longer cared. To hell with ball caps. The problem with that was, bald guys got sunburned. So he put the ball caps back on.

Monna had prepared lunch. He'd half expected Ben to handle the cooking chores, but then he remembered: this was Ben. Ben, Monna had told him defensively, was a wonderful camp cook, a wizard with a Dutch oven. Maybe one of these days, Jamison thought, he'd get to see that. He hadn't yet.

Jamison had spent the previous night at the La Quinta Inn in Dickinson, North Dakota, just off the interstate. This was a modest and welcome relief from his teaching years, which he'd spent, on his infrequent cross-country trips to visit his sister, sleeping alone in motels populated by oil field workers and their teenage wives, who smoked cigarettes from the open doors of their rooms, molded plastic chairs dragged outside, music thumping from their trucks. He'd pushed hard to get across North Dakota in one day so he could arrive in Aden at a decent hour the following afternoon.

Monna had prepared a simple lunch of mixed salad greens and spaghetti in the small galley kitchen in their home. Jamison rarely cooked in the equally small galley kitchen in his Minneapolis apartment, preferring instead to have dinner and lunch, usually alone, in one of the inexpensive ethnic cafes that dotted his downtown neighborhood. The gentle commotion of other human bodies eased his loneliness and he liked listening in on the patron's muted conversations, even if he was rarely bold enough to break into those conversations himself.

Ben speared a meatball with his fork and held it up for Jamison to see. "Bambi," he announced.

"Ben shot it off the front porch last season," Monna said. She pulled out a chair and took a seat, then put two small spoonfuls of salad and spaghetti on her plate, no meatballs. "*From* the front porch. It was in the yard. Ben hung it up in the shop. I did a couple sketches I should show you. I had him stand with his rifle next to it; sort of like Grant Wood in Montana."

Ben raised his eyebrows, expecting a rebuke from his brother in law, but Jamison, purely for show, pumped his fist. What was he supposed to say? He *liked* deer. They were all over the city parks in Minneapolis. He thought of reminding Ben, again, that he'd been deer hunting years ago in northern Minnesota with some college buddies. They'd spent most of the weekend smoking weed and drinking cheap bourbon around a campfire. The one smallish fork horn someone had shot (not him, the tree stand his buddies stuck him in didn't produce a deer) hung head down from the game pole behind them, its bloody and empty rib cage wedged open with a stick, lifeless and glassy eyed in the flickering orange light from the campfire. He'd enjoyed the drinking.

"We can put your stuff in the studio after lunch," Ben said. Jamison had packed the back end of his Honda Passport to the ceiling, which still wasn't a lot, but it would get him through the two or three months he had reluctantly told Monna he'd stay. "I'm thinking you're gonna have to watch your head for a few days," Ben said. "When I built that place, I downsized it to fit Monna. Why I thought that was such a good idea I don't know, but I did. The header in that door is only six-two or six-three, and the ceilings are a little low. I cut everything to fit. After I laid up eight or ten courses, I was getting tired of hauling logs up a gin pole and figured I'd just make the whole shitteree fit my wife, instead of everybody else, which of course is against code and probably immoral, but ask me if I care. I was twenty-eight and Monna wanted a studio. So duck your head. Those logs ain't gonna give."

"He's used to hitting his head on stuff," Monna said. "That's why he's got such a big head." She grinned at her brother. Her hand, holding a fork, flicked involuntarily, and a piece of lettuce fell to the table. She immediately placed her fork on her plate, dabbed up the lettuce with a paper napkin, and hid her hand in her lap, as if she were embarrassed, as if one of them might have seen the twitching in her fingers. "He was always doing that when we were kids, right Jamison?"

"It's true," Jamison said. "I about beat my brains out. Lucky for me I'm not using them anymore."

Ben had loaded the wood stove with pine logs from a cord stacked on the porch, and the fire crackled and hissed, sending the delicious scent of woodsmoke radiating throughout the small home. Jamison unzipped his fleece vest a few inches, which he'd snugged tight to his chin. He was rarely too warm; old, skinny guys never were. The warmth from the stove was wonderful, a small cocoon of pleasure to burrow into against the winter restlessly tapping against the house's ancient, single-pane windows.

"Okay, you've been officially warned," Ben said. "Couple guys been out here ... one of them laid himself out on that header. Remember that guy, Monna?"

Monna looked up. "Which one?"

"That plumber guy. When the pipes froze."

"Oh, yeah." Monna had resumed eating.

Jamison glanced at her hands, looking for tremors, but saw nothing more than he would have considered normal for a woman in her early sixties. But what was normal? Normal was living out your life *without* a disease like Parkinson's. Monna had never been athletic; she'd been too in love with her paints and the cloistered, devotional environs of art studios: first in a spare bedroom in their parents' home, then in the bowels of the UMN art complex in the Twin Cities, and now, for over forty years, in the studio Ben had built for her, on a hundred and sixty acres of sagebrush and barb-wire enclosed grassland halfway between the Crazy and Bridger mountains, land that was devoid of snow only when the gales that swept down in unrelenting waves from those austere palisades scoured it away. He hadn't thought the marriage would last, not to a man like Ben, who seemed to have little practical use for art, who was, in fact, unsophisticated on any number of levels that Jamison could recite. But it had, and here they were.

Monna put her fork down, dabbed at her mouth with the napkin, and turned toward Jamison. "I hadn't been painting for a while, and I forgot about the pipes. Usually I keep the wood stove in there burning and damped down all winter, and there's electric baseboard for backup. But I forgot to turn it on or something. That's what Ben says, anyway. It was winter just like now. I went out there one day and there was ice all over the floor. It was this huge mess. We couldn't figure out where it was coming from so we called up a plumber out of Livingston. He was tall, like you. Well, maybe not as tall as you, but, you know, *tall*. He hit that doorway at a brisk walk and just fell over backwards. It was like a tree going down. You should've seen the goose egg on his forehead."

"And the moral of the story is, don't forget to turn on the backup heat," Ben said. He wasn't looking at Monna.

Monna gave Jamison a fixed smile. "Ben's big on morals," she said in a stage whisper.

Ben said, "See how she is?"

* * *

As he'd known with unshakable conviction that he would sooner or later, Jamison ran into the doorway not as he walked into the studio, but afterwards, as he walked out of it. After Ben chipped away the snow from the concrete-like drift packed hard against the door—Jamison had offered to help, but Ben had dismissed him with a wave—Ben set the shovel against the wall and thumped the header with his fist as they entered: fair warning. But when they walked out again, enroute to the woodpile behind the studio he would be using to feed the stove, he'd been saying something to the back of Ben's head, not paying attention, and nailed the header dead to rights. He cursed and rubbed his forehead with the heel of his hand. Damn, it hurt.

Ben slowly shook his head. "No matter how many times I tell you guys …"

"I'll get used to it," Jamison said between clenched teeth.

The studio was pleasant. It was as Jamison remembered from his last visit: intimate and compact, with a large window facing east, and opposite it, just three of his long strides separating the two, an equally large window facing west, both framing views of the Crazies to the east and the foothills of the Bridgers to the west. Monna had installed light-blocking shades on both windows so she could fine-tune the ambient light. A tiny, separate bedroom off the living area had just enough space for a reasonably comfortable twin bed (his feet would dangle over the end of it, but what else was new?) and a cramped shower stall with a vinyl, floral-print curtain; the spray from the shower head would strike him squarely in the neck. The open kitchen had a two-burner range, a dorm-sized refrigerator, and a microwave. Monna told him she had spent entire days here, warming a bowl of canned soup for lunch or, too in thrall to her work to leave her easel, eating half a poppyseed muffin, which she bought by the shrink-wrapped dozen from the deli in Clyde Park. He wondered if she still felt that way, or if the disease had robbed her of that, the fever to create that had gripped her soul even as a child. She had said nothing to him about it.

After their phone conversation the previous month, the weather had finally moderated, and along with a modest uptick in the temperature came a resumption of the thin, scudding clouds and ceaseless wind that almost daily buffeted the north end of the Shields Valley, as lacerating against exposed skin as barbed wire. Jamison stared out the window, his arms crossed, standing where Monna had once placed her easel. The shades were rolled up, but the ingress of gray light was unsettling, the pale tufts of yellow wheat stubble to the east barely visible through drifts of ever-shifting snow, as brittle as frozen amber.

And out there: the Crazies, distant and removed, stony parapets thrust into bleak air, no place he wanted to be, no place he intended to stay.

Chapter 2

L ate at night, even after he'd banked the fire, the studio was chilly, so Jamison had asked Monna if she had anything else he could throw over his bed. She found an old sleeping bag, patched with crinkled duct tape, that Ben had stored and forgotten in the shop. Now, at six thirty in the morning, he was warm—an order of magnitude better than he'd been before the sleeping bag, which he unzipped and used as a comforter—but the fire in the stove had burned to gray ash, and he kicked himself for not bringing in extra wood the night before, knowing it was going to be cold, knowing he would find himself in exactly the situation he was now in: lying in bed with the sleeping bag drawn over his head, his wool-stockinged feet jammed against the antique brass foot rail, dreading the bone-chilling walk to the woodpile behind the studio.

He pulled the bag down from around his ears and peeked over the top. A feeble glow suffused the room, delineating the arc of the brass foot rail at the end of the bed and the watery shadow from the translucent curtain hung from the shower stall that Ben had, as a younger man, plumbed, leveled, and then lag-bolted into the logs on the opposite wall. Thus the arrival of morning.

Ben had warned him: Don't let the goddamn plumbing freeze. Jamison grunted and wiggled out from under the covers and tugged on the wool pants he'd draped over the foot rail, then pulled on his down parka and Sorels from the chair in the corner and trudged into the freezing studio, his hands thrust in his pockets, his torso goose-bumped from the cold nylon parka against bare skin. He glanced at the thermometer outside the window and walked to the stove and threw the latch on the door; beneath a soft, pewter-y blanket of ash a few red coals still glowed. That was good; he wouldn't have to start a fire from scratch.

When he opened the front door and stepped outside the cold hit his pink, exposed cheeks like a slap from a ruler. He buried his chin in his parka and trudged to the woodpile, brushed away the snow that had accumulated the night before, and began stacking his arms with wood. He saw the cat.

He heard a commotion from within the woodpile, a want-ing-to-get-out, and glimpsed the animal as it bounded away and vanished in the snow and willows along the river. Its color and size made him wonder at first if he'd seen a bobcat—he'd left his glasses on the chair in his room—but no, this cat had a long tail; even within the fuzzy boundaries of his vision he'd clearly seen it wind milling for balance as the animal leapt down the icy, eroded bank. His fingers burned from the cold, so he walked as quickly as he could back to the studio, the logs wedged between his bare hands and his chin, wondering. Could an ordinary house cat survive this cold? The temperature was seven degrees. At the doorway, he turned and backed through it, remembering, a fraction of a second too late, about the header. The impact on the back of his head jolted half the wood out of his arms and directly onto his foot, which, thankfully, his heavy boots mostly protected, although in the biting cold his pinched toe still stung like the bite of a wasp. He dropped the rest of the load next to the stove, angrily kicked the scattered logs in the doorway inside, and slammed the door.

Monna had invited him to the main house for breakfast for the first few days after his arrival, but now, two weeks on, he had long since unpacked the back of the Honda and settled in, and he found the studio comfortable, if spartan. The kitchen was sufficient for his simple meals, and unlike the plumbing, the propane refrigerator and range worked no matter how cold the weather got, although the aging refrigerator's clicks and hums and weirdly human groans prompted a reluctant mention to Ben, who told him not to worry, they were all like that. Jamison was not so sure they were all like that; the refrigerator in his downtown apartment in Minneapolis wasn't like that, nor was the refrigerator in the house he'd sold prior to moving downtown. Perhaps only Ben's refrigerators kept up running commentaries on the state of their health; but Jamison was a patient man, and in patience he would endure.

He shoved several logs into the wood stove and poured his first cup of coffee in the near dark and settled into the small sofa opposite the warm cone of heat from the stove. The stove warmed the tiny studio quickly, and the ambiance of the log walls made it almost cozy, if slightly claustrophobic, like a walk-in closet with cooking facilities. He already missed the small circle of thinkers and readers and teachers he'd grown accustomed to meeting in the inexpensive coffee shops of Minneapolis. His acquaintance with them did not extend beyond their sporadic meetings—he'd made clumsy stabs at initiating friendships, but his lifelong shyness made him appear remote, even among those few friends who had known him since college. Still, he looked forward to his coffee klatches and immensely enjoyed the comradery and interesting conversations they had. Aden had little in the way of social amenities: one bar, a general store, a part-time real-estate office, and two cafés. He'd made no commitment to Monna to stay past spring; he'd been clear about that; when the weather broke in a couple months he would return home. Still, he looked forward to getting reacquainted with his sister, whom he'd seen no more than a few days every three or four years since she'd moved west, married Ben, and took up the life of a pioneer landscape artist. He was disappointed in himself that his occasional breakfasts with his sister and Ben had already become … uncomfortable.

On her good days, Monna's symptoms were barely noticeable. But on her bad days, every movement seemed painfully considered. The laborious extension of an arm to grasp the handle of a skillet, the halting footsteps while carrying it the scant distance from shelf to stove, seemed to be taking place at three-quarters speed, like a video run frame by frame in stop-and-go slow motion. Her walk from table to refrigerator, a distance of mere feet across the worn linoleum floor, was bunched and excruciatingly deliberate, an oddly preoccupied smile on her face, as if her incapacities were more puzzling than detrimental, and when she turned to address him—did he want more coffee? Orange juice?—he was keenly aware that she was observing his reaction to *her*. But Ben, sitting opposite Jamison at the kitchen table, didn't seem to notice her difficulties, nor did he offer to help beyond a cursory rinsing of the dishes following their meal. Once, Jamison had offered to cook but Monna had politely waved him away. Ben had only shrugged, as if he'd told Jamison all along this would happen, although he had not. So Jamison nodded and said nothing, but after a week he found reason to have breakfast alone.

When the phone rang he fumbled with the book in his lap, then reached behind him and scooped his phone off the table: Monna.

"Jamison, you freezing down there yet?" She chuckled. "I was just wondering. I didn't see you yesterday."

"Nope." He tapped the door of the stove with his boot and felt the half-burned logs settle into the grate. He was comforted by the stove's cheerful warmth, which chortled and sighed as the burning logs within were slowly consumed. Outside, just beyond the warm cocoon within the studio's chinked log walls, it was horrendously cold. No matter how many layers of synthetic underwear and down he pulled on, he couldn't stay warm. It occurred to him that having an insulating layer of body fat was probably a good thing, although he'd long ago resigned himself to his scrawny physique, on which years of gulping protein shakes had not put so much as a pound. Neither Ben nor Monna were fat—his sister, in fact, had maintained a striking figure into her forties—but they weren't kids anymore and they had certainly accumulated more padding on their sixty-year-old frames than he had on the seventy-two-year-old bones that jutted from his sleeves like the skeletal wings of a bat. It hadn't escaped his notice that Ben could spend an hour in the snow with his coat partially unzipped, while Jamison had to wear a Patagonia base layer zipped to his chin, a down parka and wool scarf over that, topped with a fleece stocking cap pulled low over his shining bald pate. And still he shivered.

Shortly after his arrival, he'd dragged a barnwood end table Ben had hammered together next to the stove, got Monna to loan him a reading lamp, and after lighting a candle, spent some of his mornings and most of his evenings reading by the warmth of the fire. Beside the candle were his copies of *East of Eden* and Rilke's *Book Of Hours*; he'd brought them from Minnesota in a cardboard box in which he'd neatly stacked and alphabetically arranged two dozen of his favorite novels and poetry collections, a hedge against his sojourn into the wilds of the Shields Valley.

He'd been reading Rilke when Monna called. He closed the book and took off his glasses and rubbed his eyes. "I decided to stay inside and read," he told her. "I'm sorry I didn't swing by and say hello. I drank enough beer with Ben the other day to hold me for a while, I guess. What's up?"

"Well ..." Jamison heard his sister fiddling with the phone, then silence, then her voice again. "Can you hear me? Okay, good. The cell reception up here sucks. Somedays it just cuts out. Maybe you figured that out already."

Jamison nodded. "I have. I tried to call home the other day. Not good."

"I know. Makes me wish we still had our land line. But the reason I called, tonight is St. Patty's day at the Infirmary, remember? I told you last week. There's going to be a dance with a band, green beer, all that Irish stuff. Ben and I are going and you can hitch a ride with us. Ben's Dutch, though."

"Well, I'm not Irish, either. Come to think of it, neither are you."

"What difference does that make?"

"Right. Okay, that was kind of dumb. But I don't know, Monna, I'm not much of a dancer. I had this friend once, actually it was a girlfriend, who said that, she actually told me this, 'when you're dancing, I'm reminded of the scarecrow in the Wizard of Oz.' She had a point."

"Well, maybe you can find a new girlfriend with better taste in dancers. You'll probably get a look at about every woman your age in Aden. There aren't many."

Jamison swung his legs onto the sofa and propped his stock-inged feet on the arm rest. Heat radiated up his arm and the side of his torso nearest the stove, warming the bare pink skin on the top of his head. Opposite where he sat, beyond the east-facing window, beyond the river diminished and purling under a shelf of opaque ice, wheat stubble and sage ascended, like the stairway of a giant, in a series of rising, tiered benches to the foothills of the Crazies, and all lay asleep under an ocean of eternally drifting snow. The drifts kept an ever-shifting veil of skating, granularized snow sweeping across Highway 89, employing county snowplows from December through April. He wondered what that was like, up there above it all in the cab of a plow, watching the cars far below scurry out of the way like frightened mice as you roared past hurling fifteen-foot waves of ice and snow onto the shoulder. It was probably fun. He'd had a weird fascination with heavy equipment since he was a kid. He didn't think he'd ever told Monna that. Well.

"So, how are you feeling today?" he asked. "You're, um ..." Jamison pinched his lips together. He hated mentioning Monna's disease, as if talking about it in public validated its existence. He didn't even like the name: *Parkinson's*. It sounded like some kind of luxury sedan, not a horrible affliction that robbed people of their lives.

"I'm fine. I'm pretty good, actually. I got up this morning and noticed right off I was feeling better, I can always tell. Which is a good thing, because I'm going to the dance if Ben has to push me into the bar in a wheelchair. Besides, he wouldn't know what to do by himself. He likes to dance and he's pretty good at it, you'll see. We took some lessons from this dance-instructor lady in Bozeman, maybe fifteen years ago, before I had all this physical crap I have to deal with. We're gonna get all dressed up and stuff; besides the ro-deo, St. Patty's is a big day in Aden. Even for Dutchmen. I'll make sure Ben is nice to you."

"He's *fine*," Jamison said. He caught himself squeezing the phone. "Ben and I get along fine." They *did* get along. As always, it annoyed him that the slight tension between him and his brother in law—it was nothing more than that, a *slight* tension—seemed like such a big deal to his sister, as if he and Ben were continually squaring off in a boxing ring, one wearing white trunks, the other black. He doubted if anyone else even noticed. But she had brought this up before; she had, in fact, been bringing it up for years.

He'd certainly *tried.* He wasn't sure what it was with Ben, but he had his suspicions. Ben had attended college in Bozeman for just a year before dropping out. After he and Monna were married, he'd told Jamison he was making more money in the construction business than he ever would have made in range science, and Jamison had no reason to doubt him. Ben didn't need a degree to swing a hammer; he'd been doing it summers since he was in high school. Jamison had expounded on the benefits of working for the government; despite the drawback of being a cog in the wheel of a gargantuan bureaucracy, you would eventually retire to a modest pension. All these years later, Ben could see, he *had* to see, that at least in this Jamison had been right. Jamison's pension wasn't making him rich, far from it, but his needs were being met and would be for the rest of his life. Ben would work until he died. He had said as much. It didn't seem to bother him, but how could it not? Who wanted to work forever? Did anyone?

So Jamison, once again, found himself presenting his case to Monna. Yes, he and Ben had disagreements, like everyone else. Didn't she and Ben have disagreements? They weren't politically aligned, but that was nothing new; after several heated arguments he'd had with Ben early on, Jamison had finally figured out why Ben believed the crazy things he did: everyone he'd met in Montana was just as crazy as he was. Instead, he tried to see it from Ben's perspective. He and Monna made enough money to do what they wanted to do, Monna from the sale of her paintings and Ben from the niche remodel jobs he contracted in Bozeman and Livingston. When the economy was booming, growing cedar-sided and river-rock fireplaced subdivisions in 100-year-old farmland like sprouts in freshly planted gardens, and art galleries were arising, phoenix like, from lavishly remodeled plumbing supply stores, wealthy home owners hired Ben to add composite decking to their vast new homes and hung the walls of their tasteful living rooms with paintings by a genuine Montana watercolorist: Monna Van Hollen. If Ben and Monna wanted to take a night off to go dancing, if, on the drive home, they had a little too much beer at the Clyde Park Tavern or the Infirmary, well, they could sleep it off the following morning, having removed themselves from the tyranny of time clocks.

So Jamison told his sister what he'd always told her. "You're putting too much into this, Monna. We get along ninety-five percent of the time. Ninety-five percent of the time, we're good." Maybe this time she would believe him. But he would be fine either way.

* * *

Ben tapped the horn and Jamison scurried out of the studio, remembering to duck under the door frame and scraping the ice from the sill with his boot so he could close the door behind him. He didn't lock it; there was no lock. He'd remembered to bank up the wood in the stove so the studio would be cozy when he got back, probably after midnight, long after his accustomed bedtime. He crunched through the snow under a cold, blue moon and found Ben and Monna waiting in Ben's idling truck. He opened the door to the back seat, pushed some tools out of the way, and slid inside. The blast of light and warmth were welcome even after his brief walk from the studio to the house.

Ben and Monna were both wearing sparkling white cowboy hats, but were otherwise swathed in their heavy winter parkas from neck to knee. Monna swiveled around and grinned at him. The hats were unusual. In the summer, Ben usually wore a baseball cap or a sweat-stained straw cowboy hat, and Monna, plein-air, wore a broad cotton sombrero to protect her skin from the sun, her long silver hair falling in a thick, plaited braid down her back. She'd stopped wearing makeup years ago, but tonight, he noticed, she'd put on mascara and lipstick, subtracting a decade from her age. Maybe that was the point: a decade ago she hadn't had Parkinson's.

Ben said, "We're getting there early so we can find a place to park." Jamison couldn't imagine that little Aden, through which the sparse traffic on Highway 89 barely slowed in its haste to be elsewhere, would have parking issues, but when they got to the edge of town, their headlights revealed cars stacked along the shoulders for eighty yards north and south of the bar, exactly as Ben had predicted. Ben pulled up to Aden's lone intersection and turned right, then drove a few yards uphill and wheeled into an empty driveway. "I know this guy," he said. "He lets me use it for handicapped access." Monna rolled her eyes.

Ben killed the engine and the three of them got out of the cab. Monna carefully examined the ground, then slid out of her seat, one hand clutching the door for support. Jamison fell in behind her, his cold hands stuffed in his coat pockets and his chin burrowing into the scarf around his neck. Monna, despite her shuffling gait, seemed happy. She looped her arm through Ben's and leaned against his shoulder, girlish and almost nimble, as if she were trying to skip alongside him. Years earlier, she'd written Jamison letters—back when people still wrote letters, not emails—that had mentioned their trips to town. He wondered how long it had been since the two of them had been out dancing together. Her illness had to have cut into their dancing time; but then again, as she had told him several times, some days were better than others. Tonight, apparently, would be one of the better days.

Jamison noticed a silver Park County Sheriff's truck parked directly across the street from the bar, the only clean vehicle in a long line of parked trucks and SUV's, all uniformly filthy with late-winter grime. Ben waved at the driver, and Jamison saw the fuzzy outline of someone waving back through a steamed-up window.

"That's Gerald Metzger," Ben said. "Sheriff's department sends him up here every St. Patty's day, figuring they'll nab a couple drunks, which they usually do. Almost got me, once. Rest of the time, he patrols Aden one day a week, usually Wednesday, sorta keeps a lid on the crime wave. He's from back east someplace. He's okay, though."

The bar was shoulder to shoulder with men and women talking, drinking, laughing. Several of them nodded at Ben and Monna and grinned at Jamison with friendly curiosity. Across the bobbing sea of Stormy Kroner hats and silk bandanas Jamison saw the band setting up in the back room. Three women were tending bar and delivering drinks to the crowd. Ben draped his arm around the shoulders of one and said this here's my favorite bar wench Jessica and could they get a table. A red and black tattoo ran from the back of Jessica's neck to somewhere below, hidden in the topography beneath her flannel shirt.

She smirked. "Yeah, sure Ben. Maybe tomorrow. We've had people waiting for a table for two hours. I'll come and get you guys if something opens up. You want something to drink?" She looked at Monna and grinned. Ben ordered three beers.

"That means green beer?" Jamison had removed his fleece hat and stuffed it in his coat pocket. The mass of bodies had warmed the bar far beyond anything the propane heaters suspended from the ceiling could add, and the humidity had instantly fogged his glasses, which converted the people in the bar into a moist landscape of undulating movement, like slowly moving fish in a cloudy aquarium. He rubbed his glasses against his shirt, then held them up to the neon lights behind the bar. Despite the wintery temperature outside someone had cracked the front door for fresh air. Most of the patrons had already removed their parkas; several tables had piles of discarded coats and gloves stacked to nose height.

"You don't like green beer?" Ben said.

"No. I mean yes, I like beer just fine," Jamison said. "I've just never had green beer before. It sounds kind of … offputting."

Ben sighed. "*Offputting?* What's *offputting* is you're 72 and you never had a green beer. What do they do on St. Patty's in Minneapolis?"

"They probably get drunk and throw up like they do everywhere else. I'm English. We don't do green beer. At least, I've never had any."

"Well," Ben said, "welcome to Montana."

Monna touched Ben's arm. "Oh look," she said. "Those people are leaving. Let's grab their table."

Sure enough, Jamison saw several people putting on their coats just a few feet away. Ben darted through the crowd, slid onto one of the vacated stools, and put his hands on the stools on either side to save them. "Man," he said, when Jamison and Monna arrived. "That was lucky."

Monna slipped out of her coat, folded it in half, and laid it on the table beside her. Jamison stared.

"What do you think?" she said. "Wait till you see Ben." Ben took off his coat and hopped off his stool, his arms flexed like a body builder. Beneath his white cowboy hat he wore a bright green satin shirt with elaborate white piping. A pair of rearing quarter horses faced each other across the shirt's pearl snap buttons. Each green sleeve sported a row of spotless white fringe. His creased white slacks were carefully folded into the top of spit polished black leather boots, the shafts elaborately embroidered with black and green flames. Jamison's gaze returned to Monna. Her white, mid-length skirt was a light and airy chiffon, which floated like feathers around her bare knees. She too had white fringe on the sleeves of her matching green satin shirt, but the shafts of her black cowboy boots, which ended mid-calf, were set off with a border of campy red revolvers. She'd brushed out her long sliver hair until it shone.

"Who do we look like?" Monna was beaming.

"Like real cowboys!" Jamison said.

"No, come on! Who do we look like on television? From a long time ago. We used to watch them when we were kids, remember? Back in the olden days."

There *was* somebody they looked like, Jamison thought. On television? He tried to remember. He told anyone who asked that he'd spent most of his life reading books, not watching TV, and for what it was worth, that was mostly true. He vaguely remembered Bugs Bunny and Road Runner cartoons from long ago Saturday mornings. But there *was* something familiar about their getup; he just couldn't put his finger on it. It hadn't anything to do with cartoons.

Monna couldn't contain herself any longer. "Roy and Dale!" she squealed. "Can you see it now? He's Roy Rogers and I'm Dale Evans."

Jamison made a show of smacking his forehead.

"We started doing this about fifteen years ago, for the rodeo," Monna said. "I found this really pretty shirt at Goodwill, so I bought it. I think it was, like, three bucks. I told Ben, I said, we should dress up like Roy and Dale, just for a hoot. He wasn't on board at first but he came around." She glanced at Ben, who grinned and held up his palms: *complicit.*

"So that summer we hit the thrift shops and bought everything we could find. You can't believe what a blouse and skirt like this would cost new, you men have it so easy. We have these old pictures of Roy and Dale so we tried to copy what they were wearing. We have two or three complete outfits each, right Ben? Including the boots, which cost the most. We usually wear what we've got on right now for St Patty's day, because it's got this emerald green fabric. See?" She plucked a fold of Ben's sleeve between her thumb and forefinger and gave it a little tug, then let go and patted his arm. "We've got red-themed outfits with black and white accents for the rest of the year, like New Years and Christmas. Those are my favorites, because of the color scheme. And some cream-colored ones, too, just for really special occasions. We're sort of a tradition in Aden; people expect to see us dressed up like this a couple times a year. I think they enjoy playing make believe with us."

Jessica returned with a tray of green beer, and when Jamison reached for his billfold, Ben waved him away. "I got it," he said. "Your money ain't no good in this bar." He tossed a twenty on the tray and told Jessica to keep it. She touched Monna's sleeve. "I love your outfits," she said.

"See?" Monna said. The band had begun, and Ben began tapping his fingers in time to the music. Monna took a sip of beer, peering happily at Jamison over the rim of her glass, a thin, flecked line of greenish foam on her upper lip, the shaking in her hands so slight as to be nearly imperceptible.

* * *

On the third or fourth song, Ben crooked his arm, Monna slipped her arm through his, and the two of them walked to the dance floor, Ben tossing off a comment over his shoulder that he'd promised the "cripple" the first dance, a remark Jamison found immediately irritating. He stood, frowning, and for a few minutes watched them glide around the floor. He had to admit that Monna had been right: from what he could see—and from his admittedly uninformed opinion as a pathetically inept non-dancer—they looked like they knew their stuff. He noticed other people watching. But after a couple songs he sat back down, and his gaze fell on the beer sitting untouched on the table before him.

He took a sip and it was good, and it washed away some of the irritation stuck in his craw. He had no idea what kind of beer it was, but Ben had mentioned on the drive over that the Infirmary had a surprisingly good selection of microbrews. Jamison really did like beer; he just didn't drink very much of it, because he didn't drink very much of anything. He liked wine better than beer, and an ex-teacher he had once worked with was a single malt scotch drinker, so at the man's annual birthday party Jamison drank single malt scotch. This had ruined him for lesser bottles of blended whiskey, all he could justify on his teacher's pension.

He hunched over the table, cradling his beer and self consciously lowering his gangling frame, studying the throngs of people around him. They seemed happy to be there, happy to be out of the snow and inside, drinking green beer in the warmth of the bar, orbiting slowly around the room and the harried but patient waitresses. He saw no one who wasn't grinning or wearing a green bandana or a green shamrock pinned to a silly green plastic bowler. His anger at Ben's remark began to dissolve and soon he spied Monna winding her way back through the crowd. She was stopped twice by people she knew, but at last slid onto the stool beside him. She found the beer she'd left behind, took a tiny sip, and sighed theatrically. That, Jamison realized, had been for effect, the precursor of an impending conversation. Jamison turned on his stool and listened.

"Ben's still out there," she said. "He'll dance all friggen night. Once he learned how he loves it." She managed a weak grin.

"It sounds like maybe you don't so much."

"I used to." Monna briefly caught his gaze and then lowered her eyes. Jamison nudged her beer and she reached for it. "I get tired, is all. And tonight I feel pretty good. I wasn't sure I would, but I do. But I've got to rest. When I get tired my coordination gets all cattywampus. I can't find the beat."

"Hell, Monna, that's just Everett genetics," Jamison said. "I couldn't find the beat if someone taped a drum to my head. I lay the blame for that squarely at the feet of mom and dad."

"Did you ever see them dance?" Monna had folded her arms on the table, and one elbow touched a puddle of spilled beer. She peered at the greenish stain on the fringe of her sleeve and scowled. "I didn't, not ever. Did you?"

Jamison shook his head. "Nope. But that doesn't necessarily mean they didn't. I mean, they had to dance at their wedding, right? What did mom say?

"She never said. Probably because I never asked. All I ever wanted to do was paint. I went to some dances in college but I was never any good at it. It wasn't until Ben and I started taking lessons that it became sort of fun. The lessons were actually my idea but Ben liked them even more than I did. We were going through a rough patch and needed a diversion."

"I can see that. I would be surprised if it were otherwise."

"What do you mean by that?" Monna set down her glass, rocking back a little on her stool. "Okay. I know what you mean."

Jamison snorted in exasperation. "Monna, the things that he says to you sometimes … he called you a *cripple*, for God's sake. I felt like hitting him."

"When?"

"When did he say that? Just a few minutes ago. Right after we got here. He said, 'I promised the cripple I'd take her …'"

Monna cut him off. "I remember. Listen, Ben says stuff like that all the time. I just ignore him. Sometimes he acts like a jerk because he thinks he's trying to get me to stop feeling sorry for myself."

"Or … maybe because sometimes, he *is* a jerk," Jamison said, his lips set in a defiant line.

Monna exhaled, not looking at him, scanning the room, her eyes dark. The band had begun another set, and several dancers circled the floor, drawn like moths to the light of the music. She looked back.

"You don't know," she said. "You don't know what it's like."

Chapter 3

All he'd wanted to do was introduce himself to the horses. He'd watched them grazing on the far side of the river for weeks, jostling shoulder to shoulder around the bales of alfalfa that Ben dragged from the stable to the trailer hooked to his ATV, then towed into the pasture and distributed to the horses, who snorted and tossed their wooly heads in happy anticipation. He didn't know the horses' names. They didn't belong to Ben or Monna. They belonged to three separate individuals, so far sight unseen, whom Ben had told him paid the Van Hollens $175 a month each to pasture over the summer and feed over the winter, fair wages, he told him, for this end of the valley. There was one palomino and three sorrels, reddish and dirty, their thick winter coats dull and shaggy, their whiskers as white and profuse as the whiskers of harbor seals. Saying hello would be the neighborly thing to do.

The *intelligent* approach would have been to walk across the yard to the main house, take the plowed road over the bridge, and then walk safely to the pasture on the other side. But the river had been frozen for weeks and was no more than ten or twelve yards across, perhaps a half dozen of Jamison's long strides, and from the studio the pasture was just a stone's throw across the bank. He stepped onto the ice, tentatively stomping on it with one foot while clutching the willows behind him for safety. The ice seemed solid enough, so he took another cautious step. In six more hops he was on the far bank and pushing his way through the willows.

The horses were at the end of the fenced pasture, and when they saw Jamison they began trotting toward him, nickering and eager.

Jamison ducked into the stable, separated a flake of alfalfa from a bale, and walked out to meet them.

The horses swirled around him, suddenly possessive, stealing mouthfuls of hay from his arms, their ears laid back, their square white teeth bared at each other in jealous anger. When one of them kicked the palomino and the animal squealed in rage, Jamison threw the alfalfa on the ground and hastily backpedaled to safety.

So much for being neighborly. He followed his tracks back to the river, careful to place his feet in the boot prints he'd left in the thin film of snow on the ice, and halfway across felt the pocket of water-rotted ice beneath him give way. A split second later he was standing in frigid, burning water, one leg in the river and the other on the ice, trying to grasp what had just happened. The river instantly filled his submerged boot, and within seconds his foot was numb. He shifted his weight to his unsubmerged foot and tried to step onto the ice, but the ice broke beneath him and then both feet were in the shockingly cold water and when he tried to step out again the current threatened to suck his unlaced Sorels off his feet. He put his foot back down, the numbness in both feet now wooden and club-like.

Weirdly, he flashed on an ancient Laurel and Hardy catch-phrase from long, long ago: *Well, here's another nice mess you've gotten me into!* Now he had to think. He wasn't going to drown in eighteen inches of water. But he would certainly be risking frostbite if he didn't get out soon. He also didn't want to lose his only pair of winter boots; he'd be stuck without warm footwear for at least a couple days until he could get to Livingston and buy another pair. In the meantime, he was standing knee deep in the Shields River, icy, slushy water seeping around his soon-to-be-frozen toes, recalling punchlines from a pair of comedians who had been dead for fifty years.

"Jamison?" Monna stood on the bank, a perplexed look on her face.

He had planned to be back from the pasture in time to fix breakfast well before Ben and Monna arrived. He felt guilty that he hadn't repaid their offers of breakfast, so he had invited the two of them for coffee and toast that morning in the studio—another neighborly gesture—but that clearly would have to wait until he got himself out of the river. Ben, though, was nowhere in sight. Ben might actually be able to do something; he'd have a rope.

"What are you doing out there?"

"I fell in. I was feeding the horses. The ice was good when I walked across."

"Ben feeds the horses."

"Monna." The numbness in his feet was beginning to creep up his ankles and he was running out of patience. "I wasn't … never mind. I need a little help here, okay? Every time I try to get out the water sucks my boots off. Do you have a rope or something?"

Monna clasped her gloved hands together, as if in thought. "Hold on a minute," she said. "I think there's a long branchy thing Ben put up by the woodpile. It's for knocking the snow off the roof. Let me go look."

Jamison watched her trudge slowly back up the bank, then make her way through the snow. Despite his own frozen feet, it was painful to watch her struggle. Each stride was measured, as if she had to gauge the distance of each footstep and the balance required in shifting her weight from one leg to the next. Two nights earlier, at the Infirmary, she'd been a dancer. Now her gait was tortured, and closing the gap to the woodpile, less than fifteen yards away, excruciatingly deliberate.

When she got there, Jamison heard her triumphant yelp and saw her hoist a thin tree limb into the air. Then she began her slow, shuffling return. "I got it," she said. She was back on the bank again, just a few yards from him.

"Can you throw it to me?" He knew she didn't have the strength to pull him out of the river.

"I think so." She wound up, and grasping the limb between her hands, awkwardly tried to unwind and hurl the limb toward him at the same time. But her timing was off, and the limb clattered onto the ice a few feet from where he stood.

Again, he forced himself to think. The burning in his feet had stopped; he could no longer feel them. It occurred to him that, for once, he could use his height, the affliction that had dogged him throughout his life, to his advantage. He sat carefully on the ice, his feet and knees still submerged in the water, then lay on his back and stretched his arms above his head, groping blindly for the limb behind him. One of his hands closed on the limb and he almost smiled with relief. He slid the limb under his lower back to redistribute his weight and began slowly lifting his feet out of the river an inch at a time, careful to keep his toes pointed straight up so his boots wouldn't be sucked off by the current. In a few moments he lay free. He poked his legs into the air to drain his boots and felt a shocking surge of icy water run down the back of his legs and puddle in his crotch. Then he butt-scooted backwards to the bank and wobbled to his knees, pushing off the limb in an attempt to stand. With wooden feet and tingling ankles he could barely keep his balance. But he wasn't going into the river again; he'd crawl all the way to Aden before he did that.

Monna met him at the bank and reached for him, her hand trembling. His balance was so poor he had to lean on the limb with one hand and drape his other arm over her shoulders for support, but her forward progress was so agonizingly slow he wondered which of them needed support more. Halfway to the studio, with the prickly feeling of blood returning to his feet, he paused and tossed the limb back on the wood pile. It landed with a clatter and an instant later he saw the big yellow cat boil out from underneath and dash into the cottonwoods and willows upstream.

Jamison pointed. "Did you see that?" he said. "Is that your cat? I think it lives out here in the woodpile."

"I saw it," Monna said. "Let's get you inside by the fire."

* * *

Jamison pulled the woolen liners out of his Sorels and set the empty boots behind the stove to dry, where the leather wouldn't crack in the heat. On Monna's suggestion, he wadded up sheets of newspaper—the *Wall Street Journal*, which he'd bought at the bookstore in Livingston—and stuffed them in the toes of the sopping wet liners to draw out the moisture. She assured him they'd be dry by morning. That struck him as ambitious.

She moved haltingly around the small kitchen, pulling vegetables and eggs out of the humming refrigerator, dragging the heavy cast iron skillet onto the range, while he sat on the sofa and held his slowly warming feet to the woodstove. He'd changed into dry pants and socks, but his feet still tingled painfully. It felt like he was walking barefoot across cactus.

He apologized about not fixing breakfast himself after having invited them down, but Monna dismissed him with a herky jerky wave. "You had an emergency to deal with," she said. She cracked some eggs into a bowl and found a whisk in the drawer. "Ben said he'd take a rain check. He has some stuff he wants to get done in the shop."

Jamison nodded. He wasn't wondering about Ben. "Did you see that cat?" He began gently massaging his feet, which sent tiny electric currents shooting through his toes.

"Sure."

"I think it lives in the woodpile. I don't know how it survives out there in this kind of weather."

Monna swept a pile of chopped vegetables into her hand and dropped them in the sizzling skillet, then poured the whisked eggs on top of them. Several of the chopped vegetables had fallen between her fingers onto the counter, and after a fumbling attempt to pick them up, she swept them into her hand. She reached for the salt shaker and waved it over the skillet, up and down, as if she were patting the head of a dog. She caught him watching and he looked away.

She set the shaker on the counter. "Let me give you some good advice," she said. "Don't tell Ben about the cat."

"Why? What's he got against cats?"

"They kill his birds. That's what he thinks, anyway."

"What do you think?" Jamison's feet had warmed enough that he was able to limp to the kitchen. He knew where the coffee was and he could do that. He could set the table.

"I think Ben thinks what he thinks. I don't know if he knows about the cat or not. He doesn't get down to the studio much unless I ask him to fix something. That cat showed up this summer, probably walked up the river from town. People get tired of feeding them, they just turn them loose. It's really unfair. What are they supposed to eat? I saw it one day when I was trying to paint, a few months before you got here. I figured it had left since I hadn't seen it for a while, but I guess not. It's half wild. Maybe it does kill birds. That's what cats do. It's a pretty big cat." Monna poked at the omelet, then held the spatula upright in one unsteady hand. She'd put on a few extra pounds over the years, and her thick, insulated work overalls accentuated the slight increase in her girth, made more noticeable by her small stature. She was nearly fifteen inches shorter than him.

"So what's his bird fixation?"

"He just likes birds. We both do. But Ben, being Ben, sort of takes it to another level. He builds houses for the house wrens and puts up bluebird houses all along our property line; they're all along the road when you drive in. In winter when work gets slow he builds them in the shop. He's got bird houses stacked to the rafters out there. Anyone should just happen to need a bird house, Ben gives them one. Ben's got bird houses from Livingston to White Sulphur Springs. You want a bird house, he's Johnny on the spot."

"But has he actually seen any cats kill his birds?" Jamison meant *this* cat, the big yellow tom he'd now seen just twice, although the animal's round, four-toed tracks littered the ground around the woodpile after each new snow.

"I don't know. But like I said, I wouldn't tell him about it."

"What would he do?"

Monna had divided the omelet in half but when she tried to lift the heavy skillet it tilted precariously to one side, threatening to dump its contents onto the electric coils. She slapped her hand on the counter in exasperation. Jamison saw her frown in momentary anger, then immediately recover her composure. He gently nudged her aside, took the skillet from her hands, and slid the halves onto the two plates he'd set at the table.

"Thank you," she said quietly. She sat, scooted the chair close, and placed a napkin on her lap. "So, like I was saying. Ben would probably shoot it. He did that once right after we were married. Another big old tomcat from town, just like this one. My theory is it's learned behavior for people born on a farm, like he was. It's like that knee thingy where the doctor taps your knee with a rubber hammer and your leg jumps. Farm boy sees cat, farm boy shoots cat. I cried for two days after he killed that poor thing and he promised he'd never do it again. He hasn't so far. But that was a long time ago."

"Wild cats have to eat something beside birds, don't they? This one looks like it's pretty well fed."

Monna finished chewing, then swallowed. "Rabbits, maybe. We have a few of them around. I think they're cute. Gophers, except they hibernate in the winter. And there's lots of mice in the stable. I don't know what else they eat. I mean, they eat cat food, I know that for sure."

Jamison had finished his omelet; the cozy warmth of the studio following his immersion in the freezing river had given him a ravenous appetite. He sipped his coffee, which came from a tin can he'd found in the cupboard and was remarkably bad. He'd buy his own coffee and maybe a grinder too when the stuff Monna had stocked in the studio ran out. "So Ben's up in the shop? Maybe I'll go up and say hello."

Monna nodded. "He'd probably enjoy the company. Ask him about how he makes his bird houses if you want to get him going." She put her fork down. "But don't tell him about the cat."

* * *

Jamison heard music blasting when he was still twenty feet from the door. He recognized it immediately: Lynyrd Skynyrd. He opened the door and peered blindly into the brightly lit interior. All he could see were the flames from the open door of the crudely welded oil-drum stove and Ben's dark outline staring at him in surprise from behind a bench. He stomped the snow off his boots and stepped inside. Ben walked to the receiver and dialed the volume down. When Jamison's eyes adjusted to the light he took a look around. There were sturdy, hand-built benches against either wall, and hanging in organized rows on a perforated hardboard panel were hand tools of every denomination: saws, wood-handled chisels, combination squares and metal rulers, hand planes. A red compressor was tucked into the far corner. A portable line-feed welder sat beside it, and at the opposite end of the shop, just behind an overhead garage door, he'd parked his olive-drab ATV. There was a tall cardboard box behind the door he had entered; perhaps this was where Ben kept his birdhouses. The shop wasn't as warm as the studio, but it was comfortable, and Jamison unzipped his parka. Ben was in shirtsleeves and a Carhartt vest.

"Close the door, will you? I'm not heating the goddamn valley." Ben jabbed his finger at the door.

"Oh." Jamison pulled the door shut behind him. "You like Lynyrd Skynyrd?"

"I *love* Lynyrd Skynyrd. I hope that meets with your approval."

Jamison nodded. "It does," he said. "I used to listen to them in college. I still do sometimes. I listen to other stuff too, but I still listen to them."

"Yeah." Ben leaned back against the bench, his arms casually folded across his thick chest. "Well anyway, sorry I didn't make it down for breakfast. I told Monna to tell you I'd take a rain check. Some days I just get a hard on for shop time. You think I'd get to do that a lot, what with the work I'm in, but I don't. I got a pretty big job lined up in Bozeman next month, but not much until then. So here I am."

Jamison walked to the work bench. There were several chisels in a leather sleeve, the stamped insignia on their varnished wooden handles facing out, and the short saw that Jamison had seen Ben put down when he entered. A board was clamped in a vice. The tools on the bench were intriguing: small and precise, like a surgeon's tools. The only tools he'd ever been around were the ones in the big metal toolbox his father had kept on a shelf in the garage, a Handyman set he'd bought from Sears.

"What are you building?" Remembering what Monna had told him.

"Ah!" Ben said. He led Jamison back to the door and pointed at the cardboard box. "Take a look inside there and tell me what you see."

Jamison peered inside. The box was full of bird houses, some small, some large. He'd guessed right.

"Bird houses?"

"That is correct. I'm building a bird house. But not just any bird house."

Jamison followed Ben back to the bench. Even in the moment it took him to get there, he sensed a quickening in Ben's steps, the excited uptick in his voice.

Ben backed off the handle of the vice and pulled out the board and thumped it against the heel of his hand to knock out the sawdust, which filtered gently down onto the bench top. Large triangular teeth were cut into the board's top edge. Ben thrust it under Jamison's nose.

"See those? Dovetails. That probably doesn't mean nothing to you, so I'll explain it real slow so that even a college graduate can understand." Ben was grinning. "Dovetails are *craftsmanship*. Takes a long time to do them real good. You look at drawers in a real nice dresser, say, something from a hundred years ago, not that particle-board crap from Home Depot, and they always used dovetails on the joints. It's how you tell good furniture from shit furniture. 'Course, nowadays everyone uses jigs, but I like to cut them by hand."

Jamison searched for an intelligent question, something that wouldn't make him appear as ignorant of craftsmanship as he was certain he must already seem. "So how do hand-cut dovetails make a better birdhouse?"

"Good question! They don't! Galvanized screws work just dandy. I just like 'em that way. Nobody's got bird houses with hand cut dovetails anywhere in the valley, maybe in the whole state. Maybe in the whole world. You glue them up right, though, and they'll last twenty years out in the weather. Sheet rock screws, which is what most people use, they rust through in four or five years, especially in cedar." Ben put the board back in the vice, spun the handle tight, and touched his saw to the inside of a scribed pencil line, then began sawing with smooth, precise strokes. Jamison returned to the cardboard box beside the door. He sorted through the top layer of bird houses, examining the dovetailed corners, whistling in appreciation loud enough so that Ben would hear, although with the music on he couldn't tell. Below the first tier of houses were some that had been painted, and he pulled one out and held it to the light. Painted on three sides was a simple mural of a stubby brown bird riding a horse, the horse's haunches set in a skidding stop, the reins drawn taut against the bit. The bird held a lariat in its slender beak and had thrown a loop around the sun. Jamison showed it to Ben.

"Did Monna do this one?" he asked.

Ben glanced up and put his saw down, then slapped the dust off his hands. "Yup. She did all of them. There's more in the bottom of the box. She liked doing it. She'd spend an hour painting one birdhouse. I doubt if the wrens cared much but she did. I wish she still did."

"She doesn't paint your bird houses anymore?"

Ben shook his head. "That's not what I said. I said she don't care. She stopped. She used to love it. She's been fighting that goddamn disease for years, but lately she don't try anymore. It's like she gave up."

Jamison remembered then: He'd been on a hiatus from college, his parents hovering over him in the tidy brick home in the suburbs where he and his sister had been raised. After dinner he'd escaped to meet one of his old high school buddies in the wooden bleachers beside the high school football field, drinking the cheap beer Jamison had purchased, illegally, at a local drug store. At a head taller than everyone around him and with his hair noticeably thinning even then, Jamison had looked ten years older than he was and was rarely carded. He'd returned home after midnight half drunk, and on the way to his bedroom passed Monna's room, the light showing under her door. She couldn't have been more than nine or ten. Yet even at that age she'd spend all night in her room with her paints and her easel, lost in her art, knowing exactly what she wanted to do with her life.

"I guess I didn't know that," Jamison said. "She told me she has good days and bad days. She doesn't still paint when she's feeling good?"

"Not so you'd notice. It's why you're staying in the studio. She doesn't use it anymore."

"I appreciate that, by the way," Jamison said. "You're letting me stay there. It's nice. I can see the craftsmanship you put into it."

"Well, it was Monna's idea," Ben said, his voice measured and flat. "You should thank her." Ben bent over the vice and resumed sawing. Jamison couldn't see Ben's face under his ball cap, didn't understand why he was being dismissed, could think of nothing more in the way of conversation he could add. He nodded self consciously and mumbled something about getting back to a book and Ben kept sawing and said nothing so he backed out the door of the shop and closed it quietly behind him.

Chapter 4

Jamison strode down the shoulder in his loose-jointed, galumph-ing gait, the plastic water bottle and fleece vest in his daypack snug against his back. Monna had told him it was exactly 1.1 miles to town from where their gravel access road intersected the highway. Highway 89 had been clear and dry for over a week, a passage to town bisecting the frozen waves of snow that arose in billowing steppes on either side of it. Driving was still perilous: With the snow making the countryside all but impassable to deer, they'd been forced to use the highway as a thoroughfare, and he worried he might hit one in his car. Several had been. He counted four bodies between the studio and town, their mangled scraps of fur and twisted torsos the grisly denouement of a twenty-yard smear of frozen blood.

He'd been walking for fifteen minutes and estimated he was halfway there. Occasionally a truck would shoot by, swinging wide to give him a safe berth, the driver peering at him curiously from behind a fogged windshield. Every one of them waved.

He'd put on his light hiking boots, much better for walking than the heavy Sorels, which had taken nearly three days of stuffing with the *Wall Street Journal* to dry. But as the moisture in his boots dissipated, his peevishness at Ben's abrupt dismissal of their conversation remained. What was with the guy, anyway? Even when he went out of his way to be nice, Jamison thought, Ben wouldn't meet him halfway. Quite frankly, Ben had acted boorishly. There was no other word for it.

Jamison wanted to be fair, and perhaps Ben's behavior wasn't personal. Ben had always been a strange duck. Over the years, when Jamison brought up Ben's behavior, Monna had dismissed it with a shrug and chalked up her husband's conduct to his upbringing. He'd grown up on a grain farming operation north of Three Forks, 75 miles as the crow flies due west of Aden, on 2600 hundred acres of bottomland along the Missouri River. "His whole family's like that," she said, as if that were explanation enough.

But so what? Jamison had known any number of farm kids in college. The entire southern half of Minnesota was farm country, a *Jeopardy* fact most people didn't know: *Which Canadian border state is in the top four states for corn production?* They'd been normal, friendly kids like everyone else he hung out with in school, and later, taught in school. Not Ben. It was well within Ben's purview to moderate his behavior, conduct expected of everyone.

But Ben had been nothing more, nor less, than who he was for the forty years that he had been married to Monna, and he wasn't going to change now. Jamison had not set a firm date for his return to Minneapolis but it was out there in an as yet unscheduled future, a measure of solace, beckoning like the promise of the warm spring days Monna vowed would someday return. So Jamison had left his Honda parked beside the driveway in an SUV-sized rectangle he had cleared of snow so Ben could back out of from under the screeching automatic garage door on his way to work. Maybe, he thought, a walk in the cold air would clear his thoughts. He liked the Thoreau-esque implications of it.

He fell into a rhythm, and his gaze rose from the pavement to the land he was traversing. To the east, a low-hanging bank of clouds encircled the Crazies, but the upsloping prairie below sparkled in the cold sun breaking through; the land climbing gradually, then precipitously, as if hurrying to be closer to the sun, until it plunged into the clouds.

He stopped. He stared. In a lifetime in Minnesota, he had seen nothing as glorious as this.

When the next truck passed him, slower than the rest, he knew he was close to town. Within five minute he was at the door of the Infirmary.

He hadn't been back since the dance. He ducked through the front door, dodging snowmelt from the roof. As his eyes adjusted to the light he saw that the interior was nearly deserted. At the end of the bar, a big man in a Stormy Kroner cap nursed a beer and poked thick fingers into a plate of onion rings. Behind the bar, grinning at him, was Jessica. He walked to the bar and took off his fleece cap. He saw her gaze flick up. "Okay. I remember you," she said.

"St. Patty's day."

"I remember. You were with Monna and Ben."

"Yup. That's my sister and brother in law. I'm staying at their place for a few more weeks. They put me up in their studio."

She put a glass beneath one of the taps behind the bar, filled it, and set it in front of him. He hadn't asked for a beer.

"I guess I'll have a beer," he said.

She leaned toward him on folded arms. Jamison saw then that she had another tattoo that started at the base of her neck and meandered down between her breasts, hidden beneath a tight t-shirt. The t-shirt said, '2017 Aden Ranch Rodeo,' and had a curling lariat looping around the name 'Aden.' "How tall are you anyway? If you don't mind my asking."

"Six six," Jamison said.

"Monna's no bigger'n me," Jessica said. "How'd that happen?"

"That's what she and I want to know. We checked out all the milkmen in the neighborhood. Nada."

Jessica grinned. She was younger than he remembered, but prettier, too. Maybe a touch heavier. Maybe in her late forties. Maybe, allowing for makeup, in her early fifties. At that age, maybe she owned the bar, but other people's age, he was learning, had become increasingly difficult to gauge with his own accumulating years. It also didn't help that, so far, most of the people he'd seen in Aden where either getting into or getting out of their trucks, and so swaddled in wool that all he could see was a few square inches of the raw, wind-burned skin of their faces.

"So you moved out here, huh?"

"Well, not exactly." In fact, Jamison wasn't exactly sure what he'd done, in a way he could describe that made any sense to him, much less to someone else. He'd been in Montana less than a month, and ostensibly he'd come to help Ben take care of Monna. But Ben didn't seem to want his help; in fact, he seemed to resent it. Nor did his sister appear as debilitated as she had led him to believe; on most days she could still get around without difficulty, albeit slowly, and take care of whatever she needed to take care of.

Jamison self consciously sucked on his beer, stealing glances at Jessica as she chatted up her hulking customer. There was a football game on the screen behind the bar, but since it wasn't the Vikings, he wasn't interested. In the seven decades he'd lived in Minneapolis he'd never been to a Viking's game, but he watched them on TV, usually in a bar downtown, because he enjoyed the respite from his solitary life of books. He knew little about football and he'd never been much of an athlete himself. A lifetime earlier, as a student, he'd been strong-armed by one of his high school's basketball coaches, the man's jaw set and peering up at him from somewhere down around Jamison's knees, into trying out for the team. He'd been cut from the squad after two weeks. No one, including his parents, seemed to notice. He had returned to his books.

Jamison held his hands apart, cupped, as if holding a basketball from those long-ago days, framing his words. "I came out to help with Monna," he said. "She's sick."

Jessica nodded, frowning a little. Her eyes flicked away, and Jamison saw them settle on a painting on the wall behind him. He recognized the landscape immediately: the north to south sweep of the Crazies, the peaks white from an early snow, and far below, the yellow leaves of the cottonwoods along the river in repose over a purling current, sunlight glinting off the water.

"Monna did that one in front of the bar," Jessica said. "I love it because that's what it really looks like in October. Real pretty like that. She finished it up and took her stuff home, and then one day, I had just started working here, so it was probably ten years ago, she came in and leaned it up against the bar. I was like, 'what's this?' But she did some kind of trade with Grant, I never did ask him what for. Grant's the owner. He was going to take it back to Clyde Park, but he liked it so much he decided to hang it up in here. Said it would be criminal not to let everyone else see it."

"She told me she used to do a lot of plein air stuff up and down the road," Jamison said.

"Yup. Yup." Jessica straightened up and her t-shirt stretched tautly across her breasts, revealing another inch of tattoo. "A bunch of folks in the valley have her paintings. She and Ben have been here a long time. She used to sell 'em cheap if she knew you. Sometimes she'd do drawings, too, with a pencil. I like those the best. I've got two of them she gave me in the house. She says everyone wants paintings, no one wants the really good stuff, so she just, you know, gave them to me. I had them framed in Livingston. But I haven't seen her out painting in two or three years."

"She hasn't said anything about painting to me, either," Jamison said. "I just assumed it was because of the weather. You can't paint outdoors when it's ten below."

"Yeah. Well," Jessica said.

"You think it's the Parkinson's?"

"I don't know what else it *could* be. I've known Monna since I moved here, eighteen or twenty years ago, whenever it was. Back then she had that little red convertible she used to have, and in the summer we'd tool around like I was back in California or something. We used to drive to Bozeman to shop, except Monna was always buying paint and stuff. There was this art supply store downtown. I mean, she wasn't even into clothes all that much, not like I was, she was twenty years older than me and she was *hot* back in those days, all that gorgeous black hair. She could wear anything and just kill it. She was always getting hit on by some dumb fuck walking around up there, but she'd just flash her wedding ring and ignore them. She was probably forty something by then. I remember this one guy ..."

Jamison peered at her over his beer.

Jessica shook her head. "Nope, I'm not gonna go there. Monna would kill me. Tell you what, though. I'll bet after it was over that guy had second thoughts about doing what it is I'm not gonna tell you about."

The man at the end of the bar raised his finger, and Jessica grabbed a bar towel and ambled down to talk to him. He watched her go, trying not to be too obvious about it. He finished his beer and reached for his billfold and left ten dollars on a $4 tab.

* * *

Jamison stood outside the bar, studying the painted mural on the expansive brick façade of the Aden General Store across the street. The scene depicted a larger-than-life celebration of Aden's frontier history. There was still plenty of daylight, so the return trip to the studio would go quickly. He had timed it: it had taken him twenty-two minutes to walk to town. He stepped into the street, paused to let a truck pass—the driver waving at him as he shot by—and a moment later pushed open the door of the general store, which revealed two more doors: to the left was an entry to a café; to the right a grocery. He opened the door to the grocery, the sleigh bells on the door knob jingling. A young man in an apron greeted him from the cash register. Jamison nodded and wandered down the nearest of the store's two aisles. He soon found the produce he was seeking: baby spinach in a plastic bag (he still had half a bottle of Litehouse dressing in the fridge), red onions, carrots, and a carton of Oreos with extra filling. He kept walking, found the pet food section in the next row over and scanned the shelves. Finally, hidden behind bags of Purina Dog Chow was a single row of canned cat food. He put ten cans of *Delicious Salmon Morsels In Creamy Alfredo Sauce* in his basket, all they had. He paid for his goods with a twenty, then another—cat food was more expensive than he thought. Then he was back on the road, striding out, the full daypack bouncing off the small of his back. Shortly before his arrival at the studio he came upon a doe and her two grown fawns trotting twenty yards ahead of him on the shoulder, casting unconcerned glances back over their grey winter coats. At his approach, the trio ran into the ditch and in three graceful leaps bounded lightly into the willows along the river, their white tails flicking like pendulums, side to side.

* * *

Jamison had learned the finer points of tuning his wood stove: bank up the logs in the evening and they'd burn halfway into the following morning, which meant he wouldn't awaken to a freezing house and have to make a run to the woodpile. He had nothing against an early start; in fact, he enjoyed watching the sun come up, which he'd grown accustomed to after 30 plus years of teaching eight a.m. literature classes. But he also liked curling up under Ben's ancient sleeping bag, his consciousness slowly rising into the day like the sun-drenched chrysalis of a moth, playing the delicious game of allowing himself to remain under the covers for ten more minutes. But today would be different. Today he would arise and feed the cat.

He was opening his first can of cat food when it struck him that the cat needed a name. You couldn't just refer to *the cat*—article, noun—forever. People had names, dogs had names, so this cat, as well, would have a name. He lifted the tab on the lid and peeled it back and tossed the lid in the garbage can under the sink, then pulled on his parka. But what?

He approached the wood pile as quietly as he could, but the brittle snow crunched loudly beneath his size 13 feet, loud enough, he thought, to have given plenty of advance warning. He tried to peer down through the logs, hoping to see the cat before it ran away, but again was disappointed. He had no idea where the animal actually lived. Was there a little room down there under all those logs? He imagined a cat-sized burrow snugly lined with grass and leaves, a redoubt against the cold March nights. But there was nothing he could see, only the scores of tracks that seemed to exit and enter the wood pile at random locations. He chose a spot that was protected from the wind and tucked the can of cat food back inside, where it wouldn't be covered if it snowed. Then he loaded his arms with logs, and on the way back to the studio, started thinking again about names. Tabby? Rex?

After he had dropped the logs beside the stove, he spent a few minutes gazing out the window at the wood pile, hoping to see the cat emerge from its secret warren, find the opened can, and happily settle down to a filling, nutritious meal. He hoped the cat would realize who had fed him.

He put two logs and some kindling on the remaining coals in the stove. Flames licked hungrily up the sides of the kindling, and he decided to leave the door open so he could watch it burn. The flames, quick and feline, reminded him of the cat, and suddenly in the firelight he saw a name: *Leviathan*. It was, in fact, a perfect name for a cat of such outsized proportions.

The following morning, he again awoke early, threw on his clothes—he'd become accustomed enough to the cold that he could now make a quick trip to the woodpile without his parka—and trudged out for a look. The open can of cat food was where he had left it, untouched. He cupped his hands around his mouth and breathed through his fingers to warm them, gazing through the cloud of condensation at the frozen river. It had been well below freezing the entire previous day and into the high single digits that night; cat food was unlikely to spoil at those temperatures. He decided to leave the can for another day. But when he picked up the can he discovered it had frozen solid. So that wouldn't work.

Back inside, he put the previous day's can of cat food in the refrigerator and opened another. He had a new game plan: rotate back and forth between two opened cans, one inside the fridge slowly thawing, one outside slowly freezing, until they either went bad or Leviathan started eating them.

But on the third day, with the previous night's can of cat food still untouched, he swapped it out with a fresh can. The cat's big tracks were all around the wood pile, but Jamison couldn't tell if they were fresh. Rabbit tracks covered his snowy neighborhood in

Minneapolis; he watched rabbits from his apartment window all summer, hopping around the mowed lawn of his complex like bug-eyed yard ornaments. But in the winter, each succeeding snowfall hid the previous week's accumulation of tracks, only to become quickly covered with tracks again. He'd never looked at them closely. It had never occurred to him that there was anything to learn. Now he wished he knew how to estimate the age of the cat's tracks, something he suspected Ben already knew how to do. But at least he wasn't wasting the food; as long as the low temperatures held, he could rotate the same two cans for a week.

Monna visited two days later, after he'd finished his supper. He was stacking the cleaned dishes in the dish rack when the door swung open and she lurched in, a bottle of wine clutched between her woolen mittens. She had told him she was coming, and Jamison had puttered around the cramped interior tidying up, slapping the incessantly grumbling refrigerator once in an attempt to quiet it. She tried to stomp the snow off her boots, but could manage only an awkward rock from side to side. Jamison scurried to her side and took the wine and set it on the kitchen table, then helped her to the sofa. He helped her remove her coat, struggling to free her arms from the sleeves, and as if the effort had exhausted her, she sighed and dropped heavily into the cushions, her feet splayed unnaturally on the varnished plywood floor. Her coat slid off the sofa, but she made no move to pick it up. Jamison draped it over the back of a chair.

She said, "This is me when it's bad."

* * *

She would tell him about what it was like. In the lone bathroom in their small home, she had tried to put on makeup, but she could do no more than slash the red lipstick across her lips, giving her a clownish smile. She studied herself in the mirror and then angrily threw the tube into the sink. She knew exactly how she appeared: as if she were looking through a mask, as if the face she had just crudely painted was a disembodied parody of the rest of her.

She had trudged unsteadily through the snow to the studio, and now Jamison was handing her a plastic cup which he'd filled with the wine she had brought. The bottle had a yellow label with a leaping kangaroo. "Kangaroo wine," he said. "The good stuff."

She sat across from him, her voice barely a whisper. She tried to smile but the muscles in her face wouldn't move. Finally, she managed to twitch the corner of her mouth. "Costco," she said, pointing to the bottle. She tried to hoist her plastic cup in a toast, but the wine in the cup, which Jamison had perfunctorily filled to the brim, immediately sloshed onto the table. She set it back down again and Jamison grabbed a paper towel.

Monna tried to cradle the cup between her hands, but she couldn't will her fingers to grasp it, so she was forced to let her palms rest on either side of it, as if she were gazing into a crystal ball. "It's not like I can't talk at all," she said, her voice nearly expressionless. "But when your tongue and lips don't work it sounds funny. *I* sound funny." She saw Jamison's stricken look and closed her eyes, then opened them. "This was a good choice, the plastic cups," she said. "I'm always breaking wine glasses so I don't use them anymore. At least with plastic, it doesn't break." She pulled her cup a few inches closer, where there was less chance of a spill. "Ben said he'd buy more glasses, but why waste the money? This stuff tastes pretty good no matter what you put it in. The last wine glass I broke he cut his finger real bad picking it up." Upon seeing the blood, Ben had slammed his bloody fist into the arm of the sofa, then immediately apologized for losing his temper, solicitous of her and angry with himself at the same time. The memory embarrassed her, that she had brought him to that, that she was responsible.

"I'll be better in a couple days," she said. "That's usually how long these spells last." She hoped she sounded chipper. It certainly wasn't the way she felt.

"Is there anything I can do?"

"Just keep talking to me. I know I sound dumb. People who don't know me think I'm—they used to say retarded, but now the word is develop … develop …" Monna felt a surge of anger. Her tongue wouldn't form around the words she could clearly see. Instead, the words were lodged somewhere behind her lips, as if they were being dragged sideways through her mouth.

"Developmentally disabled," Jamison said quietly.

"Yeah. Do I sound like that to you? Be honest, Jamison."

"Of course not."

"Yes I do."

"Well, maybe a little." Jamison grinned.

Monna's eyes widened with surprise. "I'm gonna kill you for that," she said, her voice flat. But the eyes behind the mask twinkled. "Really, I am. I don't care how big you are."

* * *

"Why is Ben so pissed off all the time?" Jamison asked. He was bent over the stove. Monna watched him put his hands on his knees and stare at the flames.

She was halfway into her third glass of wine, and Jamison wasn't far behind. The alcohol was relaxing, and in her relaxation a measure of animation had been restored to her speech. She accentuated her voice with her hands, and they gave her words an enthusiastic, if sluggish, emphasis.

But Jamison's question immediately brought her back to earth.

Monna snorted, an exhalation through frozen lips. "You would be too if you had to spend all day and night waiting on an invalid."

"But you're *not* an invalid day and night," Jamison said. "You said so yourself, that it comes and goes." He took a slug out of his cup, then set it on the floor between his feet.

"Yeah, yeah," Monna said. "I know all that." She thought, *but I am.* The most infuriating aspect of her disease was the very thing everyone else thought was her reprieve from it: that it came and went, that there would be some days when she was nearly normal. In a horribly twisted way, being consistently symptomatic at least would have allowed her to adjust to the inevitability of her affliction. But suffering as she was now, this moment, was made worse knowing that it still hadn't claimed all of her, that her symptoms would recede and then return again on a date she couldn't foresee and couldn't control. Parkinson's would have its fickle way with her, and there was nothing she could do about it.

Jamison sat across from her. Monna stared past her brother at the night pressing against the studio window that had once been the backdrop for her easel. The years when she could spend all day in the studio in thrall to her work seemed a lifetime past, lived by a woman she no longer recognized. Slowly, she raised her cup to her lips. "I know how it is with Ben," she said. "But remember how much Mom didn't like it when people came over for dinner and Dad got into the bourbon and started going on about politics? First it was Goldwater, then it was Nixon. Remember? I sure do. That was the sixties, Jamison. You had to have seen some of that when you were living at home." She set her cup back on the table.

Jamison whistled. "That was a long time ago."

"Yes it was," Monna said. "But years later, I mean, when I was old enough to actually understand anything, I was home from college, I think, and I asked her about that. About why she let Dad rant and rave in front of company like that. I mean, it wasn't like everyone in the family didn't already agree with him. Mom did. She voted Democrat, straight ticket, every election until she died. But she hated it when he made their guests feel uncomfortable."

"So what did she say?"

She said, "'I love your father.'"

* * *

Jamison stood in the doorway and clumsily helped Monna zip up her coat. The wind keened, and granules of snow from the porch tumbled through the open door and skated around his stockinged feet. He thought to tell her then, before she could leave, but didn't. Long after he left home, after Monna had moved west and married Ben, he'd been invited to a dinner party at his parents' house, and one of the guests had launched into a conservative diatribe that, a decade earlier, would have triggered a passionate and full-throated defense from his father, but he had said nothing and allowed the man to vent, even smiled and nodded. Jamison had been so surprised by his father's composure he'd asked his mother about it later. She had told him this: she'd had enough.

Chapter 5

Ben banged on his door at 7 a.m., grey light backed up behind the Crazies, the diffuse glow silhouetting the peaks like a rime of hoar frost on the prow of an ancient ship.

"Tell you what," Ben said. "I'm heading into Bozeman day after tomorrow to buy some supplies for a job and Monna thinks I oughta ask you if you want to go with, maybe go shopping. Be fine with me. We can go wherever you want, long as you can roust your ass out of bed by eight. I got stuff to do in the afternoon."

Jamison stared at him, bleary eyed, his sleeping bag half off his bed, as if he'd wanted to drag it across the freezing studio with him. It had been *warm* under the sleeping bag.

"You think maybe we could have had this conversation tonight?" Jamison said.

"No."

"Right. You want to come in for coffee or something? I can put a pot on."

"Nah, I gotta get after it," Ben said. "So you up for Thursday?"

"Yeah," Jamison said. "But let me think a second." He studied Ben, who had not even put on a coat. He was wearing his dirty canvas vest unzipped over a blaze orange hoodie. No gloves. Jamison tried to marshal his scattered thoughts. Standing in the open doorway wasn't helping, it was damn cold. Lately, bent over coffee and a book, his feet to the wood stove, he'd spent his mornings reading Rilke's *Book Of Hours*, but that could wait, he'd read it three times already. After Rilke he was going to start exploring some of the local writers, maybe Harrison or McGuane or that Evan or Ivan

Doig guy who grew up a few miles north of Aden and was supposed to be good, even though he was now living in Seattle. Ben leaned against the door frame, his arms folded impatiently, staring up at him.

"Sure," Jamison said. "I've got things I can get. Maybe socks and a pair of jeans. "You have to leave by eight?"

"We can go earlier, you want. It's an hour and fifteen minutes to Bozeman."

"No, eight is fine. I'll be here with bells on."

"Dude," Ben said.

* * *

Jamison nursed a cup of coffee and watched the sun peek over the mountains and burst into the dark studio with raking yellow light. Beyond the window was the wood pile, and beyond that the river, and the river sent a chirping, burbling song, like a hundred starlings, wafting gently to his ears. But it was still cold, and each morning, the cans of cat food he put out for Leviathan were still frozen.

After a week he'd thrown out the first two cans, untouched and uneaten. They had seemed fine, ostensibly edible. Not something he would want to eat, but okay for cat food, he supposed. But reason stepped into the breech: certainly, after a week of repeated freezing and thawing, *any* kind of perishable food would be suspect. So he decided to start a rotation of two new cans. He opened the first, threw the lid into the garbage can under the sink, then slipped into his parka and Sorels.

On most mornings he swapped out the cans of cat food, checking to see if the previous day's can had been discovered and eaten. But today, for some reason, he decided to peer down through the top of the pile, as if he were peering into a dresser drawer in his apartment in Minneapolis, looking for the boxers he kept folded in half and stored beside his socks. Perhaps because of the wood he'd removed from the top of the pile over the last month, on this morning he discovered a narrow passage that led to an opening, a hidden den above the first tier of logs that was above and insulated from the frozen ground. He pushed his glasses up his forehead and cupped his hands around his eyes to shield them from the glare. There, four feet below him, a pair of greenish-yellow eyes stared directly into his. Leviathan's eyes.

Startled, he jerked his head away as if he'd been poked in the face with a needle, and the big cat bolted from its den and dashed across the snow and into the willows along the river. Jamison pedaled backwards, spun around in one direction, spun around in another, almost dancing, giddy with excitement.

"Hey!" he blurted out, aching to tell someone. "Hey! Hey!" He looked at Ben and Monna's house, but no one was watching from the windows, even though the lights were on. Ben had already left for work.

When he retrieved the can, he found it had been licked clean. He slid his glasses back down his nose and held the can up to the sun. Every morsel was gone. He put it to his nose and inhaled the strong salmon odor stuck to the tin. Certainly, Leviathan could smell the salmon too. But had he been drawn only to the scent or was there something else he craved? Jamison hoped—knowing how silly he was being, an old, silly man who had never owned a pet, not even a hamster—that somewhere in Leviathan's wild being he craved what Jamison craved: a gesture of communion, friendship.

* * *

"You help me load up some two by's at the lumberyard, we'll be out of here in half an hour and we can go wherever you want," Ben said.

"That works for me," Jamison said. Ben was merging onto the interstate, leaving Highway 89 and picking up speed in the west bound flow of traffic on I-15. Jamison had been to Bozeman only once since his arrival in Aden the previous month. The Ford roared, and the load on the 16-year-old engine produced a staccato tapping in protest. Ben ignored it. From what Jamison could see, traffic—or what passed for it in Montana—was nearly non-existent. On some days, the I-94 corridor between Minneapolis and St. Paul looked like a four-lane parking lot, rows of pissed-off commuters inching forward. This was nothing.

"You like that? Being retired?" Ben was steering with one hand, one arm resting in his lap, three fingers on his free hand holding the wheel as if he were holding a beer, the casual way he did everything. He gazed through the windshield, not at Jamison.

The question caught Jamison by surprise, as it always did when someone asked him about Life As A Retiree. He liked retirement well enough; it gave him more time to read. But he missed the kids. He missed having something important to *do*. He thought he'd enjoy being away from a classroom of raucous 16- and 17-year-olds—he had dreamed of the day he would leave—but the silence in his apartment was disquieting, not liberating, and the freedom from work made him acutely aware of the loneliness of his solitary existence.

In Minneapolis, he spent most mornings with a cup of coffee in the Naugahyde recliner in his apartment, reading. For a few hours he could lose himself in a story, his hungry mind transporting him to another world, a total immersion that he'd been able to will on demand since childhood. But then he'd close the book and find, not that he was lost, but rather, that he was still in the empty, sparsely furnished two-bedroom walk-up that held no particular meaning for him one way or another. He could no longer remember a good reason for having sold the comfortable home he had owned prior to moving there.

He said, "Yeah, it's okay. Not exactly like I thought it would be. You know."

"I *don't* know," Ben said. "That's why I'm asking."

"You thinking of retiring?"

Ben snorted. "Yeah, right. Like I'd get a pension like some people I know. Like I don't have a sick wife to take care of. I'm gonna work until I'm dead." Ben put his other hand on the wheel.

"Doesn't Monna make something from her painting? That's what she told me."

"That's what she tells everybody. She *used* to make money from her painting. Some months she made more than I did. A lot more. But she don't paint anymore. She says she can't."

"And you don't believe her."

"She won't *try*. I told you." They were passing Livingston; below them and to the north, the town clung to the side of a broad defile along the Yellowstone River. Jamison gazed toward the buildings on the east end of town, vaguely wondering if he could pick out the Rib and Chop house, the only restaurant he'd been to in Livingston since his arrival in the Shields Valley. He'd taken Ben and Monna there; their suggestion and his treat. He swiveled toward Ben, fishing around below his seat to see if he could find the lever that would move it back another two inches, an adjunct to a lifetime of riding in other people's cars with his bony knees jammed up under his nose. Now they were crossing the river, black water twisting impatiently through white ice, and Ben had stuck his foot into the accelerator to begin the long pull up the pass. The tapping resumed.

"I don't know," Jamison said. "I'd think it would be hard, trying to do something like painting when you have Parkinson's. All that fine motor skill stuff would be hard."

Ben yanked his head around. Jamison saw the anger flash from his eyes, like steam boiling off a teapot, and tried to back peddle.

"I mean, obviously, you know her better than me …"

"A *lot* better," Ben said. "We been married 40 years. I know her a *lot* better than you."

"Okay, I hear you," Jamison said. "I never meant to imply that you didn't know your own wife. Of course you know your wife. I was just posing a question. Thinking out loud. I do that sometimes."

Ben stuck his chin out. There was a cleft in the middle of it, like Kirk Douglas. "You been thinking, you would of known already," he said. "Right?" He grinned, but his eyes were bright and piercing, the anger, like heat in a closed room, still in them.

"Yes. You're right," Jamison said, turning away. Jesus, this was getting stupid. Why had he agreed to go to Bozeman? He could pick up pants and socks any time he wanted to.

"Damn straight I'm right," Ben said. He inhaled, his nostrils flaring as if he were sampling the breeze, as if a respite from Jamison's ignorance were to be found in the wind. Then he nodded once, curtly, as if an unspoken question had been answered. "I could of stayed in range management and be retired by now, like you," he said. "Working for the government. I'd of had a pension and benefits. But construction was going crazy. First seven, eight years, I made twice as much as I would of made working for the feds in bum fuck Egypt someplace. Monna's paintings were starting to sell. That's when we bought the place in Aden. It was dirt cheap. You wouldn't believe what we gave for it; but I ain't gonna tell you, so don't ask."

Jamison nodded. "Okay," he said.

"So first thing is, Monna had to have someplace to paint so I built her the studio. Wasn't enough room in that little house. Took me two weeks one summer to lay up the logs. I did it all myself, with a back hoe I borrowed. Trimmed out the inside that fall, electrical, plumbing, sheet rock. Septic system was the worst. I never got a permit 'cause I knew they wouldn't give me one but I did it anyway and it works fine. Couple years later I built the shop and then the stable so we could board horses. I still haven't got around to fixing up the house; seems like I always got paying work I got to do first. Monna says it's like that saying about marrying an auto mechanic: they can't ever get their cars fixed. She's been bitching about it for years, but I don't see any point to it, since ..."

Ben's face suddenly softened, the hard lines around his mouth easing. He looked away. The change was so abrupt it was startling, It would not last.

"Since what?"

"Since *what?*" Ben slammed the flat of his palm against the wheel. "You know what *fucking* happens to people with *fucking* Parkinson's Disease?" Ben was nearly shouting. The softness, the pain, had vanished, and in its place was rage, anger at an abyss he could neither fathom nor navigate around, at a blind and unknown future to which he refused to surrender.

Jamison stared at him, eyes wide.

"Do you? I'll tell you what happens. You push them around in a goddamn wheel chair! You gotta feed them, take 'em to the, to the …" Ben slammed his fist into the steering wheel again, and the truck swerved wildly into the other lane. Jamison yanked his head around, looking through the back window and praying there were no oncoming cars. Ben jerked the steering wheel the other way and swerved back into his lane.

"You take them to the bathroom," he said. Ben had put both hands back on the wheel, but now his shoulders sagged, as if the outburst had exhausted him. "They can't even wipe themselves." Almost whispered, as if he hoped he wouldn't hear.

* * *

"You want some pizza?" Ben asked. "I want a pizza." Jamison was fine with pizza; it was close enough to lunch to suit him and he wanted to get out of the truck. They'd stopped at the lumberyard and loaded two by sixes onto the rusting iron rack bolted to the pickup bed; a couple husky college kids who worked in the yard had done all the heavy lifting. Ben grabbed a carton of metal gussets and two boxes of sinkers, eights and sixteens, for his nail guns. "Lumberyard will deliver this stuff," he explained, "but about every third trip they get their signals crossed, and I got to send it back and sit on my thumb half the day with nothing to do. So for small loads I'd rather pick it up myself." They'd stopped at Murdoch's on the way home so Jamison could buy a pair of work pants, which he planned to use for hiking in the mountains, or hiking *near* the mountains, if, as he was beginning to suspect, the snow in the mountains never actually melted. That would be something: eternal winter. Ben had waited for him in the truck.

They slowed on the outskirts of Aden and a moment later Ben edged the truck against the curb opposite the Infirmary. Behind them, the mural on the Aden General Store loomed. Jamison saw

Gerald Metzger's patrol truck parked a few yards down the street. Metzger waved at them.

Ben hopped out of the truck, slamming the door behind him. He jerked his chin toward the bar. "They built the addition and the restaurant in the back just a few years ago," he said. "Grant wanted me to give him a bid, but it was too big for me. That's why I usually don't do commercial stuff. I'm a one-man operation. Contractor did it come out of Livingston. I could of saved him some money I'd of taken the job, but it didn't turn out too bad." They walked to the bar. "Anyway, used to be just bar food in here. Now the pizza's pretty good. But you can let me know what you think." After his outburst that morning, Ben had seemed almost embarrassed, as if he'd revealed more of himself than Jamison had a right to be privy too, and now it seemed that Ben was going out of his way to keep the conversation upbeat. Which had been a relief. Jamison hadn't known how to react to revelations about his sister that he wasn't ready to think about; he'd read about the symptoms of Parkinson's, of course; he read about everything. Cloaked in abstract medical terms, the descriptions seemed antiseptic and almost bland. But it was an entirely different game when it was your sister who was afflicted, the child squealing with delight you had pushed on the swing in your parents' backyard in Minneapolis; the grown woman who had married a man who, however superficially, was someone you had known half a lifetime.

Several people were sitting at the table closest the door, and Jessica was taking their order, her back to Jamison and Ben. They walked behind her, Jamison's self-consciousness ratcheting up a beat when she turned and smiled at him.

Ben slapped his hands on the bar and slid onto a stool and Jamison sat on the stool beside him. He glanced in the mirror, noticed the warm light in the bar glistening on his bald head and put his hat back on. He checked his reflection again and removed his glasses. Jessica delivered two glasses of beer unasked and Ben grinned. "Now, *that's* service," he said. Ben ordered the meat-lover's pizza and Jessica disappeared into the kitchen. Ben watched Jamison watch her go.

"She's best friends with Monna," Ben said. "They go to Bozeman, go shopping, whatever. I don't care what they do. I think it's good for her to get out."

"That's what she told me last time I was in here," Jamison said. "She's, um, a little younger than Monna, right? The makeup."

"Lot younger. Forty-six. Moved here from L.A. about nineteen, twenty years ago. I know her exact age because a bunch of these cowboys were buying her drinks couple years ago after the rodeo, trying to get her drunk enough she'd show them her tattoo. She said she was celebrating her birthday. Birthday's a month after the rodeo."

"Did she?"

"Yup, sure did. Climbed right up on the bar and took her top off. Man, you should of heard 'em howl. That tattoo on her back is a dragon goes all the way down her ass and then some. Wouldn't take off the rest of her clothes. The one on the front is a phoenix, that bird that rises from the ashes. She didn't take off her bra, either, 'case you were wondering."

"I thought you said you never saw her tattoos."

"Oh, I saw them. Everybody in the front of the bar did. That's just what I told Monna. She was in the back dancing with Grant. Grant owns this place. I told her I was in the head and missed the show. The band was pretty loud so she couldn't hear what was going on. I had plausible deniability."

Jamison took a sip of beer and put it down. Good stuff, whatever it was Jessica had poured for them. He was not optimistic about the math. Jessica at forty-six was 26 years younger than him; not exactly salutary odds. He'd been out of grad school three years before she was *born*. He swiveled around on his stool so he was facing out, his elbows behind him on the bar. There were four customers at the front table, two more seated at the table beside theirs. With him and Ben, that made eight, which is what he assumed amounted to the lunch rush chez Infirmary. He took another sip of beer and wiped his mouth on his sleeve. He set his glass beside him on the bar and slowly rotated it in the pool of condensation puddled around the base. Then he spun back toward Ben. "Did you ever hear of the legend of the phoenix?" he said. "In Greek mythology?"

"Didn't get much into Greek mythology in range science, no," Ben said.

"Ah! So. According to Pliny the Elder, Herodotus, *et. al.*, the phoenix was a bird associated with the sun; like a lot of academics, I've always interpreted it as embodying the persona of the sun. It was a huge bird, as tall as a tree, with giant talons and magnificent plumage, like nothing mankind has seen before or since. It would live for 500 years, and then went out—you could think of it this way—in a blaze of glory. It burned up. Burned to a crisp, until there was nothing left but ashes.

"But the phoenix never really died; its death in flames was a precursor to its resurrection. At a certain point, it would arise anew from the ashes and begin another 500 years of life. From a Christian perspective, the allegory of Christ's resurrection is clear, I think."

Ben nodded, frowning. "Yeah, well, clear to you, maybe."

"What do you mean?"

"I mean, that's mythology. The Bible's not mythology; Bible's fact."

Jamison thought, don't go there. He nodded, considered Monna's painting on the opposite wall, and took a different tack: "You think Jessica knows about the legend of the phoenix?"

"Well, she had it put on 'bout seven or eight years ago, so maybe the tattoo guy put it on in Billings explained it to her," Ben said. "But I wouldn't hold my breath."

Jessica arrived and deposited a steaming tray of pizza buried under pepperoni and hamburger. Ben tapped his glass with his finger. Jamison was barely half way though his own beer and declined another. After she left, Jamison said he'd sure like to see that phoenix. Strictly research, wink, wink.

"Should of been to the rodeo," Ben said.

* * *

"See that? Where the river bends in toward the road? That's where Monna's car got pushed in." They were just south of Aden, the truck picking up highway speed. Beside them, the Shields curved to the west, then pooled into a placid, deep glide and finally, as if freed of the constraints of geography, accelerated into a broad riffle directly below a large home overlooking the river. Ben pointed at the house. "That used to be just a little old stick-framed ranch house, been there probably since the forties, long as our place has. Then somebody got a hold of it and remodeled the shit out of it and now it's *that*. Probably some rich guy from California."

"Maybe you should have done it," Jamison said.

Ben chuckled. "I would of. Done a better job, too. And I would of charged them up the yin yang to do it. But anyway, that's not what I was saying. That pool down there's a lot deeper than it looks."

"What happened to Monna's car? You mean the truck? This truck?"

"No. Monna's *car*. *The* car. Back when she was making good money painting, long time before she got sick, she got this wild hair she had to have a convertible. She never told you about that?"

Jamison shook his head.

"Well, she did. Couldn't talk her out of it. What are you gonna do with a sports car in Aden? The only paved road in town is the highway. But by God, she wanted a convertible. A red one. Didn't even care what kind, long as it was red." Ben peered over at him. "You ever figure out how women think, you just let me know, 'cause I'm still in the dark.

"So I wasn't gonna waste money on a car you could only drive five months out of the year, that's for damn sure. And I told her that. So she said fine, she'd do it herself. And she did. Found this '66 MG Midget, I think in Billings or Sheridan. Not all that much money, even. Guess what color it was?"

"Red."

"Correct. You ask her why, and she'd always say, 'Red is the fastest color,' then laugh like crazy. But I'll tell you what, when it ran, it was fun. She made me keep it in the garage all winter. Sometimes, it was like she missed driving around in it and she'd just go out and sit in it—you know, just fiddle around with stuff. But summers, we'd fold down that rag top and take it on trips to hot springs all over this half of the state, long as there was a paved road going to it. I don't know how many times we drove it up to White Sulphur Springs. 'Course, a couple times a summer it'd just die someplace, and I'd have to go out and get it running again. Socialist countries make shit cars. But they were pretty simple back then and I could usually figure out how to get it going. She loved that car." Ben eased his foot into the gas and the motor tapped lightly under the hood and then faded out.

"So one day, she's driving up the highway, right back there where I just showed you, and the engine just quits on her like nobody's business. There was enough juice left in it she got it pulled over back there by that pool. Then she got out and started walking home, figured we'd drive down the next day and I'd get it running again. No traffic those days, so we figured it wouldn't hurt to wait 'til morning. Next morning, we drive down, and she starts getting all panicked. Says the car's not there. I pulled over and we got out to look. And there it was, at the bottom of the river. A foot of water's running over the top of it. You can see it underwater, clear as can be, like it was encased in glass, like somebody drove it up there from downstream and parked it. Maybe going fishing."

"What happened?"

"I never did figure that out. But somebody had to push it in, probably some drunk high school kids up from Livingston. Probably thought it was funny. Monna cried all day. Seeing her like that, I'd of killed them. It still pisses me off, thinking about it. By the time we got a tow truck down there to pull it out it had been underwater for two days. You think English cars are bad, try starting one that's been soaking in river water for two days. I set it up on blocks in the yard and pulled the oil pan and the plugs and distributor cap to drain it out, but there was water and grit all through it. Could of parted it out but I just towed it to the junk yard. I had to get it out of Monna's sight."

Jamison folded his hands behind his head and stared out the window. He'd never known his sister had the slightest interest in cars. He couldn't imagine Monna in an open MG, her long black hair whipped into knots, tooling up Highway 89, the pumpkin-seed-shaped car skittering around the trucks and semis on the road; couldn't imagine Ben in the passenger seat, grinning like Theodore Roosevelt, the hot summer slip stream making quick, short furrows through his cropped hair. His hair would have been black then, like Monna's. River water under the bridge.

"Maybe you should get her another one," Jamison said. "A red one."

"I ain't got the money," Ben said. "Cars were cheap back then."

"Yeah, but ... couldn't you buy a used one or something?"

Ben flicked on his turn signal, swung the truck sharply right and dropped onto the access road to their house. "That's not it," he said. "She can't drive one anymore. She can't make her feet work a clutch."

Jamison glanced through the windshield, saw Monna standing in the driveway, holding something in her hand, smiling. Ben slowed to a stop and rolled down his window. "Give me your hand," she said. She reached for his hand, clumsily opened her trembling fist above it, and dropped a single yellow dandelion blossom into his palm. "Spring!" she said.

Chapter 6

Jamison stood before the studio window and marveled at the snowmelt pouring off the roof. It had been melting for half a week, yet still it came. When he'd gone out to feed Leviathan that morning, he'd noticed that all but a narrow band of snow trapped behind the snow stops had melted away. Ben had not installed gutters, so a cascade of dripping snowmelt beat a rhythmic tattoo on the puddles below both eaves, the sheet of falling drops like a beaded curtain hung across a doorway.

Spring was happening more quickly than he could have anticipated. His Sorels were stashed in the corner behind the stove; he had stopped wearing them over a week ago. Now he was back in his light hiking boots, which were adequate for the puddles he would encounter on the short walk up the gravel drive to the Van Hollen's home, where Monna had invited him for coffee cake. In Minnesota, he'd grown accustomed to weeks of dreary weather marking the onset of spring; on this morning sunlight announced spring's arrival in the Shields Valley as from a procession of heavenly trumpets. The north-facing slopes of the Crazies were still covered with a mantle of white snow, but there were patches of brown on the exposed southern flanks that grew larger each day. When he studied them through his binoculars, he saw tinges of green, shoots that had germinated under the snow reaching for the sun, the color promising new life, as the blush of dawn promises the day. He wondered if this was what Monna saw when she painted, if this was the wondrous light she had spoken of so often.

Jamison put on his jacket and walked to the Van Hollen home. He let himself in—Monna had insisted he do so, despite his polite objections—and tossed his coat over the back of a chair. She scooped two squares of coffee cake out of the foil pan onto a pair of plates. She seemed to be moving with relative ease, relative, at least, to how she'd been just a day or two before. He told her as much.

She nodded. "I noticed right away when I woke up," she said. "I usually do, you know. When I know I'm going to have a good day." She slid a coffee cup and a plate across the table to Jamison, his long legs crossed loosely at the ankles and extending a foot past her chair, his black-rimmed glasses perched on the tip of his nose. He took them off, squinted through the lenses and rubbed them with the tail of his shirt and then put them back on. Monna sipped her coffee, holding the cup with both hands. Jamison had grown accustomed to his sister's shuffling walk and painful muscular rigidity, and on the days her symptoms manifested themselves less obtrusively, she seemed light and airy, transformed, almost as if she were dancing.

"Did Ben go to work?" Jamison set down his cup. He touched the handle with his finger and pushed it a quarter turn.

Monna shook her head. "He's in the shop. He decided that since I was gonna have a good day he was gonna have a good one with me. We'll see what he means by that. He said he'd be back in a little while, give us a chance to catch up. I think he might want to talk to you about something."

"What would that be?" Jamison wasn't used to Ben asking him about anything; Ben usually *told* him about this, that, or the other; delivered in declarative sentences.

"I don't know. Something about a job he has coming up. He thought you might be interested."

"Okay," Jamison said. "Maybe. If he needs help on something I'll be glad to help. I'm not too handy with tools, though."

"I think he knows that."

Jamison chuckled and slid his cup forward. *Everyone* knew that. Monna rose, grabbed the coffee pot from the burner, and topped off his cup, then returned to her seat. She'd dolled up a little this morning, put on mascara and a skirt. Jamison hadn't seen her in a dress since the St. Patty's Day dance. It struck him that his sister would still be considered attractive by most men; from his high-school years forward, he'd been told he had a pretty sister by all his male friends, some of whom, to his red-faced uneasiness, had openly flirted with his then teenaged little sister. Now, Monna told him, she was an "unreconciled" 63, and the ensuing decades had added a pound or two and ringed her eyes with faint dark circles, undetectable, he noticed, beneath her makeup. The restorative power of cosmetics never ceased to amaze him.

He hadn't awoken that morning with plans beyond a cup and a chat with his sister. On the days that Ben worked and she was beset with symptoms, he'd tried to help her around the house—preparing lunch, shoveling what little snow remained on the concrete sidewalk between the garage and the house, running her to Clyde Park or Livingston to shop. Yet, despite her disease, on most days she didn't seem to want much help, his raison d'être for having driven to Montana in the first place. On many afternoons and evenings, unneeded, he found himself retreating to his studio to read, to gaze out the window, to plan hiking adventures in the mountains as soon as the snow melted. He'd bought a guide book in Livingston, *100 Great Day Hikes Around Bozeman and the Greater Yellowstone,* and had book-marked a few of the easier hikes he thought he might want to try. But he was apprehensive about his relative lack of fitness; although he'd done some hiking in Minnesota, outdoor recreation there tended toward more sedentary canoes. Now that he was in the Shields Valley—for how long, he had yet to decide—maybe he'd join a hiking club, perhaps make some new friends in the time that remained. Monna had told him there was a club in Bozeman.

She was studying him. "You ever know anyone else with Parkinson's?" she said.

Jamison nodded. "A couple guys I knew of in Minneapolis had it. One was a school principal I worked for. But I've read about it. When you told me you had it, which was ..."

"Six years ago."

"Yeah. So I went to the library and checked out some books, pretty technical stuff, and studied up."

"I knew that's what you'd do. Mom used to say you were born with your nose in a book. You could have just asked me."

"Uh huh." He lowered his gaze, suddenly uncomfortable, at a loss for the words he had spent his life living in. How do you talk to your sister about her incurable disease? How do you ask her what it's like to be trapped inside a rigid, trembling body you can no longer control, a prisoner within a sarcophagus of flesh? Jamison awkwardly put his finger on the table, tracing a line in a thin layer of dust.

Monna patted his hand. "I'm not trying to make you uncomfortable, Jamison. I'm just saying, you could have. You could now."

"I didn't think people liked talking about that, about their, you know, afflictions."

Monna snorted. "Ben's the same way. Men are so stupid. Why wouldn't I want to talk about it? What *don't* I talk about? You were always the quiet one in the family, Jamison, not me. I told Ben, I said, 'We better talk about this. I'm stuck with it for the rest of my life, which if there's any justice in the world will be short. Who wants to live forever as a cripple?' I told him he better get to flapping his lips."

"Okay," Jamison said. He frowned, drew himself up in his chair, and formally clasped his hands in his lap. "Let it be known that on this eighth day of April, in the year 2017, I am formally inquiring of one Monna Christine Van Hollen, a party with a vested interest in, but not expressly limited to, the disease known as Parkinson's, what it is like to have said affliction, also known as Progressive Supranuclear Palsy."

Monna stood, leaned across the space between them, and punched him in the chest.

* * *

"I was painting one day in the studio," she said. She scooted to the edge of her chair and rested her elbows on the table, her legs tucked to one side, animated, wanting to talk. "I had these great photos of the river I'd taken that week, and I was anxious to get to work. It was beautiful out, just a beautiful summer day—you'll see for yourself what it's like here in a couple months if you stick around. I had all the windows open; I remember it was just so lovely outside and I wanted to go and take a walk along the river, but I wanted to paint even more, so there I was, working. I always wanted to paint more than anything.

"Sometimes my hands would tremble a little, but I hadn't given it much thought because I said, you know what, I think I was 56, everyone trembles a little when they get old. I know lots of people who have shaky hands; it's not, well, it's not normal per se, but in your fifties you're not 23 anymore, you know what I'm saying? And it kind of runs in the family, right? Gramma Everett had shaky hands. I was always scared I'd get it too, so I kind of suppressed the thoughts I had about all that, like if I didn't think about it, it wouldn't happen to me. And besides, the shaking had never been much of a problem before and it always went away after a few minutes. But that day it was really bad. It was ruining my work. I could barely hold the brush, and my strokes were all wrong. I was using some pretty expensive cold-pressed paper and I didn't want to ruin it, watercolor's tricky enough as it is. Ben and I were down at the Infirmary the night before, and he thought maybe it was the alcohol, something like the, um, what's that thing called? *Delirium tremens.* Me too, that's what I thought. So I finally cleaned my brushes and took a walk, which is what I wanted to do anyway. When I got back a couple hours later, my right hand was still shaking. That's when I knew."

"You knew you had Parkinson's?"

"I knew. The shaking had never lasted that long before. We went to a neurologist in Bozeman and he took a bunch of tests and then he sent me to a specialist in Salt Lake and they took a bunch of tests and a couple weeks later that's what they told us. I had two weeks to prepare myself. I think I knew deep down that the diagnosis wasn't going to be any good, so I'd sort of accepted it. But Ben kept telling me it was nothing, they weren't going to find anything, he didn't want to hear me say that I thought it was bad. *Knew* it was bad. So when we got the official diagnosis it just hit him really, really hard. Harder than me, I think. You have to remember, I *knew*. He wouldn't let himself know. He walked into the living room like he was in a trance and sat on the sofa and turned on the TV, never changed the channels, just stared at it, like the same show had been running for two weeks and he was just now able to see it and it wasn't even his favorite show."

Monna paused and looked at Jamison and then down at her coffee cup. "Oh," she said. "I need a refill. You?" Jamison nodded. Monna got up and retrieved the pot. She filled his cup and set the pot on the table on a wooden coaster. The coaster had a painted house wren peeking out of a painted house.

"So after that, the symptoms went away for a couple months," she said. "No hand tremors, nothing. Ben kept saying I was cured, like if I just believed it enough it would happen. I kept telling him to stop but he wouldn't listen. The doctors warned us that's the way it was, that in the beginning stages you get the symptoms for a little while and then they go away for a long time but they always come back. They came back a few months later and Ben took it harder the second time around than the first. I think by then he'd really convinced himself I was cured. He sure was trying to convince me of that. I finally gave up and went along with him because he was so miserable even though I knew he was fooling himself, except maybe I really wanted to believe it a little myself. You never give up hope, right? Now I realize that was a mistake. I shouldn't have let him. But it's not like I didn't have issues of my own I was dealing with."

Monna sipped from her cup. "This is good," she said. "It's French Vanilla." She leaned back in her chair, crossing her legs. "So anyway, to get to the question you didn't ask, thank you very much, there are five stages of the disease; five is terminal, or might as well be. You can't get out of bed. They tell me I'm probably somewhere between stage two and three. Some days like today I'm almost normal, I feel like my old self. Other days, well, you've seen me."

"And there's no cure." Jamison, a statement.

"Nope. But it isn't like I'm going to die tomorrow. I'll live long enough to wash the dishes, if that's what you're worried about. They tell me this can go on for years." Monna smiled gayly and tilted her head, as if she were still the kid giving him the same knowing smile after she'd caught him in the garage drinking beer with Toby Endicott, his one enduring friendship in high school. It had been hard to put one over on Monna, even when she was little.

"And there's this other thing," she said. "Hallucinations. Some people get them, some people don't. Unfortunately, I do."

Jamison bent forward. "You mean, you see things? Like on LSD?" Jamison had taken LSD once in grad school. He neither regretted it nor had any intention of ever taking it again.

"I don't know what LSD hallucinations are like," Monna said. "Don't you, like, see little green people and stuff? I get them every few months, they seem to come in clusters. For me, it's like, everything moves. You know what I'm saying? Everything—the house, the whole living room, the river, the highway, the horses—everything *moves*. But not like they're supposed to. Different. I can't explain it any better than that."

"Moves around? Moves from here to there? What?"

"It just moves," Monna said. "Some things sort of expand and contract, but it's not exactly like that, either. It just *moves*. I don't know what else to say. It might be the meds."

Jamison heard Ben stomping his feet outside and then the back door opened. Ben took off his vest and slapped the dust off and hung it behind the door. Monna winked at Jamison and then turned toward her husband. "Darling," she said, grinning.

* * *

Monna insisted Ben take a seat. She glanced at her empty cup and he quickly reached for the pot and filled it for her, then slid it back on the burner. But instead of returning to his seat, he stood behind her, his hands resting on her shoulders. She squeezed his hand, letting it linger a moment before returning it to her lap. They were staring at him.

"Monna says you might want my help on something?" Jamison said. Ben glanced down at his wife.

"I told him you might need some help on that Bozeman project," she said.

"Oh, that." He had begun gently massaging his wife's shoulders. "Yeah, I might. It's an addition, which is no big thing as far as the framing goes, but I got to pour a foundation and set the trusses. I can't do that by myself anymore. You ever do any construction work, anything?"

Jamison shrugged. "I helped some friends build a kennel once, for their dog. We built the doghouse, too, if that helps. And then I helped some friends who were remodeling their house put up some of that white wallboard stuff. But that was a long time ago."

"Sheet rock. Okay, that's about what I thought. I'll get back to you in a couple days. I gotta pencil this all out."

"I mean, I'm happy to help, if you need a warm body. I'm good at taking orders."

"Yeah, okay. I'll get back to you. I can't do anything until it warms up."

Monna was smiling at him, the corners of her mouth flickering in an amused grin.

"Anything you want me to read?" Jamison said. " I could study up on it." Oblivious.

Ben frowned, exhaled, then strode without a word into the bedroom, trailing impatience like exhaust from the tailpipe of a car. He strode back carrying a yellow legal pad and a pencil, which he slapped down on the table. "Okay, I'm gonna sketch it out real quick. This is all you got to know." He bent over the pad, his pencil poised. He drew a rectangle that filled the bottom half of the page, bisected by vertical lines. "Those lines there, those are the wall studs," he said. Then he drew two closely parallel lines beneath the rectangle. "And those, that's the foundation. It's a slab so I'm gonna grade it out myself, rent a Bobcat." He drew some triangles over the rectangle. "Those are trusses. There's seven of them. Been better to break on eight, lots better, would of saved on OSB, lumber, sheet rock, other stuff when you trim it out, but it's in this guy's backyard and he don't have the room. Seven's not enough for them to send out a crane, I got to set them by myself. Except you can't set them by yourself. Takes two guys to set a truss by hand." He stabbed the tip of his pencil into the legal pad, tore off the sheet, folded it in half, and slapped it against Jamison's chest. "There. You're good to go. That's all you're gonna need. I've done this a million times. That's an exaggeration, but not much."

Monna was standing now, leaning back against the kitchen counter, and Ben moved to her side. Again, they were staring at him.

"Jamison, Ben and I need to talk about something," she said. Jamison saw her slip her arm around her husband's waist.

Jamison glanced from one to the other, and the clouds began to part. "Oh," he mumbled, color surging to his cheeks. He felt like smacking his forehead with the palm of his hand, just for effect. He stood and waved the paper Ben had given him and folded it in quarters and put it in his shirt pocket, then pushed his chair back under the table. It made a loud, grating screech on the linoleum. "The coffee cake was … *exquisite*," he said. He spun on his heel and took two hasty steps toward the door.

"Good bye, Jamison," Monna said.

"Good bye, Jamison," Ben said.

Jamison closed the door behind him and Ben's fingers slid down his wife's hips and found her hand.

"*I'll* show you exquisite," he said.

Chapter 7

Jamison strode by the studio window, caught a glimpse of yellow out of the corner of his eye, and backpedaled for another look. Unbelievably, Leviathan was sitting on the woodpile, gazing at him through the window as if he were watching an animated television screen, as if, Jamison thought, the big cat were waiting for a speech. Jamison stared. He hadn't seen Leviathan in weeks, and knew he was still living in his secluded warren only because the tin cans of cat food he put out every morning were licked clean by the following day. The cat's tracks, gone with the melting snow, had long since disappeared.

Jamison stared, as spellbound as if he were watching a Bengal tiger in the jungles of India. Before today, he'd seen the cat only in glimpses, as it dashed for the safety of the willows along the river. Leviathan was older than the dashing, Disneyesque creature he had imagined, its fur matted and scruffy, its face scarred from countless turf battles. But even from this remove, he could see how large the cat's feet were. As if he had read Jamison's thoughts, Leviathan leaned to the side, lifted one big paw and put it down again, as if testing his own weight. Jamison stood before the window, rivetted. And then remembered: he'd forgotten to replace the can of food that morning. He backed slowly away from the window and hurried to the kitchen, his heart racing, hoping he still had food left in the cupboard. To his relief there were two cans remaining; he'd have to make a trip to the General Store soon. He grabbed one, quickly peeled back the lid and slid into his hiking boots—too excited to bother with his socks—and eased out the door, tip-toeing as quietly as he could around the far wall of the studio that hid him from view. Then he peeked cautiously around the corner.

Leviathan's green eyes were staring directly into his. As slowly as he could will himself to move, Jamison extended one foot, then another, easing into full view from behind the wall. Equally slowly, the cat sank until his head was resting on his paws, the tip of his tail flicking nervously back and forth, as if in sync to his beating heart. Jamison took another step and still Leviathan remained. Now Jamison was within fifteen feet, the animal gazing into Jamison's astonished face, its eyes feral and wary. Jamison held out the open can of cat food. "Here, kitty, kitty," he whispered.

It was too much. Leviathan sprang to the ground and retreated in a nervous trot toward the safety of the river. Just before he disappeared over the bank, he glanced over his shoulder. Elated, Jamison found the empty can from the day before and bent down to replace it and was seized with a notion: why not put the new can on the studio side of the wood pile, the side from which he could see the mountains, the side from which he could watch the cat—*his* cat—and the cat could watch him? Separated only by a pane of glass, they could begin the process of getting to know one another. He walked to the near side of the wood pile, checked the studio window to make sure it was within viewing distance, and placed the new can at his feet. Then he returned to the studio, taking one last look at the bank of the river, at the spot from which the cat had vanished. Leviathan, hidden in the grass, watched him.

* * *

Jamison heard the blare of the stereo before he rapped on the door of the shop. He let himself in. Ben was bent over a howling machine and didn't look up. Nor did he turn down the music. Ben shut off the machine and straightened up, his face hidden behind a dust mask and safety glasses, and placed the mahogany trim he'd been routing on a stack of several similar pieces. Jamison pointed at the receiver and Ben nodded and turned down the volume. A lot.

"I gotta have it loud so I can hear over the router," Ben said. "It's kind of obnoxious, but not as obnoxious as this." He slapped his palm on the router table and a cloud of dust spurted into the air. "You gonna be in here for long, you should put on one of these." He tossed Jamison a dust mask and Jamison stretched the two elastic bands over the back of his head. The mask pinched his nose uncomfortably. His breath immediately fogged his glasses, and he slid them down his nose so they would clear. Ben waved his finger in the air, leaving faint, gauzy trails in the dust drifting down. "This shit'll give you lung cancer," he said.

Jamison walked over to the stack of wood and picked up the piece of mahogany Ben had routed and turned it over in his hands. The piece had been expertly shaped with fluted grooves. "Looks like fun," he said, doubtfully. He put it back down.

"Actually, it kind of is," Ben said. "I always liked making stuff." He tapped the pile. "This stuff here, that's to trim out a window I'm swapping out. You can't buy that profile anymore, it don't fit any standard profiles they make anymore. Anderson, Pella … good windows, but they don't do custom profiles, or it costs like a mother if they do. But I got enough bits for my router I can make anything, long as it's not *too* exotic. It's one of the ways I out-compete the big outfits; big outfits can't afford to pay some guy shop time to shape custom profiles. Plus, the dimwits they hire don't know how. And second, the ones that do suck at it, probably don't even know how to keep a piece of wood from hitting a knot and blowing up. I know of one guy almost lost his eye that way. Me, the cost of custom profiles is included in the bid, if it comes down to it."

"So now I know about shaping profiles," Jamison said.

"Yup."

Jamison held the mask away from his nose for a second so he could breathe, then let it snap back in place. Warmed by his breath, the filtered air behind the mask was hot and moist, like the inside of an unventilated bathroom after a shower. He wouldn't want to be stuck in one of these things for hours on end, as he'd seen Ben do in his shop, and hoped he wouldn't have to wear one on the theoretical job site that Ben was theoretically going to need help with at an unspecified future date. He thought about asking, then changed course, remembering that he'd come to make amends for his thick headedness the morning before, feeling anew the same tongue-tied awkwardness.

"So the other day …" Jamison said, letting it hang.

Ben took off his safety glasses and waited, amused. Ben, Jamison thought, was the only person who could look down on a man who was a foot taller than him. But Jamison would not react. "I mean, I may be slow, but eventually I get it," he said. "Consider it a learning disability."

Ben grinned. "Oh man, we had a good time with *you*," he said. "I told Monna, I said, 'next time we decide to do the wild thing, let's just paint up a big old sign, big old capital letters, and stick it right down in front of him. Maybe he'll get *that*. I know he can *read*."

Beneath the mask, Jamison felt his cheeks burning. "No one ever accused me of being good at taking a hint," he said.

"That's for shit sure, Sherlock." Ben slid his mask down around his neck. "You can take that thing off now. They get hot." He walked around the router table and picked up a dust pan and brush. He worked the brush along the base of the fence and then along the top of the table and then swept the accumulated dust into a neat pile, which he nudged into the dustpan and carefully slid into a galvanized garbage can so the dust wouldn't roil back out. Then he hung the pan and brush on hooks beneath the table.

"When was the last time you had a girlfriend?" Ben asked.

Jamison blinked. He thought about the woman who had told him, apologetically, that he was too emotionally distant. That reading books was not the same as living.

"That would be five or six years ago, maybe more like six," Jamison said. "Actually, maybe more like seven or eight. We did the Match.com thing and dated for a few weeks, nothing serious. She was a science teacher, but from another district. I was getting ready to retire. Nice enough lady."

"If she was so nice, why'd you only go out for a few weeks?"

Jamison gazed at the pegboard tool rack behind Ben, at the tools hung in orderly rows. "I don't know. Why does anyone only date someone for a little while? It wasn't working. No chemistry, maybe. Chemistry's important."

"Okay, yeah." Ben said. "What you just said, that's what I'm talking about." He folded his arms and stared at the floor. "So it's like, you know … with me and Monna, it's been a long time." Jamison could barely hear him over the drone of the stereo. "Too long. The Parkinson's …" And couldn't finish, looked at Jamison for just an instant and then away.

Jamison found himself blinking, nodding stupidly, waving to cut him off, please let's not talk about *that*. For god's sake, she's my *sister*.

"I know," he said, too loudly. "I know." But Ben had put his mask back on and switched on the router and Jamison wasn't sure he was still listening.

* * *

Leviathan did not appear the next morning, or the next. But he was clearly still around; the cans of cat food Jamison had stocked from the Aden General Store—he'd bought out their meager supply and ordered more—were empty each morning, licked clean no matter which flavor he bought, consumed with a feline gusto Jamison couldn't fathom. The opened cans smelled like salmon-scented excrement to him, and didn't look much more appetizing.

Monna's streak of nearly symptom-free living extended into the week. One day, while Ben was holed up in his shop, she drove his truck to Livingston to purchase supplies for spring. In a rush, she drove from location to location: buying flower seeds for the halved, whiskey-barrel planters on either side of the front door, oil seed for the bird feeders Ben had hung in a half dozen locations around their property, a barely rusted True Temper spade and a nearly new garden rake she bought for three dollars apiece at a garage sale. Jamison asked her to buy more cat food and please don't tell Ben. Upon her return, she put the cat food inside the door of the studio.

Monna had given Jamison a folding lawn chair she'd retrieved from the stable, found behind the saddles and tack that belonged to the horse's owners. Jamison propped the chair against the back of the studio, the better to view the snow-capped Crazies in the distance. It was quite pleasant, halfway through April; the temperature in the high forties, the sun absorbed by the logs behind him and warming his perpetually chilly bones as though he were swaddled in a blanket. Jamison gazed at the sky. The warmth radiating from the logs was like the warmth of his sleeping bag in the morning, like the warmth of a car left in bright sun on a cold day. Even the stark spires of the Crazies seemed supple and generous, as if the snow reflecting the blazing afternoon sunlight were sending its rays directly to him. Across the river the horses grazed, plucking new shoots of grass from between their hooves. Monna had told him that, with rain, they had enough grass in their two pastures to carry four horses through the summer. In the fields beyond the Van Hollen's quarter section, Jamison spied whitetail deer. Occasionally one would raise its tail, prance several feet in mock alarm, and then, as if satisfied that all around had noted its concern, resume grazing.

Jamison, drowsy with warmth, closed his eyes, and when he opened them again Leviathan was sitting before the woodpile, staring at him. At the same moment, he heard the back door of the main house open, and saw Ben, fifty yards away, on the graveled path from the house to the shop. Ben saw him, waved, and then continued on, without another backwards glance. Leviathan watched, no more concerned than if he had been observing the horses in the pasture or the placid deer beyond.

Jamison wondered what Ben had seen, if the cat was even visible at that distance. If Ben had been looking for a cat he certainly would have seen Leviathan; with last year's brown grass flattened by the winter's snow, the cat's yellow coat would have been easy to spot. But Ben had shown no sign of recognition other than his cursory wave.

Jamison returned his gaze to Leviathan. He knew he'd put the cat's food out that morning; Leviathan was sitting just a few feet from the empty can. Slowly, Jamison bent forward in his chair, trying to make himself smaller and less intimidating. He put his hand on the ground and slowly ran his fingers through the grass. "Kitty, kitty," he said quietly. This time, instead of crouching in alarm, Leviathan arched his back, his tail upright and curled over playfully. Jamison said, "Kitty, kitty," and Leviathan paraded back and forth along the wood pile, languorously rubbing his back, his tail arched, his eyes never leaving Jamison's. But when Jamison slid out of his chair and got on all fours the cat froze, his innate wildness returning, and stared with unblinking eyes. And then, in a twinkling, he leapt to the top of the woodpile and disappeared over the other side.

"Well," Jamison thought. "Progress."

* * *

He knew it wasn't optimal to be visiting the shop so soon. Visiting too soon might betray his anxiety about Ben having possibly discovered Leviathan, revealing his hand. But Jamison had never been a good poker player; in point of fact, he was a lousy poker player and everyone back home knew it. He decided to go. Casting about for an excuse, he found a plausible one: a bird house.

Ben was standing over a cabinet saw, cutting the trim he'd been working on when Jamison had last visited. Jamison found the dust mask where'd he'd left it on the router table and pulled it over his nose and mouth, then took off his glasses and slid them in his pocket. Ben cut four lengths of trim, turned off the saw, and slapped the pieces down on the outfeed table, fitting them together in a rectangle, tight and true. "Perfect," he said.

Jamison slid his mask down around his neck. "I saw you coming out here," he said, "and thought I'd stop by for a visit."

"Well, you're Johnny on the spot. I'm about done. Tomorrow I can frame out that window I been working on, then finish trimming the room out, then call the painters in, then get *paid*. Getting paid is *good*. I keep hearing about a construction boom but I ain't seeing one. No work all winter. Winters I usually get kitchen and bathroom remodels and painting jobs, which I hate—I *hate* painting. But I'm heading into spring running a deficit. Like the government."

"Yeah," Jamison said. "Well, like I said, I saw you going to the shop and thought I'd run up for a visit."

Ben walked past Jamison and said excuse me and retrieved the brush and dustpan from beneath the router table. "You never seen me go to the shop before? I go to the shop two, three times a week. I could, like, ride my bike or something, make you happier. I got a bike."

"You have a bike?"

"Nice one."

"I left mine in Minneapolis," Jamison said. "There was no room for it in my car. I didn't have a bike rack."

"You want to ride my bike, you can ride my bike anytime you want. It's over there in the back, between the wire feed and the quad. Might have to put some air in the tires. Monna was using it a couple years ago to work on her balance until that stopped working. Bike fits both of us. I'm taller'n her but she's got longer legs."

"Actually, that's not what I came up for, but I'd love to borrow your bike sometime, if it's not too small, maybe as soon as it warms up. They're talking about another storm moving in, maybe when that's done I'll see if I can raise the seat and make it fit. Actually, I came up to ask about your bird houses. I was wondering if maybe I could buy one?"

Ben braced his arms against the router table, as if surveying the terrain. "You want to *buy* a bird house? Nobody ever wanted to *buy* one of my bird houses before. How much you want to pay for a bird house?"

Jamison hadn't got that far. "I don't know. I mean, whatever's fair. Whatever you want."

"Hmm," Ben said. "You want a bird house, huh? Just exactly what do you want a bird house for? What kind of bird?"

"I don't know. There are different houses for different birds? What would you recommend?"

"Well, let's see what I got," Ben said. He picked up the cardboard box behind the door and carried it to the outfeed table. Then he began pulling out the bird houses within: some were tall and rectangular, some short and compact, some painted, some not. "Okay, you got your two basic species at this end of the valley. I'm assuming you want to put it up next to the studio, right? You got your house wrens and you got your western bluebirds. They both live in houses. But bluebirds are kind of snotty about the company they keep, so I'd go with the wrens. Plus, they have a real pretty song."

Ben held up one of the wren houses so Jamison could see. It was squat, and like several of the others, rendered in bright primary colors by Monna's artistic hand. The house Ben held had a southwestern theme, a red sun setting over a green saguaro, a tiny brown bird perched on one of the cactus' arm-like branches.

The setting was wrong but Jamison liked the colors. "How about that one?"

"That one's pretty special," Ben said. "Only one she painted like a desert. Don't ask me why. But that makes it a one-off."

"Okay, cool," Jamison said.

"You know how to put these things up, right?" Ben peered at him. "No, I can see you don't. You look around our place, probably all the houses look like I just threw them up at random. But I didn't. Bluebird houses you put on fence posts 'cause bluebirds like open space all around. But wren houses you put in the trees because wrens like to hide in trees. It's like those houses I got outside the bedroom window. Put them up too high and the hawks see 'em, wrens won't use 'em because they're scared of the hawks. Then again, you put them too close to the ground and you run the danger of ..." Ben flicked the bird house with his finger. "Cats." He looked at Jamison.

"I haven't seen any cats," Jamison said.

"Me neither. I'm just saying. You want house wrens, do it like I'm telling you."

Jamison's heart ticked up. He could feel his pulse throb a little and wondered if it showed. "Actually," he said, "I was thinking of giving it to someone. Sort of a gift, actually. Nothing special, just, you know, a friend."

"Now you're talkin'," Ben said. "A *present*. Presents cost more, 'specially presents going to women, 'cause women are just naturally more expensive, 'case you haven't figured that out already. What kind of present would this be?"

Jamison shook his head with exasperation. This was getting tiresome. "C'mon, Ben! I don't know! Enough of the third degree, already. What do you want for a goddamn bird house?"

Ben held out the bird house and Jamison reached for it and Ben yanked it away. Ben smirked and Jamison rolled his eyes. *God*. Ben held it out again and Jamison ignored him.

"Go ahead, take it. Really."

Cautiously, Jamison held out his hand, palm up, as if expecting rain. Ben placed the bird house in it. "This one's free," he said. "Special introductory offer. Give your girlfriend a big wet kiss for me."

"She's not my girlfriend!" Jamison protested. "I just said a friend! Jesus! Friends that are women don't have to be girlfriends, you know."

"Uh huh. Right."

"Anyone ever tell you you're a dick, Ben?"

"Yeah," he said. "Monna."

* * *

Jamison put the bird house into his daypack last, so he could get to it without having to fish through the rest of the stuff he'd put in there. The weather forecast had been hinting at a spring storm, so he brought his raincoat and pile vest along, just in case. But at the moment it was pleasant: pushing fifty, calm and bright. Far above the pocked asphalt on Highway 89, thin rows of clouds marched across silent sky, a ghostly halo ringing the sun. Jamison could see it only by glancing obliquely in the direction of the light; when he looked at the sun directly the halo disappeared, as if direct eye contact burned it away. *It is ever thus, in this world and beyond*, he thought, not unpleased with the way he'd put the words together, the philosophical bent of his mind.

Maybe he'd ask Jessica for a pen and paper so he could write it down. Then he'd add it to the plot twists and scene descriptions he scribbled on a yellow legal pad he kept in a leather briefcase at the foot of his bed, in which he kept a smattering of notes and the sparse chronological narrative he'd been expanding for the 13 or 14 years he'd been planning to write The Book.

The Book was his novel. The plot thus far was a star-crossed story about a high school English teacher and his much younger lover, the teacher's rebellious former student. Years earlier, in a burst of inspiration, he'd hatched the idea and written the opening chapter, and in a celebratory mood, he bought the expensive leather briefcase to store future notes. But somehow the rest of The Book never materialized. He had papers to grade and real students to teach; and in the summer, when he had two and a half months largely at his disposal, he filled his lonely hours with books other people had written. It occurred to him that he might never finish The Book, but the thought was deeply unsettling—he had been *trained* for this—and he swatted it away. You didn't rush art. Books were written when the muse was perched on your shoulder.

Jamison felt the birdhouse pressing lightly against his back and adjusted the daypack's straps until it settled comfortably between his shoulder blades. Then he kicked up his stride to cruising speed. It was 22 minutes to the Infirmary from the studio; he hoped to shave off five minutes and fit in a cardio workout, as well. The snow had only recently cleared; like everyone else in Aden but Ben, who plowed through any weather in his dirty orange hoodie and canvas vest, Jamison had been housebound for weeks. It felt good to be on the road, walking.

There was an uptick in traffic today. The women drivers smiled at him; the men lifted a finger from the wheel with no change in expression. Jamison happily waved at them all.

When he approached a bend in the road he saw a small group of mule deer grazing in the ditch. One, a yearling, had wandered up to the roadside and cautiously begun to cross. When a car approached, it spun around on its hind legs and ran back toward the shoulder. But a truck from the opposite direction hit it head on, the impact shattering the passenger-side headlight in a screech of tires and tinkling glass. Jamison heard the yearling groan, a mournful wail, as if in terrible comprehension. The truck skittered down the highway, the creature trapped between the bumper and the road, the head on its broken neck bobbing like a rag doll. The driver finally was able to stop and boiled out from behind the wheel in a fury. Cursing, he examined the shattered headlight, then dragged the deer from under the bumper and kicked it into the ditch. Then he got back in his truck and sped away.

The entire episode had happened in an instant. Jamison followed the trail of blood and hair to where the animal lay head down in the ditch, a rope of twisted guts flung from its exploded belly. There was no last breath, no movement. It was dead.

At the Infirmary, still shaken, he told Jessica what he'd seen.

"It's evolutionary," she said. She pulled the beer tap over a glass, filled it, and set it before him. "We've only had cars for a hundred years, something like that. Deer have been around for eons. Another million years or so, they'll figure it out. You could have claimed that deer, you know, if you'd called up and got a permit. They just passed a law says you can do that."

Jamison shook his head. "Ben and Monna have got all the venison I want. I'm getting used to it. I can't say I'm a big fan yet." Still hearing the impact, the flesh against steel.

"That's about par for the course," Jessica said. She was wearing a silk t-shirt, the top of her phoenix and dragon tattoos, front and back, peeking at him above a lacey neckline. "Most of the men that aren't from around here say they like it, and most of the women I know don't. Even the ones born here. *Especially* the ones born here. I, personally, can take it or leave it. Depends on how it's cooked."

"*Life* depends on how it's cooked," Jamison said.

"Amen." She grinned and disappeared into the kitchen. Several men were seated in the dining area in back but the bar was empty. He spun around on his bar stool and gazed at Monna's painting on the wall behind him. She had told him she'd painted hundreds of landscapes, some including animals like elk, deer, wolves, coyotes. He wondered if his sister had ever painted a dead deer. He doubted that a painting of road kill would sell, no matter how gruesomely artistic. He got up from his stool to examine the painting more closely and was surprised at the intricacy of the details, what he'd heard her describe as 'the creation of form through brush work.'

"Not bad, huh?" Jessica was back behind the bar. He returned to his stool, nudging the daypack below him with his toe.

"It's not bad at all," Jamison said. "I never really looked at her stuff that much before. When she was growing up, I just took it for granted that she was good. That's what everybody said. I was always pretty good at writing, never had to work at it that hard, so I didn't. I keep thinking I'm gonna …" He tapped the bar with his finger, then shook his head. "It's like, when you take your talent for granted you run the risk of not paying attention to it. But she was never that way. Monna never quit trying to get better. She's only got a couple of her paintings up in the house, and none in the studio where I'm staying, where she used to do all her work, and she doesn't talk about it much. But people like her usually don't. They don't have to."

Jessica folded a bar towel in half, then again. "She's always been like that. We'd drive to town in that little red car of hers—God, was that ever fun—and talk about everything: men, who was screwing who, where we were gonna eat for lunch, everything but painting. I used to think it was just because it never came up. But after a while I saw things different. I'd be like, 'that's a really nice painting, Monna!' and she'd just kinda shrug and smile, not say much. Like she didn't have anything to add to what she thought was obvious."

Jessica leaned her elbows on the bar. "For a long time, I didn't get that. You take me, I never shut up. I'll talk all day about anything. But now I think Monna didn't talk about her painting because painting is what she *lived*. Like some people don't talk about their kids because they're just too close to them, can't imagine themselves as separate from something they love that much. They *are* their kids, just like Monna *is* her painting."

Jessica made a perfunctory swipe with the towel. "I don't know if that makes any sense at all," she said.

"Yes," Jamison said. "It does."

* * *

Jamison ordered a beef and bean burrito, the sole item of Mexican food on the menu. Jessica delivered a gargantuan plate of food ten minutes later. Half the plate was covered by a mound of shredded lettuce; a huge burrito, still sizzling, lay beside it, smothered in enchilada sauce and cheese. Buried under the shredded lettuce was a heaping ration of refried beans. There was more food here than he could eat in two days.

Jessica chuckled. "Nobody ever starved to death in this bar," she said. "I told Grant we're feeding people way too much. They fill up and don't have to come back for a week."

"I can see why," Jamison said.

"Might put some meat on your bones," she said. "Wouldn't kill you to add a few pounds. You're stringy as a jack rabbit."

This was not news. No matter how much he ate, the scale refused to budge, and his long, toothpick arms remained long and toothpick-like. Now, officially a senior, he'd developed a small, annoying pot belly, which was unnoticeable fully clothed but flopped over the elastic band on his boxers when he perused his scrawny physique in a mirror. He wondered if some inscrutable law of physics, a science he'd never understood, might explain belly fat one could physically see that nonetheless didn't register on a scale. Was it analogous to the theory of relativity, where time travelers on a journey returned before they had begun? Or was it smoke and mirrors? His foot brushed his daypack, and remembering the bird house, he hoisted the daypack onto the bar.

"Hey," he said, "I have something here for you, if you want it." He fumbled with the drawstring and reached inside, immediately self-conscious. What kind of gift was a painted bird house? A *stupid* gift. He pulled the bird house from his daypack and set it on the top of the bar. "Ta da," he said.

Jessica picked it up and held it to the light slanting through the window. "It's *beautiful*," she said. "The desert."

"Monna painted it. Ben made it but Monna did the artwork. See these?" He tapped the ridgeline. "Those are dovetails. Only bird house in Montana with hand cut dovetails." It pleased him that she seemed pleased; maybe a birdhouse wasn't such a stupid gift after all. "Ben's got a whole box of them in his shop," he said. "I liked this one the best and he said I could have it." Then he mumbled, "A pretty bird house for a pretty lady." The instant the words left his mouth Jamison felt his face turn crimson, and he blushed so deeply that his image in the mirror behind the bar, magnified by the soft light, made him look beet red and distorted, as if Monna had painted his face in fat strokes with a red brush. Jesus, he couldn't believe he was going on like this.

"Aw, that's so nice of you," Jessica said. She leaned across the bar and pecked him on the cheek, embarrassing him further. "I'm going to put this in back, where it won't get scratched or anything. I have a perfect spot for it at the house."

Jessica walked into the kitchen, the birdhouse cradled in her arms, and then Jamison remembered: Monna and Ben were going to the hot springs in White Sulphur Springs tomorrow and had invited him to go. Monna's symptoms had returned, and the hot soaks helped. For a moment Jamison considered his options: perhaps Jessica would want to go. There was plenty of room in Ben's truck.

But giving her the birdhouse had exhausted his small reserve of courage. When she returned, beaming, thanking him again for the wonderful gift, he could only nod and smile, too self-conscious to utter another word. He hoisted the daypack over his shoulder, quietly slipped a twenty dollar bill under his glass, and waved good bye as he walked out the door, the half eaten burrito cooling on his plate.

Chapter 8

"We've done this what, about a million times?" Monna turned slowly to look at her husband, who sat across from her in the driver's seat. After a week of largely symptom-free living, the sudden return of her affliction was startling. Jamison sat behind them in the crew cab, his legs shoved awkwardly into the cramped space behind the passenger seat. He'd noticed her deterioration the minute he'd opened the door to their home, Ben's truck idling just outside the garage, the automatic garage door lowering an inch at a time and protesting loudly as though giving voice to Monna's silent, tortured movement. She had struggled with her coat, but peevishly turned her back when Ben offered help. Both men watched in uneasy silence as she wrestled with first one sleeve and then the next, as helpless as if they'd been watching a dying fish circle an aquarium. Once her coat was on, she forced a smile. "It's only about forty-five minutes to White Sulphur," she said, as if answering Jamison's unspoken question. "It's kind of a cool little town. I used to paint there. Wait'll you see the hot springs." Ben handed Jamison a towel rolled around a loaner pair of swim trunks; Ben's thick waist meant the trunks would be at least an approximate fit on Jamison's bony hips.

They were silent for the first ten minutes of the drive. Ben stared through the windshield, his lips pursed, one hand on the wheel, the other resting in his lap. He did not look at his wife, who seemed absorbed in the landscape streaming by the passenger window. Jamison, watching the two from the backseat, cast about for a way to ease the tension. Finally, he found one. "Look!" he said.

Ben and Monna looked where he was pointing and Monna's furrowed brow relaxed. "Elk!" she chirped. "Oh look, Ben."

A small herd of elk was milling anxiously behind a barbed-wire fence a dozen yards from the highway; several had already leapt over the fence and were trotting across the road in single file. None so much as glanced at the approaching truck. Ben slowed to a crawl and then stopped to let them pass.

Jamison counted eleven elk, none with antlers. "Are they all females? I don't see any males," he said.

"Bulls throw their horns in March," Ben said. "I've seen a few still have horns this time of year, but not usually. You can check the size, though. There! Look at that big guy in back. That's the bull. You're lucky. Bulls are usually off by themselves this time of year, don't want nothin' to do with the cows. Guess he figures on getting himself some before he has to fight for it." He grinned and looked at Monna, who rolled her eyes.

The elk seemed to loosen Ben's tongue. He pointed out the town of Ringling, a cluster of tin barns and dusty homes woven together in a net of unpaved roads, all of which seemed to terminate at an ancient bar fronted by an elaborate wooden façade. "Jimmy Buffett, he wrote a song once about that place right there," Ben said. "Used to be on the jukebox at the Murray in Livingston. Probably still is, they still got juke boxes anymore. When I was a kid, bunch of us would drive all the way over here from Three Forks just so we could get drunk in the Ringling Bar and cut loose on that song. Can't even remember if we had fake ID's. Nobody cared."

Monna gazed at the mountains to the east. They had passed a brief declivity at the northern end of the Crazies, a breach in an unbroken line of rugged spires, and now another series of peaks arose from the prairie, less precipitous than the mountains to the south. One peak stood above the rest, still capped with snow.

"Which ones are those?" Jamison asked.

"Those are the Castles," Monna said, "and that tall one's Elk Peak. Kind of appropriate, considering what we just saw."

"They're really pretty," Jamison said.

"I think so too," she said. "I used to come up here all the time to paint. But nobody wants paintings of quiet places like the Castles. They want paintings of places they know, like the Crazies and the Bridgers, big, dramatic peaks with roiling storm clouds. Drama's what sells. Nobody ever goes to White Sulphur, unless they're going to the hot springs."

"Those two landscapes we got in the house, those are the Castles," Ben said. "Hung in a gallery for a year and nobody bought them, so we took 'em back. If Monna'd put in somebody getting shot like Charlie Russell they'd of sold in five minutes."

Monna tried to turn her head part way around, straining to realign her body so she could see Jamison, her discomfort and frustration at being unable to perform such a simple act revealed in the set of her jaw. She pushed her clawed fist against the dash to gain an additional inch. "Yup," she said, her voice nearly lost in the rumble of the engine.

The road branched and they swung east and in a few minutes they arrived on the outskirts of White Sulphur Springs. Ben wheeled the truck into a modest motel complex whose rooms bordered two sides of an asphalt parking lot. "This is it," he said. He killed the engine and glanced through the windshield at a brooding sky. "Speaking of roiling storm clouds," he mumbled. He hopped out of the cab and gazed at the sky and then studied the cloud-shrouded mountains beyond while Monna pushed open the passenger door and slowly lowered one foot and then the other to the ground. Ben's aggrieved eyes caught Jamison's.

Jamison was surprised at how elaborate the hot springs was. He left his clothing on a bench in the dressing room beside folded stacks of jeans and boots and pearl-snap shirts from the dozen guests already in the pool. Outside, the complex surrounded a court yard and two large pools. A hand painted tableau on the motel's wooden walls rendered Indians, grizzlies, elk and buffalo existing cheek to jowl in pre white-man union. Jamison eased into the water as quickly as he could, conscious as always of his white, hairless torso, then frog-kicked to where Ben and Monna were already leaning against the side of the pool, the steam from the aqua green water fogging his glasses and blurring the edge of the world.

"This is nice," he said. He took off his glasses and swished them in the water, then put them back on. "Does the hot water help?" He sat opposite his sister, only his head and neck exposed, his arms waving languorously through the water like seaweed in a current. He felt the anxious knots in his shoulders loosen.

"A little," she said. "Nothing makes it go away. I'm still glad we came. It's pretty here."

"Pretty pricey," Ben said. Monna shrugged.

Jamison had thought the $7 admission a steal. In Minneapolis, it would have cost three times as much to do just about anything. Listen to a string quartet at the university commons. Attend a good play. Or buy a single bottle of the good cabernet some of his former students liked to buy, anxious to meet him after work, still calling him Mr. Everett despite his insistence that they call him Jamison. Tiny drops of condensation had begun speckling his glasses, and he took them off and shook them, a little annoyed, then peered at the sky. It was snowing. "Guess we got here just in time," he said.

"I knew this was gonna happen," Ben said. "Forecast said snow *tonight*. They never get it right."

"I think it's pretty," Monna said. "See if you can catch a snow-flake on your tongue." She stuck out her tongue and Jamison stuck out his, his head back, watching the snow spiral down from the immeasurable heavens in a feathery, gentle blanket of white, an infinitude of flakes vanishing like dreams the instant they hit the water.

Ben watched them. "You know," he said, "wind picks up, it ain't gonna be any fun driving home in this."

Monna lowered herself in the water until just her head was showing. "It'll be okay," she said. "Just relax."

"I am relaxed. I am. But you get a warm front like today, wind usually picks up and it can get nasty out. I ain't lived in the north end of this valley forty years not to know that. *You* know that, Monna. Jamison here, Jamison's blissfully ignorant. I'm not."

Jamison sank back into the pool. He felt the hot water lapping his chin. "Should we leave?" he asked. "We just got here." He didn't want to leave.

Ben sighed and folded his arms. The snow was heavier now, falling in fat, wet flakes into the steaming water. "No," he said. "Monna needs to soak. Not unless she's ready to go. You want to go, Monna?"

"Monna don't wanna," Monna said.

Ben shrugged. "So I guess we ain't goin' yet," he said. He took a deep breath, ducked under water, pushed off the side of the pool, and swam halfway across beneath the surface. He came up sputtering, shaking his head, and wiped the water from his eyes. Then he pointed at the far end of the pool. "I'm going to the steam room," he said. "Either of you want to go?"

Jamison shook his head. Monna slowly lifted one hand out of the water, her fingers bent, and waved goodbye. Ben looked from one to the other, said "okee dokee" under his breath and hoisted himself out of the pool and walked to the far end. Jamison noticed for the first time how bowlegged he was. Ben yanked open the door to the steam room and disappeared.

"I don't think he's enjoying himself," Monna said.

"I'm picking up on that," Jamison said. "What's wrong?" He had his ideas.

"I don't know. Coming here was actually his suggestion. He just wants to do anything that helps. He thinks the hot springs helps me with my muscle soreness, and sometimes it does, but it usually doesn't last long. But I do like it here; I always have. It's nice." She tried to smile, the corners of her mouth fixed in a porcelain grin, as if painted on the immobile face of a doll. "Someday I won't be able to do this at all. Maybe six months, maybe six years. The doctors don't know. Nobody knows anything. If I just *knew*, I could make some plans. And then I have good days like last week, and I think, 'it's gone.' Even though I know better, even though I've been through this a million times, I still think that. You can't help it. It seems unfair because it *is* unfair. I think that's what Ben feels, that it's not fair."

"But you're the one with the stupid disease, Monna! You're the one that has to live with all this shit!"

"You've never been married, have you?" she said, quietly. It wasn't a question. Behind the unmoving expression, behind the dead muscles, her eyes bored into his.

"Okay, I get that," Jamison said. "I'm sorry. I just don't, you know … I just don't understand how you guys deal with all of this."

"Neither do I," Monna said.

* * *

East of Livingston and north to Clyde Park and still north, ongoing; past the town's small homes and small green lawns and the single, two-pump gas station, the sweep of country is beautiful beyond any words fairly described and the new growth is lush and green even as the cottonwoods along the river burst into foliage. Then Aden. And a growing sense that the balance has shifted toward desolation, that presence recognized but not spoken of; the landscape austere yet achingly beautiful, austere as the beauty of the desert is austere, as is beautiful the encompassing loneliness of all unvisited regions where only an enduring handful of families can eke out a modest living from an exacting land. Beautiful from a distance.

The Shields River skirts Aden and then, diminishing upstream, wanders north and east before dissipating into parched, thirsty soil. To the west, between Aden and White Sulphur Springs, are forty miles of sagebrush and mountains and barbed wire, none an impediment to the gales that funnel out of the Castles and the Little Belts and the Big Belts and scour the valley floor, blowing sheets of granular snow across the highway that blind uncovered eyes and sand exposed faces raw, and which even now were clawing at the tightly closed windows of Ben's truck. Jamison jabbed his thumb into the window button, lowering the window two inches to get a good run at it, then ran it up again, the brief blast of cold air dusting his legs and the seat beside him with snow. But the howling around the edges of the windows continued.

Ben tried to bore his truck through the swirling white-out, his jaw set, cursing under his breath. Jamison, in the front seat on Ben's orders, bent forward in tense vigilance, both hands gripping the dash, searching for landmarks, road signs, snow poles, anything that might tell them where they were, whether or not they were still on the road or approaching a shoulder where they might unknowingly drive into a ditch from which they would be unlikely to get out, trying to grasp the ferocity of the blizzard that had erased the world before his eyes. That morning, when they'd left Aden for White Sulphur Springs, it had been sunny.

"Can you see the road at all?" Monna, sitting behind Jamison, was resting both hands on her knees, oddly impassive, her voice barely audible. As if this were an inconvenience.

"I can't see shit," Ben said through clenched teeth. He had slowed the truck to a crawl. Jamison could just make out the speedometer: 10 miles per hour. "I knew this was gonna happen," Ben said. He flicked on the lights, but they were instantly reflected back at him in the white maelstrom outside. He turned them off again.

Jamison heard a vehicle approaching from behind and in the next instant a semi roared past five feet from the driver's side of Ben's truck, throwing up a solid wall of snow that forced Ben to a complete stop. "God *damn* it," he said, slamming his fist into the wheel. "God *damn*, god *damn*."

They sat in an ocean of moving, swirling white that obliterated everything, so disoriented that it was as if the truck were in a monstrous glass snow globe, shaken by a giant hand and then set back in place, the whirling blizzard within blinding them all. Jamison felt disembodied, as if, freed from his seat belt, he might discover he was actually upside down.

"This ain't working," Ben said.

"Maybe we should wait it out," Jamison said. He knew it was a bad suggestion the moment the words left his mouth.

Ben jerked around to face him. "You see that truck just came by? We stop in the middle of the highway and one of those ass-holes'll be on top of us before he can hit the brakes and that's all she wrote."

Jamison nodded grimly and thought, we could pull over, get to the shoulder. But he said nothing and stared straight ahead. He had never seen anything like this. It was terrifying.

Ben glared at him and then ahead, through the windshield. He turned his lights on again and cursed and shut them off. Then he nudged the truck into the snowbank on the side of the road and put it in park and swiveled around in his seat.

"This is what we're gonna do. What we have to do. I'm gonna get out and walk ahead of the truck and try and keep us on the road. Jamison, you're gonna drive. You think you can do that? You hear what I'm saying, Monna?"

Monna said she heard.

Jamison felt a tiny spurt of electricity surge through his chest. "Sure," he said. "I can do that."

"It's automatic so you don't have to worry about a stick."

"Either way," Jamison said. "You might want to move the seat back a little."

Ben moved the seat back and then opened the door and slammed it shut behind him. Jamison opened his door and stepped into the wind and the blinding snow and walked around to the front of the truck to where Ben was standing. Ben had put his hoody up and Jamison couldn't see his face. He passed him and got into the driver's seat and reached down to see if he could move the seat back more and then Ben was out front, waving him forward.

Jamison's focus was exhausting. Ben would walk forward a few feet, then hold up his hand to stop, and Jamison would instantly hit the brakes, afraid of hitting Ben, whose seething anger Jamison half expected might melt the massive iron deer guard bolted to the frame. Then Ben would walk forward a few more feet at a different angle, motioning impatiently for Jamison to follow. They had left the hot springs at one, and the next time Ben motioned him to stop,

Jamison took a quick glance at his watch. It was now past three. He had no idea how long they would have to inch ahead through the storm; it seemed as though they had never *not* been crawling through a blizzard, undifferentiated white everywhere he looked, a world without color or gravity or shadow.

Monna sat in the back seat in silence. Jamison glanced over his shoulder, thinking of saying something upbeat, a word to ease the tension, and when he turned back Ben was gone.

He slowed the truck and then stopped and frantically looked to his right, to his left, behind him, wondering if Ben had wandered off and fallen into a drift, fighting panic, disbelieving that in the small arc of visibility in front of the truck, Ben was no longer there. He said, "Monna, do you see Ben?"

Monna shook her head.

"He disappeared someplace. You absolutely sure you don't see him?"

"No," Monna said.

"I've got to go find him," Jamison said. When he opened the door, the blast nearly wrenched it from his hands. He stepped into the gale and slammed the door shut with both hands and plunged forward, his head down to protect his face from the stinging pellets of wind-driven snow. He felt pavement beneath his boots and understood that he was still on the road, that the truck was still on the road, although whether he was on the right side of the road or in the lane of oncoming traffic, he had no idea. "Ben!" he called. "Ben!"

Jamison tried to think what to do. He decided to walk up the road as far as he could while keeping the truck in sight behind him. At ten yards out he could still see the truck, although barely, a dim gray outline in the all-encompassing white. He took a few more steps and suddenly Ben appeared before him, surprised. "What the hell are you doing out here?" he said.

"You disappeared. Monna was worried. We didn't know where you went."

"I was *peeing*," Ben said.

Jamison gaped at him and then looked away, put his hands under his armpits. His fingers were freezing.

"You think I should just stand there and whip it out in front of the truck?" Ben said. "Monna'd love that."

Jamison shook his head. "I don't …" He could think of nothing further to say. He turned and walked back to the truck, Ben on his heels. When they arrived Monna was not in the truck. Ben strode in three quick steps past Jamison and yanked open the crew cab door and Monna was not lying down out of sight, napping, as he had pointlessly hoped, as he had known she would not be.

"What'd you tell her?" Ben said, trembling with anger. "What'd you say to my wife?"

Jamison raised his hands in dismay, not believing this was happening again, sick at heart, distraught that he might have missed a cue, that he might have foreseen this. "Ben, I didn't tell her anything. She hasn't said a word since you left the truck. We didn't talk. I was following you."

Ben walked to the front of the truck and put his elbows on the hood and put his head in his hands and stared past Jamison into the raging storm, as if he could see her out there, clothed in white like an angel or an apparition, beyond the highway and the snow and the wind where no one could see anything.

"You better goddamn figure out where she went and you better goddamn find her right now," Ben said.

"Tell me what to do," Jamison said.

Ben's fists were clenched, white from the cold. Jamison noticed for the first time that he had taken off, or lost, his work gloves. "She can't be in front of us, we came from there," Ben said. He looked at the snow under his feet, bent over, then jabbed his finger at the ground. "I got tracks," he said. "Barely. She walked off into the ditch."

Jamison blindly followed Ben down and into the borrow pit, looking over his shoulder to keep the truck in view, certain he wouldn't be able to find it again if he lost it, sick with worry about his lost sister. "Monna!" Ben called, but his voice was obliterated by the wind. The snow was deeper in the ditch. Ben stooped, his hands on his knees, studying the rapidly filling tracks with intense concentration. They had begun to meander, crossing back over themselves, and the depth of the snow made it impossible to determine Monna's direction. Ben stood and cupped his frozen hands around his eyes and stared into the blizzard and then plunged up the opposite bank. Monna was sitting with her back to a barbed wire fence, watching them. The knit stocking cap she'd been wearing was in her lap, and the snow gathering on her long hair and eyelashes gave her a wizened look, as if she were an ancient crone, a sorceress alone with her potions.

"Monna," Ben said softly. He knelt and grasped her hands and pulled her to her feet. Jamison awkwardly took her arm, uncertain of what to say, ashamed of himself for no reason, uncertain if he should speak at all.

They held her between them and walked her back to the truck. Monna moved haltingly, one dragged foot at a time. She did not struggle, nor did she seem relieved at having been found. Ben and Jamison had plowed a wide furrow through the snow and the back trail to the truck was easy to follow. Ben opened the passenger door and helped her inside, lifting her legs one at a time onto the floorboard, then reached across her shoulder and buckled her seat belt. Monna said nothing and stared straight ahead through the windshield at the storm, which miraculously had begun to abate. Just above the still swirling ground blizzard, Jamison glimpsed blue sky, a tear in the white shroud that encompassed them. The storm had descended to just a few dozen yards above earth. Jamison got in behind Monna and Ben took the wheel and in less than a mile the worst of it was over, tufts of harmless, cottony snow slanting down, the shoulders and ditches sheathed in white but the highway wet and clear. Jamison heard Ben flick on the turn signal and spied the turnoff to their home. They had almost driven by it.

Ben pulled the truck into the driveway and stopped in the front of the garage, the motor idling, fingers tapping under the hood. He took his hands off the steering wheel and turned, facing his wife.

"What were you doing?" he said.

Monna shook her head.

"You could of froze to death. Could of died, we hadn't run you down. You know what it's like out there, that kind of weather."

"It was nice," Monna said.

"Nice," Ben said. He pivoted around and stared at Jamison, incredulous. "Nice. She says it was fucking *nice.*"

Monna slowly swiveled toward her husband, one hand clawing for purchase on the back of the seat. Her frozen features struggled to form a grimace but her eyes blazed from behind the immobile mask of skin. "Why didn't you just leave me?" she said. "It was *nice.*"

Chapter 9

"Guy says he wants $14,750 for it, firm," Ben said. He smiled and shook his head. "That's what they always say. We get down there and wave some cold, hard cash under his nose, I'm betting he'll come down a little. I'm thinking twelve five, maybe even twelve."

Jamison tried to absorb the thrust of this new conversation. Ben was planning to drive to Denver to buy Monna a car for her 64th birthday, a 1972 MGB Roadster he'd found on Craigslist. Cherry red.

"Ben, can we discuss this?" Jamison said. The sudden acceleration of Ben's plans, and Jamison's apparent inclusion in them, had left him with a case of cognitive whiplash. He'd been reluctant to talk to his sister about exactly what had happened during the storm; in the week since her near loss, he had stayed close to the studio, nursing a gnawing sense of guilt for something he couldn't quite put his finger on, afraid to broach the subject with her, uncertain whether he had done anything to be ashamed of. Yet that is exactly how he felt. He had thought that leaving the truck to look for Ben was the right thing to do, and he had wanted to do the right thing. Then Monna had disappeared, shuffling deliberately into the maw of a raging blizzard, and Jamison remembered only his panic, his confusion, his fear. Why had she left the truck? What had she wanted? The answers to those questions lurked in a locked room behind his thoughts, pressing under and around the door he'd closed against them like water seeping through a crack in a dam. Now he wanted to find a way to make amends—for acting badly with good intentions, to apologize for a mistake he wasn't sure he'd made.

"Fourteen thousand bucks is a lot of money," he said, spinning the numbers in his head, light suddenly showing at the end of a murky tunnel. "And then you have to add in what it's going to cost you to drive to Denver and back. So let's say five hundred bucks for both of us, gas and motel and food for a couple days, maybe three. Now you're talking fifteen thousand and change. I don't know, but I'll bet they didn't cost that much new."

"They didn't," Ben said. "I looked."

"So?"

"So the guy's redone everything from the ground up," Ben said. "Ring job and had the tranny rebuilt. Custom wire wheels, which aren't cheap. Reupholstered the interior. Canvassed the top. It's his hobby, takes in old cars and restores them mostly by himself, although he had the tranny done but he says he's got the receipt. Gave me some recommendations to call and I'm probably gonna. But it sounds clean. This ain't the first used car I ever bought."

"Uh huh." Jamison hadn't bought a used car in years, not since before he began teaching. He found new cars he liked—the least expensive he could afford, after diligent research—then kept them forever. Ergo, the Honda Passport he'd driven cross country to Montana, which he'd owned for nine years. He'd keep it for another nine, if he and the car lasted that long. Why on earth would Ben buy Monna an almost fifty-year-old car? He had no sense that she was pining away for a sportscar to relive the wild days of her youth. But then, he remembered, he'd barely spoken to her in a week and not nearly enough, to his disappointment, since he'd first arrived. He had assumed they'd spend evenings over a glass of wine talking about their shared past, about her plans for the future, the adjustments she'd had to make to her life since the onset of her disease. But, as often as not, he learned how Monna was feeling, what Monna was doing, what Monna was thinking, from Ben.

A week after they'd returned from the hot springs, Ben had informed him that Monna's symptoms had again begun to ease, and that morning, wanting to get out of the house, she'd felt well enough to drive the truck to Livingston for groceries and lunch with Jessica. Now he and Jamison were parked on lawn chairs on the bank of the river behind the house, the water churning with milky brown runoff a few yards from his feet. Two of the horses in the pasture were grazing and two, including the palomino, were idly studying them from the far bank, their ears swiveling lazily in the warmth of the day, a warmth Jamison couldn't have imagined two months earlier when he'd arrived. Beyond the pasture, beyond the green blush of winter wheat in the fields that rolled to the foothills of the mountains, the Crazies gleamed, snow-covered spires thrust toward a blazing sun. It was, Jamison mused, simply a lovely day. He had never thought he would see the valley, and this view, in quite this way.

Ben rocked forward in his chair and peered at the ground, then, standing, took two steps and bent over. He slapped his palm on the ground, then held up a small grasshopper between his fingers. The insect wasn't moving, its stiff, motionless legs dangling from its body as if arrested mid-hop.

"Hopper," Ben said. "That's the first one this year."

"Is it dead?"

"Nope. Froze. Another hour in the sun and it'll be hopping around like a Mexican jumping bean." He walked to the river and tossed the bug in the water. The hopper pirouetted downstream like a tiny green cork. "Thought maybe a trout would grab it, but it's too muddy," Ben said. "Hoppers are like prime rib for trout. Me, I like to feed 'em to the wrens, when they get back, which oughta be any day now."

"I'll bet that's cool, feeding your wrens."

"It'll be really cool if it ever actually happens," Ben said. "I've been trying for years to get one of them to take a hopper out of my hand, but no such luck. They're goosey little suckers. I keep trying, though. But we were talking about Monna's car."

"Back to that," Jamison said, still weighing the options in his head. "I'm thinking about something. But just for my own edification, do you happen to have fifteen thousand dollars lying around?"

Ben leaned back in his lawn chair and clasped his hands together, fingers and thumbs steepled, as if in thought.

"No," he said. "I got nine thousand in CD's, or whatever they're worth now. I bought them about five years ago when I was flush from a job. Monna doesn't have anything, last painting she sold was better'n three years ago. I can get a loan. They know I'm good for it. Never missed a payment yet."

Jamison was astonished. "All you have saved is nine thousand dollars? How are you going to retire on that?"

Ben snorted. "Who said I was gonna retire? I took social security at 62, would of been stupid to wait. Monna's still waiting on her government money, but when she gets it it's gonna help. I'm still healthy and I can still work. I never figured I was gonna be able to quit. Can't, so it's a moot point."

"Yeah but, Ben …" Jamison threw his hands in the air. "You can't just work until you die. Nobody works until they die. Sooner or later you have to quit, you'll be too old. I mean, look at me."

Ben shook his head. "No. That's wrong. I know this old geezer'n Bozeman runs a trim crew with two other guys and he's pushing eighty. Trim's easy work. He mostly manages stuff, says he never picks up a nail gun unless he has to. That's gonna be me in five or six years. I'm already moving in that direction. Trim work pays pretty good. And we can always take on more horses, we got plenty of grass."

"Nine thousand dollars." Jamison said. "That's it?"

Ben rested his arms on the arm rests and gazed at something across the river, maybe the horses. Three of the four had resumed grazing. The other ambled lazily toward the stable, stopped, shook its head, and continued.

"Yup," he said.

Jamison nodded once or twice and said that was good to know and settled back into his lawn chair and studied the muddy water churning at his feet. He had once asked Ben if he were worried about flooding and Ben said he was, but what was he gonna do about it? Jamison asked him if it had flooded before and Ben said it sure as shit had. Couple of times it got up to the foundation. But this year didn't look too bad; so far the snow pack was coming off nice and slow.

Jamison had sold his house in Minneapolis around this same time of year, early May, when the snowpack in his own yard had long since melted away. The Mississippi ran right through the middle of town, but he lived on a safe incline on the west side and flooding was not a threat, a selling point that he'd never considered but his realtor had. The house sold in less than a month to a young couple who had lived next to the river and had had enough of its moody fluctuations.

Jamison hadn't really needed the money—his modest pension supported him well enough and he picked up pocket money from his teaching gigs at continuing ed., but it was reassuring to have a couple hundred thousand dollars in index funds, which each year grew steadily, if not spectacularly, in value. He couldn't imagine gazing into the future from the imperceptibly slight vantage point of nine thousand dollars in CD's. He didn't know what a car loan would cost, but he suspected it was more than Ben and Monna could realistically afford. Monna had told him that they'd paid off their place a dozen years earlier—a smart financial move—but the increase in savings they had hoped to realize had somehow never materialized. She didn't know why.

Jamison didn't need to do the math: buying another car, and driving to Denver to do it, was a foolish idea any way you penciled it out. But he could easily afford this.

"So I've been thinking about Monna's car," he said. This time, he would do the right thing. "What are they going to charge you for a loan? It seems to me car loans aren't cheap."

Ben shrugged. "They're not that bad anymore. Recession knocked interest rates back down. It'd be a personal loan, not a car loan. Three to five years, like that. But I was always the type paid things off early."

Jamison pulled down the bill of his cap and grinned, enjoying the suspense. "Daddy Warbucks to the rescue," he said. "Have I got a deal for you."

* * *

North of Aden, Highway 86 runs west through the Bridgers, the road leisurely curving through bottomland on either side of a purling Flathead Creek and continuing past the settlement of Sedan, 99 souls still extant, before swinging south and cresting Battle Ridge, pickup campers and orange tents in the campground there, then descends in broad curves past the ski area and summer homes of recycled timber and river rock. Then Bozeman, a city as removed from its farming roots as the three-quarter ton Ford Monna was driving was removed from the long ago car she had loved.

This was the route she and Ben had chosen when she'd owned the MG, when they wanted to make a day of it, only later taking the interstate home to avoid the glassy-eyed deer on highway 86 that made nighttime travel in the frangible, bullet-like roadster a nerve-wracking game of Russian roulette. But today, in Ben's truck, she would not be going nearly so far. She spied the gravel road branching west and reflexively hit the turn signal, no car behind her for miles. She drove a hundred yards onto the road and pulled to the shoulder and killed the engine. She felt the tires settle into the incline that fell away into the ditch, where she wanted to be, where she'd been a hundred times before. Directly ahead was the northernmost spine of the Bridgers, the rifle-sight notch of Flathead Pass framed by the windshield. She had painted countless landscapes from this very spot. Beside her, a pad of Strathmore paper and a box of pencils lay on the seat.

She would try this one more time. As she had tried one more time before.

Monna propped the folding easel Ben had built for her on her lap, then clamped a sheet of paper to the top. She rested her hand on the pencils, willing the trembling to stop. She'd had some success with this, sometimes. But it was becoming more difficult.

She could not remember when she had finally known she was an artist. She had wanted nothing else but this; she could not remember in all her life when she hadn't been drawing or painting or wanting to learn about drawing or painting, but that was different from knowing you *were* an artist, that your work was who you had become, no less who you were than the way you spoke or the way you made love or the way you danced. Even into her early thirties she had not known.

But that had changed. That moment: looking back from the vantage point of a certain day she couldn't pinpoint in a certain year that had merged with all the others and realizing that nothing had changed nor would it because she already was and had always been what she had sought to become. That epiphany like the awareness of true color, that the sky had forever been blue exactly like this, only now she *understood*. She took a pencil from the box and began to sketch, her fingers thick and halting.

Thin lines for the mountains, broad strokes for the trees in the foreground, shading the parts hidden from the sun, adjusting the light, knowing intuitively how to do this. But something was wrong. The colors she saw in her head were not in the shadows nor were they in the trees nor in the mountains she was sketching. The color wasn't coming through the course lines of her pencil because the color wasn't there.

Learning she had Parkinson's had been devastating, as much for Ben as for her. But not knowing how much longer she'd be able to paint, or to sketch the studies that preceded her paintings, had forced her to bitterly reevaluate who she had become. She had withdrawn into silence while Ben raged. She had wanted to know how much longer she could paint but had been afraid to ask the doctors. And when finally she did, they had offered only vague answers; it depended on this, or on that. Well, now she had an answer.

Monna tore the paper from her easel and laid it beside her on the seat and placed the easel on top of the paper. Then she opened the door of the truck and walked to the opposite side of the road and threw her pencils into the ditch and drove back to Aden.

* * *

Upon seeing the big cat, Jamison felt a small, happy surge of excitement, as if he were greeting an old friend. For several weeks now, he could count on Leviathan waiting on top of the woodpile to be fed each morning. On the days he wasn't there, Jamison worried. Ben had told him that owls killed cats and he'd got on his laptop to check it out. When he found it was true, he wondered if an owl—even a great horned owl, notorious cat killers—could carry off a cat as big as Leviathan and decided it was extremely unlikely—Leviathan had to be pushing 15 or 16 pounds—but he worried nonetheless, particularly after Ben mentioned that he'd seen great horned owls in the cottonwoods along the river.

"Usually show up about now," Ben had told him, gazing at something across the room.

Jamison vowed he'd protect Leviathan from owls, and having made that intention his apprehension eased, although he had no clear idea how he would fulfill his vow. As a boy, Jamison had tried half heartedly to convince his parents to let him get a pet, cat or dog, but they'd been resolute that animals were a bother and besides, he'd be in college someday and then who would take care of it? His mother letting the question hang. Jamison didn't press the issue.

So, he was surprised at how much he looked forward to seeing Leviathan and how much he worried on the mornings the cat wasn't there. It concerned him that he'd be gone for three days while he and Ben drove to Denver, but then he reminded himself that the cat had been living on wild rodents and birds for years and a few days without Salmon In Creamy Alfredo Sauce probably wouldn't kill him.

And now Leviathan was crouched contentedly on top of the woodpile, his tail flipping languorously from side to side. When Jamison tapped on the window, the cat stood and arched his back, squinting in happy anticipation. Jamison pulled a fresh can of cat food from the cabinet above the sink and peeled back the lid. He walked out the door and around the back of the studio, then sat with his back against the wall, facing the woodpile, waiting. Leviathan watched.

Jamison had tried to get close enough to feed the cat by hand, but Leviathan had always bolted when he got within arm's reach. Jamison knew the exact moment it would happen: the cat's expression would change from happy anticipation to cautious wariness, its innate wildness overriding its hunger. Leviathan's green eyes would widen, staring into Jamison's with distrust, gauging the extent of his intentions. And then, as Jamison tried to narrow the distance with a last, hesitant step forward, the cat would spring from the woodpile and vanish into the willows, the limit of his tolerance as definable as a line scuffed in the flinty soil. He would return to the opened can of food only when Jamison had retreated a safe distance away.

Today, Jamison decided, he would see if the cat would come to him. "Here, kitty kitty," he said softly. Leviathan peered at Jamison's face and then at the can of cat food on the ground beside him. "Here, kitty kitty," Jamison said again. Leviathan hopped off the woodpile and butted his head against a log and purred.

"Look what I've got, Leviathan," Jamison whispered. He touched the can of food with his finger, then slowly moved his hand safely back to his lap, sensing the gesture would be seen as less threatening. Leviathan took two steps toward him, then flopped on his back and peered at Jamison from upside down, rubbing his back against the earth and squinting with pleasure. Jamison touched the can again. Leviathan rolled back to his feet and trotted toward him, then sat. He was now just a foot from where Jamison sat, Jamison's long legs uncomfortably crossed and holding his breath, his back just touching the sun-warmed logs of the studio. Leviathan stared at the can of cat food at Jamison's side and twitched his tail. Jamison heard the cat utter something from within, the first time he had heard it express anything that could be interpreted as a "meow." It sounded to him like a question.

"Meow," Jamison said.

Leviathan stretched a paw toward the open can, tentatively, as if gauging the extent of the fear that kept him from the food he desperately wanted. And then, in a twinkling, he swapped ends and sprang over the woodpile and vanished. In the next instant Jamison heard Ben's heavy footsteps approaching from the opposite side of the studio. He squeezed his eyes shut and sighed, hid the can of cat food under the grass, and walked around the studio to meet him. Ben was on the porch.

"Oh, there you are," Ben said. "Head out tomorrow at six, that's okay with you. I got the coffee. It's a long ways to Denver."

* * *

Jamison felt the Honda lurch a foot toward the median and then back again, as if the car had been bent like a sapling into a bow and then released. The wind south of Casper was ferocious. He thought the ongoing gales in the Shields Valley were the worst he'd seen, but they were nothing compared to this. It was as though the light-weight Honda was being passed between two giant hands, a marble flung in terrifying jags from one shoulder of the interstate to the other. Jamison was glad it was Ben's turn to drive.

"This right here's why I don't live in Wyoming," Ben said, as the car lurched another twelve inches to the left. He had, as usual, his hands in his lap, the fingers of one hand resting lightly on the bottom of the wheel, relaxed. "Back in the seventies, early eighties there was this oil boom going on, you probably remember, and they were screaming for carpenters in Casper, people moving into the oil patch from all over the place. Paying seriously good money. So I came down here looking for a job and that's when I discovered the wind and I eighty-sixed that idea right then and there. From here to Wheatland it's always bad like this, 'specially in the spring, when it starts warming up. Few years later I drove down to pick up a camper trailer we bought, Monna and me, full-size twenty-four footer, which back in those days should of been heavy enough to stabilize things. Monna and I decided we were gonna do some lux-ury camping.

"So I get down to the RV dealership in Denver, this was before they had a good dealership in Montana, and the guy says, you know, he says where am I from? I tell him I'm from Montana and he proceeds to tell me to watch my ass towing my rig from Wheatland to Casper, wind can be just a little bit stiff up there.

"I get up to Wheatland and gas up, and then on the radio I hear that north to Casper there's gusts up to 50 miles per. I asked the gas station guy about it and he says, shit, 50 miles per hour is *calm* in Wheatland. So I decided to go ahead. Stupidest thing I ever done.

"I get back on the interstate, and there's campers and 18-wheelers sideways all over the place. I saw one flipped on its back like a turtle. Every time I got hit by a gust, top of that camper I was towing would lean over a good two feet and go to fishtailing. I finally had to drop it down to about thirty, thirty five, just to keep it from tipping over and taking my truck with it. I finally got to Casper and I felt like I'd been in a war. All keyed up like that. North of Casper all the way home it was beautiful."

"What did you do with the camper?"

Ben chuckled. "That's the thing. We used it a few times and then Monna decided she'd rather sleep in a tent, like we always did. She always liked doing things like that, camping, hiking. Never would hunt, though. Only woman I ever met likes to sleep in a sleeping bag. So we kept it around a few years and then I sold it. Got back almost what I put into it, too. Another thrilling episode in the life of Ben Van Hollen."

"Makes me wonder about driving the MG back in wind like that," Jamison said. He imagined the little car skittering sideways across the interstate like a water bug on a wind-whipped pond.

"Naw, it'll be fine," Ben said. "MG's real close to the ground. Lot closer to the ground than a camper. We'll be fine. But I'll drive it through this stretch, you want."

"That works for me," Jamison said. This kind of wind was something he'd rarely seen in Minnesota, where every open expanse was hemmed in with tier upon tier of wind-absorbing trees. The wind in the mostly treeless Shields Valley had been a rude awakening, the austere loveliness of the place tempered by it, as a great meal is tempered—but sometimes ruined—with too much salt.

Ben and Jamison drove in silence, gusts periodically slamming into the side of the Honda, plastic grocery bags impaled on the fences bordering the interstate waving like frantic, shredded pennants.

Jamison said, "Tell me again about why we're driving down here. What you told Monna."

"We're hitting a builder's convention," Ben said. "You're coming along to help with the driving, 'case we end up driving at night. Monna thinks my night driving vision isn't so hot anymore. Probably isn't."

"And she bought that?" It didn't sound like a particularly convincing lie to Jamison.

"Sure. She don't care. She probably doesn't want to know. Probably happy to get me out of her hair for a few days. I actually used to go to builder's conventions every couple years, so it works for whenever I want to get away for a few days."

Jamison tried to recall a passage he'd read about the small lies inherent in enduring relationships. Who had written that? It had been a good writer he'd read long ago, a woman. He slid his hand down the side of the seat and tried, again, to find the lever that would slide it back, giving him more leg room. He'd adjusted the driver's seat of the Honda on the day he bought it and left it there. But now that he was sitting in the passenger seat of his own car, everything felt out of place. He couldn't remember if there was a button or latch he had to push, and pushed and pulled everything his groping fingers found, but still the seat wouldn't budge, leaving his long legs uncomfortably bent. He'd find the latch when they stopped for gas; he wasn't going to ride all the way to Denver with his knees shoved up under his chin. Ben, who claimed to be 5'10", but who in Jamison's appraisal was probably closer to 5'8", would have no such problems. He wondered, again, about what it must be like to be of average height, to not have to shop at the online Tall and Big Man's store to find pants that fit, to sit in a car without having his head and legs curled in a semi-fetal crouch. Like Ben. Ben, who was now watching him out of the corner of his eye, who discovered Jamison had caught him watching and self-consciously returned his gaze to the interstate rolling under the Honda's wheels on a windswept corridor of asphalt.

Ben cleared his throat and said I want to thank you again for the loan.

"It's not a loan," Jamison said. "I'm donating it to the cause. You pay for the trip, I'll cover whatever the car costs. Like I said." He didn't really want to talk about it. Being thanked by Ben made him uncomfortable in the same way being hugged by one of those crazy mixed martial arts guys on TV would have made him uncomfortable; not because it was improper, but rather, because it seemed so awkwardly out of character. Certain people didn't do certain things.

"Well, I just wanted to thank you for that. I can pay you back."

"It's not a loan," Jamison said. "Like I said."

Ben nodded, frowning. They drove. Ben shifted in his seat. "I hope she likes it," he said.

"I don't see why she wouldn't," Jamison said. "You told me she loved that car before it got pushed into the river. This would be like the rebirth of the car she lost all those years ago. Think of it like Jessica's phoenix."

Ben grinned. "Monna knew I was thinking about Jessica's tattoos, she'd cut my legs off. Or something else. You can't hide nothing from women."

He might be right about that, Jamison thought. There had been times when he thought that perhaps Monna had summoned him to Montana in the capacity of older-brother-who-imparts-pearls-of-wisdom; someone that much closer, in this golden rendering, to his own demise, and therefore possessed of the insight that accrues to the aged. Jamison almost laughed. His age had proved two things: that it was bad for hair and a lousy excuse for giving unwanted advice. He had no earthly idea how anyone could look into a ruined future without hope of remedy, a prisoner within her own body, with the same quiet acceptance Monna seemed to possess when looking into hers. Despite his research—he'd read everything he could about the disease when she first told him of her diagnosis—he understood nothing about Parkinson's that really mattered, nothing about what it was like to live while slowly drowning. Not in the way Ben understood.

And Ben wasn't talking. As if ever he would, as if talking would remake a universe aligned against him.

"So yeah," Jamison said. "Speaking of that." He cast about for a coherent line of inquiry, wanting an answer, maddeningly, to a question he couldn't quite put his finger on. "Monna's affliction. Is she … no, that's not it." He jammed his finger into the dash, trying to jolt his thoughts into order. "What do the doctors say?"

Ben seemed to tense up all at once. "They piss me off!" he said. "You can't get them to make any predictions, only that it's not gonna get any better. Nobody knows shit. They keep coming up with these new medications and Monna keeps trying them and sometimes they work real good and we think, *okay*. And then the symptoms come back and they're worse than before. Now they say we gotta put these electrodes in her brain. But then what? We got to make *plans*. You can't just go on forever not knowing anything. Monna can't. She doesn't want to. I don't either. It ain't even close to being fair, nothing fair about it. I did things the right way all my life and so did she. So she loved that crappy MG she used to have? I mean, I used to have to sweet talk that stupid English piece of shit just to get the engine to turn over. But I'm gonna buy her another one. Fuck them."

Jamison stared out the windshield at brown grass fluttering in violent, rippling waves, wind-whipped tumbleweeds and splintered stalks of sage skittering across the pavement like stones skipped across the obsidian surface of a river. This was wind that presaged a storm. He gazed across the brown prairie, new green growth pushing up around last year's clumps of dead bunch grass. Far to the west, like a gathered curtain about to drop across a stage, a low bank of black clouds roiled. But the metal nose of the Honda was still pointing southeast, toward the light. Soon, they'd be in Wheatland and then beyond, where he hoped it was calmer, where it *had* to be.

Jamison said, "Monna asked me to come to Montana so I could help you guys out. Seems like I've been sitting on my thumb since I got here. Seems like I ought to be doing something productive. I can help if you tell me what to do."

Ben lifted his chin ever so slightly, his lips closed in a firm line. Then he seemed to diminish and almost imperceptibly he settled back into his seat. He glanced at Jamison and then away, at the road ahead. He pointed at the horizon. "You can just barely see it, but that blue-colored line to the south, that's the Rockies, that's Colorado. We'll hit it in about three hours. Colorado's a whole different mindset from Montana. Everybody thinks Colorado, it's all mountains and ski areas, stuff like that. But Colorado's mostly flat. Flatter'n Montana, anyway. All the mountains are to the west of the interstate. That's for your own personal edification." He punched the button on the radio and a twangy country song blared. "You got any rock and roll in this thing? I hate that country crap."

Jamison pushed another button and Ben nodded and said that was better, that was fine. He rubbed the side of his nose. "I hear what you're saying," he said quietly. "I'm not in the habit of taking favors, but I appreciate it."

Chapter 10

She had come to dislike painting when Ben was around; he would hover in the background, anxiously waiting for her to produce something, anything, on the expensive white paper before her. She'd splash on a wash of blue or orange, just to make him happy, and then, satisfied and deceived, he'd touch her shoulder and abandon her to her thoughts and frustration and despair.

In her old life it had never been this way, but the Parkinson's had changed all of that. Monna's painting had sprung from her heart. No discordant uncertainty between feelings and image; no conscious manipulation of the brush or the hand that held it. What she saw and her expression of that had been connected like a taut violin string between tuning peg and bridge, harmonious and perfectly pitched.

But she would try again. She retrieved the easel and stool she had stored in Ben's shop and the paper and paints from the spare bedroom and set up the easel and stool away from the direct light from the window. She had two more days before Ben and Jamison returned from Denver.

When she'd first been diagnosed, after she'd recovered from the shock of having the doctors confirm what she had long suspected, her work had not been badly affected. On the days when the tremors in her hands made painting impossible, she'd clean her brushes as best she could and wait until she could paint again, listening to the river, hearing the house wrens sing from the bird houses Ben had hung in the trees in the yard, the ambient music of her life on their quarter section of grass and cottonwood trees easing her impatience. It had been a difficult adjustment, much harder than she had let on to Ben, but what choice did she have? At least she could still work some of the time. She was still selling her paintings then and even had a modest backlog of orders.

The hallucinations had started later, after she'd finally learned to accept the rhythm of her disease and how to channel her passion into the reprieves, and they'd added another degree of uncertainty to a once predictable future, like finding a new pothole in the rutted surface of a road long memorized. She sensed their onset in the way epileptics sensed a seizure: peripherally, lurking somewhere behind her and just out of sight, a presence felt that disappeared when she tried to confront it directly. It was, she supposed, like Jamison's phantom-like yellow cat, which she had glimpsed just once perched on top of the woodpile behind the studio, Jamison hovering in the background, watching the cat in the same anxious way Ben watched her. What was the name he had given it? *Leviathan.*

Maybe she should give her hallucinations a name and call them out. For today they were in the house, invisible and unbidden, tugging at her sleeve.

She stapled a sheet of paper to a board and placed it on the easel. She wouldn't need a sketch; the landscape she had in mind was committed to memory. South on 89, just before the highway's short swing west onto the interstate, was a steel railroad trestle that paralleled the road and crossed the Yellowstone River. She'd painted it countless times: in the winter, when brittle gray ice clung to the banks and the water ran sluggish and obsidian black; in the summer, when the dusty green cottonwoods along shore had the contented and floppy-eared laziness of the horses in their pasture; in the spring, when sprigs of grass in hues of yellow and sienna and cadmium red burst through the luminous, living green undergrowth. She set her tubes of paint in a half circle around the ceramic dinner plate she used for a palette and arranged her brushes between two plastic cups of water and a stack of folded paper towels and then felt in crushing resignation that the hallucinations had begun coming into her in the same way that the first raindrops of a storm are felt before the storm arrives, when all that will become the storm is still distant. She sensed the paper on the easel moving. She pressed her finger against the paper to stop it from moving but it didn't stop as she had already known it would not. She folded her hands in her lap and gazed over the top of the easel and out the back window that illuminated the small living room. Beyond their home, Ben's shop seemed painfully expressed, limned by a heavenly light that pulsed and sparkled. At any other time, beyond what she understood was happening, it would have been beautiful.

* * *

Jamison tried to wrap his head around how quickly the transaction had taken place. They'd met the owner of the MG at the door of his modest suburban home, and after Ben drove the owner and the car around the block and popped the hood and the two of them made the appropriate noises—Jamison, clueless—Ben agreed to the full asking price. The owner, a man about their age with a head of thinning silver hair combed straight back, seemed as startled as Jamison was. Startled but not foolish. He slapped a pen into Ben's hand and Ben handed it to Jamison and Jamison cut him a check on the spot, so much for negotiation.

Ben's delight with the little car, and his eager anticipation of Monna's surprise upon receiving it, lent him an almost childlike exuberance. Jamison tried to reconcile this new Ben with the old Ben: the Ben whose moments of forbearance extended only to those within the confines of their homestead in the Shields Valley; whose judgement of the world at large, like the five-strand fence that hemmed in their land, was barbed and unforgiving. He couldn't have imagined that the purchase of a car would spin him around like this; Ben was a like a kid buying his first girlfriend a cherry coke.

Since they still had several hours of daylight left, they decided to drive to Cheyenne and spend the night, then make the long, ten-hour push to Aden the following morning. Ben hopped into the

MG and drove briskly through the neighborhood before roaring off into the traffic on I-25, and Jamison had to punch the accelerator on the Honda to keep up with him. The afternoon crush was horrendous, but he'd spent all his adult life navigating gridlock in Minneapolis, so he wasn't particularly concerned when the MG was swallowed up in the miles of crawling, bumper to bumper traffic on the interstate. Occasionally he'd catch a glimpse of Ben darting across lanes like a pumpkinseed-shaped beetle skittering out from beneath the shadow off a pickup, his right arm slung over the passenger seat and his left hand resting casually on the wheel, a beatific grin on his face, the top down and the slipstream riffling furrows through his close-cropped salt and pepper hair. Two hours later, Ben phoned and told him that they'd be staying in the Quality Inn south of Cheyenne and gave him his room number. Ben had paid for separate rooms.

Ben pounded on Jamison's door minutes after he arrived. "Man, it runs like a *top*," he said. "I'll tell you what, that guy was a straight shooter, and that's the god honest truth. Shifts tight and clean, almost no play. No shimmy, doesn't pull, everything works real good. That's pretty amazing considering it's, like, fifty years old." He did the arithmetic, canted his head, frowned. "Forty six years, to be exact," he said. "Almost older'n you."

"Same age as Jessica," Jamison said, wondering why he was thinking about *that*. They strode into the lobby and out the front door of the motel, Ben's high spirits caroming off the walls like a handful of gravel flung against a board fence.

After Ben had walked around the MG, put up the top and checked and then double checked the locks, he hopped into the Honda and directed Jamison to a steak house a few blocks up the road, turning to gaze at the MG until it blinked out of sight behind a corner. Over drinks, Ben outlined plans for their arrival home the following day.

"So I'm thinking Monna's gonna want to go for a ride first thing," he said. He tapped his finger on the table top as though it were the tip of a pencil, tracing the route home through Casper and

Sheridan and then into Montana and west through Billings and Big Timber and finally to Aden. "It's gonna be hot after ten hours on the road, even if I keep it at sixty five, which is about all these English cars will do without overheating. Ten hours is a long time, so maybe we'll just stop before we get home and give it a rest, spiff it up a little before we get to the house. Also, let the engine cool down just in case. Pulling up to the house with the radiator boiling over wouldn't make a good first impression."

Jamison agreed that it wouldn't. He knew next to nothing about cars. "Where were you thinking?"

"The Infirmary's about right. Grant or Jessica or somebody'll give us some bar towels so we can wipe off the bugs. Take fifteen or twenty minutes, long as it takes for a beer. But the important thing is, how're we gonna do this? We got to come up with a good presentation. We got to think about that. It's got to be perfect. Ain't every day you get a sports car for your 64th birthday."

Their waitress had disappeared, and Jamison cast about for her, wanting another glass of wine. Ben's lofty plans had put him in a celebratory mood. He finally waved down another waitress who took his order. She apologized for the previous waitress' delinquency. "I think I saw her out behind the kitchen having a smoke," she said. "I'll let her know you're looking for her."

"I'm okay," Jamison said. "She's fine." He hated being a bother. It was best to get along, to accommodate people. He turned back toward Ben. "When exactly is Monna's birthday? I'm embarrassed I don't remember. We used to send cards back and forth when we were younger, but somehow we got out of the habit and now I can't think of the exact day. I know it's right around now, though."

"Day after tomorrow," Ben said. "May 19th, exactly one week after Mother's Day. We got a lot of mileage out of that, seeing as how we never had kids."

"You guys never wanted any?"

Ben didn't answer. He picked up his menu and opened it, said he thought he might get something to eat, even though it was early.

"Okay," Jamison said.

Ben closed his menu and set it before him. "I wanted them," he said.

Jamison found a spot on his glasses and took them off and cleaned the glasses on his shirt and put them back on. "Well," he said, "not everybody wants kids."

"Not everybody," Ben said.

Jamison changed the subject. "Okay," he said. "Okay. How are we going to surprise Monna? What is the official plan?" Fingers making air quotes around "official."

"I been thinking about that all day," Ben said, growing animated once more. "So what I got is we pull into the driveway real quiet, don't blow the horn, nothing like that. And you go inside and get her and bring her out. I'll just be sitting there in the driver's seat real casual, like guess what I found honey, that car you loved got pushed into the river. Like that. Or something like that. And then I'll get out and bow or something and hand her the keys. She's gonna pee in her pants. Then we'll go for a ride. She can drive, she's up to it. But probably I'll have to teach her how to use a stick again."

"That sounds perfect," Jamison said. "If we had a big yellow bow, we could stick it on the hood like it was gift wrapped, just to get the point across. Except we don't have a bow."

"Nope."

"But I still think it's a good plan," Jamison said.

"Me too," Ben said. "I've been thinking about what I was gonna do all day." He drank his beer and wiped his mouth on his sleeve and gazed around the room. Their waitress had returned. Jamison saw her talking to the waitress that had taken his order, then glance their way.

"I sure hope she likes it," Ben said.

"Jesus, Ben," Jamison said. "She'll *love* it! *I* love it and I haven't even been in it yet. It's consummately gorgeous."

"Yeah, but she was in her thirties then, maybe just hit forty. We were just kids. It's different when you get old."

"Ben, they don't make cars like that MG anymore, either," Jamison said. He had no idea if that were true, although it probably was.

"I'll tell you what, they don't, and by god that's the truth," Ben said, brightening. "Her first MG was a midget; this is an MGB so it's a little bigger'n that first one, a little more kick under the hood, but she won't know the difference. Important thing is, it's the same color red she loves. She's got I don't know how many shades of red she paints with, but this is the one she says she *loves*. This exact shade. This is best idea I ever had. 'Course, most years I buy her dinner in Bozeman for her birthday. Guess she's just gonna have to live without dinner this year. New car's better'n dinner at Applebee's."

"Maybe she'll buy you dinner," Jamison said.

"Yeah," Ben said. "Never thought about that. Maybe she will."

* * *

Monna lay in bed, the heavy flannel sheets pulled to her chin, and listened to the robins sing from the trees outside the partially opened bedroom window. Distinct from the robins' cheerful trilling but delicate and lovely, like the dulcet undertone of a flute in a musical ensemble, was the liquid warble of the house wren that had arrived on the same day Ben and Jamison had left for Denver. Ben had hung a cluster of bird houses in the grove of aspens outside their bedroom just so they could listen to this. She could see one of the houses from her bed. Ben would be happy to know his tiny birds were home.

Her gaze found the crown molding between the ceiling and wallpapered walls, then fell to the elegant mahogany dresser Ben had hand crafted decades earlier, when he still indulged his passion for woodworking. In the light of that morning, the dresser stood defined and unmoving in the sunlight streaming through the window, no ethereal halo of golden light, no pulsing movement. Sometime as she slept the hallucinations had gone away. Today, perhaps, she could make the colors work.

The house was quiet without Ben in it, knocking open the cupboard doors, his short, broad frame banging into corners that she glided around, as if the shortest distance between two points was through any object that refused to get out of his way. Jamison, she mused, was a study in opposites. She saw him most often from a distance, cradling a cup of coffee and a book, reading in the aluminum lawn chair she had given him on the sunlit patch of dandelions between the wood pile and the studio. She sensed that, over the decades, he had become more like her and less like Ben: not a man to bang into things, approaching the day not, perhaps, with reverence, but with the stillness of someone who listened. But why wouldn't he be like her? They were the same blood.

She knew change was coming. She felt it as clearly as she felt, each October, the onset of winter, coiled patiently in the mountains that loomed over the valley, waiting. But now she wanted to paint.

Monna wasn't hungry. She wrapped herself in her flannel bathrobe and walked into the kitchen and put water in the coffee maker and then sat at the kitchen table and waited for it to perk. The sun warmed the table top and she put her hands on it to feel the warmth. She saw the wren dart past the window with a twig in its beak, a diminutive brown arrow of purpose and straight-ahead intention, the tiniest of nest-builders. When the coffee pot was full she filled a cup and walked to her easel.

The easel and her tubes of paint and her brushes were where she had left them the day before. Monna picked up her wash brush and dipped it in water and washed in the skyline in broad, quick strokes, extending the wash three-quarters of the way down the paper. But her brush was too wet and water dripped down the paper and when she tried to dab it dry with a paper towel her hand jerked and the drips ran down the paper and puddled in the tray. She rotated the easel flat to stop the drips and then sat back and examined what she had done. The drips were annoying but the wash was still usable. When she painted the trestle and the river she could paint over them. This wasn't what she had planned, and she would have preferred a wash with no careless drips, but this was acceptable, this would work. She was determined to make it work. She wanted a painting to show Ben.

She tilted the easel up and picked up a round brush and worked up the sky: manganese blue, ultramarine blue green shade, yellow ochre; a touch of thinned alizarin crimson. The brush shook but the wet paper blotted up the colors and spread, bleeding into each other, hiding her unsteady hand. That would do for now and she rotated the easel all the way to vertical, then backed away from the paper to examine what she'd done. No one would be able to see that it wasn't right. She had learned that in art school: when her paintings were critiqued by other students, no one ever noticed her mistakes; and over time she came to believe that her own evaluation of what she created was the only real measure of its worth, which renewed her determination to perfect her technique—as if she needed more passion, as if that had ever been in question. After college, she gave away all the paintings she had made in school; she did not consider them worth keeping.

She picked up a #4 round and dipped it in water, then pulled it through the brown paint on the dinner plate, splaying the sable fibers on one side and then the other, loading the belly. She began brushing in the form of the bridge, using the brush almost like a pencil, twisting the tip for a thinner line. When her hand trembled and the paint wouldn't go where she wanted it, she picked up a #8 and recharged the brush and tried again. Maybe, with more paint, she could hide the tremors her strokes betrayed. Instead, she was reduced to stabbing at the paper with the brush, unable to complete a single continuous stroke, her eyes beginning to well with tears of frustration. Finally, she jerked the brush through the water in the cup and blotted it dry on a paper towel and then set it aside and walked to the living room window, wiping away her tears with the sleeve of her robe.

She gazed across the highway at the greening prairie. She had often thought that spring green was the loveliest green, with the yellow and orange undertones ripe with life and fecundity. Ben had called early that morning and told her they would be arriving around five and had asked twice if she was going to be there. Of course she was going to be there, where else would she be? She'd make something for dinner if they were hungry. Mac and cheese, he liked that, with a nice salad. Jamison was invited, too. Ben said

Jamison would be plenty happy about that, see you at five, we'll have drinks and get a head start on your birthday. She'd forgotten about her birthday.

Monna shuffled back to her easel. Over the years, her symptoms had become worse and the respites from them more sporadic. She picked up a brush by the tip of its wooden handle and held it upright at arm's length, trying to will the brush to be still, but the brush magnified every tic in her hand, every involuntary spasm, weaving and jerking at the end of her fingers like a fat, tethered bumblebee. She would not do this again.

For two hours, she stabbed and hacked at the paper with her brushes, the colors wild and uncontrolled, the trestle and river taking form in chaotic, rigid thrusts beneath strokes she could scarcely control. By midafternoon she was close to exhaustion, emotionally spent and hungry. She decided to take a break and fix herself something to eat. She had not eaten in a day.

She spread peanut butter on a slice of whole-wheat bread and returned to the easel and sat unbalanced on the stool and studied what she had done, the uneaten bread beside her.

The painting was not her. There was nothing about the painting that was her. The perspective and composition were adequate but the colors were wrong, their application wrong, the mood, *wrong*. It was as though someone had Scotch-Taped together a disconnected montage of images that had come from the petulant hand of an angry child. She recharged her brush and tried to soften the lines but the lines and the images remained angry, accusatory, rebellious. *This is the last one,* they told her. *You knew.*

* * *

Gerald Metzger ran his hand over the hood of the MG, nodding. This was the first time Jamison had seen him, and he was younger and considerably more muscular than he had envisioned, perhaps in his mid forties. His light brown hair was flecked with grey but his face was still unlined. He carried his pistol, taser, handcuffs and radio in a black leather holster that creaked in pleasant cadence to his steps.

Metzger stepped out of his patrol truck when he saw the MG make a U-turn and pull in behind him, one big hand on the doorway and the other on his pistol, his biceps bulging in his sleeves. He relaxed when he recognized Ben and hooked his thumbs in his belt. Jamison had parked opposite the Infirmary and crossed the street to meet him. Metzger stuck out his hand. "Gerald Metzger," he said. "Are you the guy that talked him into this?"

Jamison shook his head. "Nope. I don't usually think that far ahead. This was entirely Ben's idea."

"Monna's birthday present," Ben said, proudly. "She doesn't know it yet; we just got here. She had a red MG just like this one twenty years ago. That would have been the late nineties. Probably before your time."

"I was still in diapers in the late nineties," Metzger said. "That's only a slight exaggeration. But I think Jessica said something about her and Monna riding in that car once or twice, kind of like that movie *Thelma and Louise*. I'm going to keep an eye out for you two. No drag racing down the middle of Aden. Go to Big Timber if you want to do that. Different jurisdiction."

"I'll relay that important information to Monna," Ben said, rubbing the back of his neck and smiling. He was happy, enjoying this. A cream-colored moth fluttered toward them from across the street, momentarily arresting the three men's attention. It landed on the canvas top of the MG and fanned its wings, then folded them, as if testing the little car for warmth. Metzger flicked it off with his finger.

Inside the Infirmary, both Grant and Jessica were behind the bar. Jamison had never met Grant, and when Ben introduced him as the owner of "this dump," Jamison mentioned that he had enjoyed the St. Patty's day dance and shook his hand. Grant told them the next dance would be after the rodeo, and to be sure to come, they'd hired a really good band from Bozeman.

"Wow," Jessica said, making big eyes at Grant. "We got both of these dudes at once. I'm blessed." Ben slapped a twenty on the bar and ordered two beers. "Monna's got herself a new car," he said. "A 1972 MG. Like that one you and her used to drive around in."

"Really?" Jessica said. She seemed genuinely thrilled. "When do I get to see it?"

"How about now?" Ben said. "Monna hasn't even seen it yet, it's a surprise for her birthday. It's right outside. We just drove in from Denver. Want to take a look?"

"Shit yeah," Jessica said.

Jessica walked around from behind the bar and followed them outside, gently poking Jamison in the ribs and smiling up at him when he opened the door for her. Jamison flushed in spite of himself, and his embarrassment turned his pale skin redder still. He followed her out the door, his eyes locked on the gently undulating tattoo peeking above the scooped back of her camisole.

Jessica rounded the corner of the Infirmary and spied the car. "Oh my god, she's gonna love this," she said. "She's gonna *love* this. Oh my god, it's gorgeous. It's just like the old one. I am *so* jealous."

"Drove it all the way from Denver without a hiccup," Ben said, beaming, grinning so broadly Jamison thought his face would split open. "Totally restored from the ground up. I checked it out. Monna can take you for a ride soon as I get her lined out."

"Oh my god," Jessica said.

* * *

Monna tried to pull the staples out with a staple puller but her fingers wouldn't work and finally in anger she ripped the painting free. One edge tore in a jagged line a third of the way across the paper. She dropped the torn painting on the kitchen table. Unsteadily, she dumped the two cups of water in the sink, then threw the empty cups into the waste basket. She put her brushes and tubes of paints back in the Plano tacklebox she had used since college and folded the easel under her arm and returned the easel and tacklebox to the darkest corner of Ben's shop, away from the bright fluorescent lights where he kept his tools, and put them on a stack of cardboard boxes and old clothing and broken household appliances. She looked down at them. Then she shuffled slowly back to the house to await Ben, her head down in defeat and resignation, her despair raging behind a frozen face that could not form the shape of her crushing sorrow.

So. This was the end of it. She had thought—or indulged the thought, she could no longer tell the difference—that the culmination of a lifetime of passion for her art would merit a blaring of trumpets and a proclamation from someone official and important, but now that idea seemed unbearably pointless, for the only measure of her ascent in this world was that which she no longer had.

She and Ben had lived in their small frame home for four decades. She walked inside and took a seat at the kitchen table and pushed the painting away from her. She did not want to look at it.

Jamison and Ben arrived at precisely at 5; Ben must have timed it. She was rising slowly from her chair when Ben burst through the door. "Happy Birthday!" he sang.

Monna tried to smile. "Tomorrow," she said. "My birthday's tomorrow."

"I know that, Monna, but you're getting your birthday present a day early. What do you think about that?"

"I don't know, Ben."

Ben took a step toward her and reached for her arm and then his eyes fell on the painting on the kitchen table and he stopped. He bent over the paper, his hands flat on either side of it, then slowly rose. "What's wrong with it? It doesn't look, you know ... it's not like what you do."

"I painted it for you," she said. "It's that railroad trestle over the Yellowstone. Down the road. It tore when I took it off the board."

"But you can fix it, right? It's not a very big tear."

"I can fix it," Monna said.

"It's really nice," Ben said quietly. She turned away from him and he saw then that she had been crying. He reached for her arm again but she pulled back, her arms rigid at her sides. "Monna," Ben said. "I got you your birthday present. Don't you want to see it?" He reached for her arm once more and helped her up from the chair and led her past the painting and out the front door of the house.

"Close your eyes," he said.

"But I'll trip, Ben. I'll fall."

"No you won't. I'll catch you. Close your eyes."

Chapter 11

Ben backed the Bobcat Skid Steer off the back of the rental trailer and drove it around the house to the backyard, through the opening where they had yanked the chain-link fence out of the ground and pulled it to one side. Jamison heard the muffled and frantic bark of a dog. He peered at the house and saw a small brown dog hurling itself in fury against the sliding glass doors overlooking the concrete patio. Ben put the rumbling machine in neutral, hopped out, and swung his arm dramatically toward the seat, as if presenting a banquet table to an esteemed guest. "Hop in," he said. "You're gonna drive. You gotta stop and pee, go against the back fence. They don't want their dog to get out."

Jamison's eyes grew wide. "Ben, I've never driven one of these things. I haven't got a license or anything."

Ben cocked an eyebrow. "You don't gotta get a license to drive a fucking *Bobcat*. It ain't exactly rocket science. Get in."

Jamison climbed in, feeling the motor vibrate through the seat. "Okay, see that there?" Ben pointed down and to the right, about the level of Jamison's knee. "That switch there is the throttle. Turn it toward that little rabbit picture and you'll get more engine speed, 'case you hit a hard patch. Up there to your left? Those are the gauges. You can leave those alone; they're already set where I want 'em. You got all that so far?"

Jamison nodded. "I think so." Happy little spurts of adrenaline mixed with apprehension surged through his legs and chest. Ben had hired him as a laborer; he had no idea he'd be trusted to run the heavy equipment. It was something he'd wanted to do since he was a boy. But he was deathly afraid he'd screw up; he envisioned a runaway bobcat plowing a path through the back fence, across the alley, and into the living room of the house across from the job site.

"Okay," Ben said. "Now the important stuff. Those two gear-shift things on either side of you, those are the joy sticks. That one on your left controls the loader—forward and back and left and right. That's why they call it a skid steer, 'cause the machine will pivot wherever you want it. That joystick on the right raises and lowers the bucket. Trick to that is, don't try to take too big a bite. Just skim off a little and dump it and then skim off a little more."

Jamison nodded nervously. Before the bobcat were four wooden stakes connected with string that delineated the rectangular perimeter of the excavation site. Ben pulled the string off and wadded it into a ball and tossed it into the yard.

"Most important thing to remember is, you get in trouble, take both hands off the joysticks and the machine will just stop. Just drop them both. Even you can't screw it up. Okay, want to give it a try?"

Jamison nodded grimly.

"Lift the bucket!" Ben said. Jamison paused, grasped the right joy stick, and after a couple of tentative attempts, the bucket lifted slowly in the air. Jamison pumped his fist.

"Good," Ben said. "Okay, back 'er up a little. Good, that's good. Okay, now come forward toward me." Jamison eased the left joystick forward and the loader crept towards Ben's feet.

"Stop!" Ben barked. Jamison's eyes grew wide and he stared at Ben in alarm. "Drop the sticks!" Ben barked again. Jamison took his hands off the joysticks and thrust them above his head as if he were the bad guy in a cowboy movie. The Bobcat stopped in its tracks.

"See what just happened? You drop the sticks, you stop. You can't get sideways in these things." Jamison exhaled through his mouth and tried to calm his rocketing pulse. He looked at Ben and then gazed over his head, at the tops of the roofs behind the wooden fence that separated the back yard from the alley. Halfway down the block, another addition was going up, partially sheathed in bright new OSB. Ben saw two men on the roof and heard the staccato whump! of a nail gun.

Ben hooked his thumbs in his pockets and chuckled. "Didn't mean to scare you like that," he said. "But now you know what to do, something happens."

Jamison's heart rate began to modulate. "I sure hope you have insurance for this beast," he mumbled.

"No insurance," Ben said. "You ain't gonna do nothing I can't fix. So here's what this job entails. Those stakes there"—he pointed at the stakes that had been attached to the string he'd just removed—"those are the approximate corners of the slab. You're gonna take off a foot across that whole area. Edges don't have to be perfect, don't worry about that, but the depth's gotta be dead nuts, so get out and check it with your tape measure to make sure. Twelve inches. You take off too much, we have to backfill with extra gravel, which costs me money. I don't have much wiggle room on this bid."

"What are you going to do?" Jamison asked.

"I'm gonna watch until you get the hang of things, then I'm going to run out and pick up some stuff we're going to need for tomorrow. Be gone an hour or two at most."

"Okay," Jamison said, not at all sure he was ready to solo. "That's okay, but, I mean, maybe you should stick around a little longer? In case something happens?"

"Nothing's gonna happen," Ben said, as if he could already envision a perfectly level, twelve-inch deep excavation in a way Jamison could not yet imagine, as if smooth sailing behind the joy sticks of a Bobcat were foreordained. "I showed a hundred guys how to operate these things. I even taught girls. Monna, for instance."

"Uh huh," Jamison said.

"You're gonna do just fine," Ben said. "You get in trouble, get too close to the fence, something like that, just let go of the joysticks until you figure out how to back it up. Or whatever. If you really get in trouble, just shut off the key. I'll fix it when I get back. But you're gonna be fine. Really."

* * *

Jamison tried to remember the first time he'd driven a car. It had to have been the summer of 1963, when he turned 16. His father had taught him. He couldn't remember if he'd been this apprehensive; that had been a long time ago. He did remember one incident that had stuck in his head all the ensuing years: he and his father had been driving down the road on their block. Some neighbors were having a lawn party, and there were cars parked on either side of the road, narrowing the passageway through, although there was more than enough room for his father's Pontiac. His father, gently encouraging him from the passenger seat, seemed to be enjoying Jamison's intense concentration as Jamison slowed to a crawl, peering anxiously out both sides of the vehicle, trying to navigate between the parked cars.

"You think you got it?" his father said, grinning.

Even then, Jamison was so tall he had to hunch over the wheel to get a clear view through the windshield. He nodded, a quick jerk up and down, too nervous to risk talking. But he got it.

He was going to get the Bobcat, too, by god. Once the surges of panic with the machine's every lurch and wobble began to abate, he started to relax, and in much less time than it had taken him to master his father's Pontiac, he was flying. He found he could spin the Bobcat on a dime, forward and back. He could push, lift, tamp or flatten the growing pile of dirt and sod he was excavating and put it anywhere he wanted it. He could chop off a section of sod with the blade of his bucket and then scoop it out in one piece, lifting it from the earth as though he were sliding a spatula into a pan and lifting out a slice of chocolate pie. It was all just fun as hell.

He didn't notice Ben had returned until he backed up the Bobcat to take another run at a stubborn boulder in the mostly rock-free topsoil he'd been excavating. Ben was standing behind him, watching, a white paper bag in each hand. Jamison held up his finger as if to say "watch this," then goosed the throttle, canted the bucket, and took a run at the boulder, feathering the blade up just enough to pop it from the ground. The boulder rolled free, leaving a basketball-sized divot in the earth. Jamison scooped it up and dropped it on the pile of dirt beside the excavation, then released the joy sticks and killed the motor and climbed out of the cab.

Ben whistled. "God damn," he said. "I turn you loose on a skid steer and when I get back you're putting on a show for standing-room-only crowds."

Jamison beamed with delight. "That was *fun*," he said. "It makes me feel guilty about what you're paying me."

"Oh, you don't got to worry about that," Ben said. "I'll get my money out of you. Fourteen bucks an hour is not exactly executive wages."

"It seems pretty good to me," Jamison said, rubbing his glasses on his shirt. Perspiration had flecked the lenses. "It's about three or four times what I was getting slinging hash when I was writing my thesis in grad school."

"Oh yeah? So what was the thesis?"

"*Filmic Adaptions Of Joseph Conrad's Lord Jamison, 1925 Through 1965*. 'Filmic' is kind of a pretentious word, so let's just say I was trying to make the subject matter sound important. But anyway, they went for it. So here I am. Ta da."

Ben handed him one of the white paper bags. "Ta da," he said. "For what I'm paying you, I figure I can spring for lunch. Hope you like Taco Hell." He walked to the shade of a maple tree and sat down, folding his legs beneath him, then took off his sunglasses and propped them on the bill of his ball cap. Jamison sat beside him. He peered into his bag and saw that Ben had bought him two huge burritos and a giant cylinder of diet Coke, far more food than he could consume in one sitting. Maybe he'd share one of the burritos with Leviathan.

For a few minutes, they ate in silence. Ben set his burrito on the grass and slurped his Coke through a straw. He mentioned that since it wasn't worth what the Bobcat cost to swap out the bucket for a couple hours' work digging footers, they'd run it back to the rental shop and then clean them out by hand, call it a day. Tomorrow morning, Ben said, they'd form up the slab and call for a pour so they'd have a few hours to trowel the concrete while it cured. Concrete had to be perfect or someone would bitch. Ben tapped Jamison's boot with his foot. He was gonna need rubber boots or the concrete would eat through those pretty hiking boots. They could pick up a pair at Murdoch's on the way out of town, figure on thirty, forty bucks. They'd come in handy for ranch chores, assuming, you know, Jamison ever got around to doing any ranch chores. Eyes darting from Jamison's face to something over the fence.

Jamison took a bite of his burrito. *Ben.* A watery chunk of cheese and refried beans dribbled onto his hand, still hot. He flicked it into the lawn.

"I almost forgot," Jamison said. "How does Monna like the car? I've been holed up in the studio for the last few days, not doing ranch chores. I'll bet she was excited. Jessica told me she loved that first one."

Ben stopped chewing, then made a barely perceptible shrug. He finished his burrito and stuffed the wadded wrapper into his paper bag and pulled out another burrito and slowly began unwrapping it, lifting up the tape that held it closed, pulling apart the folds. Refolding the wrapper.

Jamison studied Ben out of the corner of his eye, aware that his attempt at small talk had had exactly the wrong effect. He balanced his half-eaten burrito on his leg, wiping both hands on a napkin he fished out of his bag, silently berating himself. It was as though he'd been walking across a level lawn and stepped into a hole he had always known was there, the predictable surprise of having done that. "I guess I didn't see you guys go," he said, too casually. "I was probably in the middle of a book and didn't hear the engine. When I get like that, I'm oblivious. You know me."

"She hasn't driven it yet. She ain't even been in it."

Jamison set his Coke down. "But why?"

"She's sick. You saw her that day we got back, all stoved up like she gets. I told her I'd drive but she said she just wasn't up to it.

Wasn't *feeling* like it." His jaw was set, his face clouded, angry. He gazed at the burrito in his hand and then put it on the grass beside him. "You don't got to *feel* to ride in a fucking car," he said bitterly. "All you got to do is sit there."

"What did she say to that?"

"She didn't say anything. Just looked at me. Like I was in the way or something."

"But Ben ..." Jamison shook his head in exasperation. He didn't know what to say. This was all so silly. What had got into his sister? And then he realized, with abrupt clarity, that he simply didn't know, couldn't know. That he couldn't know because he had never known his own sister and never would. It was Ben, after all, who had spent the last forty years of his life with her, not Jamison; Jamison had gone away to school when Monna was still a child. He'd taken out-of-state jobs during his summer breaks from college, so he'd watched her grow up only on his infrequent visits home. They'd corresponded via phone and mail and then email, correspondence he'd treasured. But they had become, Jamison realized, more pen pals than relatives, she a person whose joys and accomplishments and small insecurities he learned about second hand through the genealogical bond of email, her earnest narratives filling the corners of his inbox as if they'd been painted there with a brush, yet once removed even so; as a print is once removed from a painting. At no time in their adult lives had they been in physical proximity for more than a few days at a time—a Christmas visit, every few years or so; his sporadic road trips west. Until now.

"She likes the car," Ben said. "I know she does. She's *got* to. She loved that first MG we used to have. Used to drive it all up and down 89 with the top down. I led her out there that day we got back, her eyes closed, you remember, and then she opened them up and I thought she was gonna love it. You were *there*. You *saw* her. And it was like, 'that's so nice of you, Ben.' Like I just bought her dinner or something. Maybe I should of bought her dinner instead. Would of saved you some money."

"Don't worry about that," Jamison said. "She liked it. That's what I thought, too. Who wouldn't like a birthday present like that?

You might have misread her. It's hard to tell with the Parkinson's. And she was having trouble walking. It was one of her bad days. You have to consider that."

Ben nodded and rocked forward a little, as if he were going to rise to his feet, then settled back. He picked up his burrito and put it back in the wrapper and put it in the paper bag, then folded the bag closed and held the bag at arm's length and let it fall.

"It's more than that," he said. "She's changing. Or maybe she's already changed. I mean beside the disease. Used to be she looked at it like it was, you know, driving through that snowstorm we got in coming back from White Sulphur. That sucked. I been driving through shit like that my whole life and I still hate it. Ain't nothin' good I can say about white-outs. But I knew we were gonna come out the other side sooner or later. You probably did too. Monna *used* to think like that.

"But now she thinks different. Like there is no other side. You saw her that day in the snow."

Jamison remembered. Just beyond his feet, he spied an up-side-down grasshopper clutching a blade of grass and watched it nibble tentatively at the blade that supported it. He wondered if it would chew through all the way and fall, or if grasshoppers at some implicit level understood the consequences of their actions, that unsupported weight always upset the balance of things.

"She'll come around," Jamison said. Maybe she would. He *hoped* she would.

Ben was going to say something but didn't and rubbed his sleeve across his eyes and for a while kept his arm across his eyes. Jamison stared at the Bobcat. When he turned back Ben had rolled to his feet. He slapped the grass from his pants and plucked his lunch bag from the ground. "Let's hit the road," he said. "It's a long drive to Aden." He held out his hand and Jamison took it and Ben pulled him to his feet. Ben was grinning.

* * *

"You got a minute? I want to see something up here." Ben flicked on the turn signal and swung up a gravel road that joined the highway just north of Clyde Park, a pitch that rose sharply and then crested on wheat fields that unfurled in silent yellow waves to the horizon. Ben had gassed up in Bozeman and bought a six pack and the pocked gravel road jostled the six pack against Jamison's new rubber boots. Ben pointed out a pair of sandhill cranes standing motionless and erect in a pasture bordering the river below them; exceptionally fine birds like sandhill cranes, Ben said, called for another beer. Ben clinked his bottle to Jamison's and Jamison marveled at the birds' size. He had never seen cranes before, and from a distance they looked like large, furry pterodactyls, their exquisite calls haunting and primordial.

The road bisected one edge of a vast bench and now a new panorama lay before them: a bright red, meticulously maintained barn in the near distance; several uneven clusters of grain silos and pole barns leaning over unadorned, single-story homes on the distant skyline. Ben swung north onto a dirt road and then drove under a welded iron arch topped with the silhouette of galloping prairie animals: deer, elk, antelope, moose, bears and a cowboy on a horse, cut with an acetylene torch into sheet iron, arrested in flight as if frozen midway through a continuous loop of film. He poked his thumb at the roof of the cab as he drove underneath. "Always liked those," he said. Ahead of them and beyond, the Crazies, still dusted white, fell away in the hazy blue distance, a world at tree line of cold nights and cool summer days a season behind the rapidly warming basin of the Shields River valley. Here, two hundred feet above the highway, it was warm and very nearly hot, into the high seventies where it wasn't supposed to be, and when Ben switched off the key the motor ticked, cooling fitfully.

They had stopped in a cemetery. Weathered granite monuments leaned into the sparse grass, as if longing to rejoin the earth. Clusters of bleached plastic flowers stood erect, garishly cheerful, in rust-pocked wire stands. Ben opened his door and hopped out and walked to a gap in the headstones at the far end of the five-acre enclosure. He was holding a beer. Jamison followed.

Ben stopped and stuck his free hand in his pocket, the wind pressing his t-shirt against his thick chest. He scuffed the flinty soil with the toe of his boot.

"This is where I'm gonna end up. This plot right here. Monna bought it for me for my birthday about eighteen, twenty years ago, long time before she got sick. They were only a few hundred dollars apiece back then, probably about the same as now. I never could figure out if it was supposed to be a joke or what. She bought one for her, too, right next to mine. Like we were going out on a double date to heaven, 'cept I'm not so sure about the heaven part." Ben sipped his beer and gazed back down the road. Somewhere below the crest of the hill was the river and in a pasture beside the river were the cranes. He could still hear them.

"I always just assumed she'd want to be buried back in Minnesota where you and her came from," Ben said, "but I got it wrong again. She said we should be together, she wanted to be buried next to me. They got a cemetery up in Aden but it's even worse'n this one. You seen what the weather's like up there in the winter, not that it matters any if you're dead. But down here, it's nicer." He set his bottle on the ground between his feet and straightened up and crossed his arms.

"Anyway, you can see for yourself it still ain't much of place to rest for eternity. But on the other hand it's real pretty up here on this bench, I always liked it up here. Guy owns that red barn over there used to let me hunt along the crick. I never give much thought to where I was gonna be buried so I guess this is as good a place as any. One less thing I got to worry about."

"Well," Jamison said, "you've always got the cranes."

"You're right there," Ben said. The thought seemed to make him happy. "I'd rather have a crane standing over me than a headstone. Maybe if I planted some grass or something they'd move in. They're omnivores. That means they'll eat anything. Bugs, seeds, crawdads and minnows in the river."

Jamison knew what "omnivore" meant.

Ben squatted on his haunches, plucked the beer bottle from between his feet and stuck his finger in the open end, swinging the half-empty beer bottle from his finger like the clapper in a bell. "I

used to try to figure out why she bought these but I never got anywhere with it. It sounds kind of sinister but it was never like that at
all. If she wanted to kill me off she would of done it a long time ago.
I guess it was one of those things where you just had to be there."

"Did you ever ask her?"

"No," Ben said. "Never. It's not exactly how we make small talk
where I come from. I said, 'thank you for the beautiful cemetery
plot, dear.' Next year she bought me a custom rifle case out of saddle
leather she had made for this tack-driving Sako I used to own, had
my initials carved on the side. First couple months after Obama got
elected gun prices went through the roof so I sold it for twice what
I got it for but I wouldn't sell that case for anything. I still got it."

"Sounds like she figured something out," Jamison said.

"Yeah," Ben said. "She figured out I'll never figure out women.
'Specially her."

Chapter 12

Jamison and Monna watched Ben from the shade on the back side of the house, their lawn chairs tucked up under the eave and out of the sun. Halfway between the house and the river, Ben prowled the unmown dandelions and crab grass in the lawn. Every now and then he'd stop, stoop, and slap his hat over a grasshopper, then carefully unscrew the lid of a Mason jar and drop it inside with its captive brethren.

"He'll never give up," Monna said. "He's been doing this since we were first married. He's just bound and determined to get a wren to eat out of his hand. It's like this fixation with him."

"Has he ever done it?" For some inexplicable reason, Jamison found Ben's quixotic quest to feed a house wren charming. It was so unlike what he had come to know of the man that it was pleasantly unsettling, as if Ben had taken the mike at karaoke night at the Infirmary and belted out an operatic rendition of Arturo in Bellini's *I puritani*.

"Not that I've ever seen," Monna said. "And I'd be the first to know."

Monna had brought out a bottle of red wine and two glasses—it was late afternoon—and Jamison raised his glass then let it dangle lazily from his fingers. "You seem better today," he said. "Better than a week ago, anyway."

Monna hoisted her glass. "Miracle elixir," she said, grinning. "But no. I *am* feeling better. I knew it when I got up this morning. That's been one of the hardest things to deal with, feeling better but knowing the symptoms will get worse; and then feeling worse but knowing eventually you'll feel better, only not as much as the last time. There's this beautiful pen and ink illustration I saw once of a ring of fish, each with the tail of the fish in front of it in its mouth, a circle of death and rebirth that never ends. Having a reprieve from my symptoms is like a rebirth, even if only for a few days."

"And the descent into symptoms is like …?"

Monna thought about that. She pinged her glass with her fingernail. "Everyone knows where all this leads," she said quietly, meeting Jamison's eyes. "My, aren't we serious."

"I'm sorry," Jamison said.

"No. It's good for me to talk about it. I can't really talk about it with Ben. I try but we're just too close. Sometimes I think he feels like it's happening to him instead of me."

Jamison set his glass on the uneven earth beside his chair, his hand hovering just above it. The glass wobbled unsteadily for a moment but didn't tip. Jamison's eyes returned to Ben. Ben walked slowly through the grass, the jar in one hand and his hat in the other. He paused, shaded his eyes, and then continued walking.

Jamison wondered, then, if the desire to know was sufficient justification to ask a personal question. Monna's MG was still in the garage where Ben had driven it on the day they'd brought it home; Ben hadn't spoken of the car again since their first day on the job site.

"That's a cool car," Jamison said. "That MG Ben got you for your birthday."

"Best birthday present I ever got," Monna said without emotion. She swirled the wine in her glass.

"I would have, you know … I would have thought you'd have taken it out for a drive by now," Jamison said. "Or something." He reached for his glass.

Monna wedged her glass between her legs and folded her arms and watched Ben. Ben had stopped on the bank of the river and was studying something in the willows on the opposite bank, shading his eyes with his hat. The river, having scoured its bed of silt during the previous month's spring runoff, was rapidly clearing. Monna had told him that that's when the fishermen began showing up.

"Are you and Ben going for a ride in it? Someday, maybe?"

Monna shot him a glance. "He's been talking to you."

"No," Jamison said. "But it's kind of hard not to notice. The car is still in the garage. Ben thought you'd be excited to get it. He was like a kid in a candy shop. You should have seen him."

Monna settled back then, as if her bones, weary from the effort of supporting her failing muscles, had collapsed into the framework of the chair. "That morning ... it had to be *that* particular morning," she said. "It was a really bad day. I was feeling terrible, but I wanted to paint, I wanted to *try*. You and Ben were in Denver so I thought I could focus, like I used to. But something about it was like waking up from the dreams I used to have. When I was little, I was always dreaming I could fly. I never told Mom and Dad, they already thought I was half crazy. But it was so real! I can remember skimming up and down the driveway and all around the house, a few feet above the ground, my arms held out like wings. I'd see the grass go skimming by underneath me. Flying! And then I'd wake up and lie in bed and for a few minutes I still thought I could fly if I could just get back that feeling. The *right* feeling. I don't know how to describe it any better than that. But after a few minutes I'd realize that it was just me, Monna, and I couldn't fly after all. I'd be terribly disappointed but eventually I'd forget about it until it happened again, and of course nothing ever changed. When I got a little older the dreams quit coming."

Monna stared into her glass. "So that day you guys came home, I wanted to paint like I could before the Parkinson's, I wanted the *right* feelings back. But they weren't there. Instead, I had to look at some things I'd been avoiding looking at for a long time. I had to look at my 'new and improved feelings'"... Monna held up her hands in air quotes, her hands trembling only a little—"thanks to this wonderful disease God has given me. It was just really hard for me, Jamison. And so Ben, my sweet Ben ... Ben shows up with the car, and I knew that on any other day I would have loved it, but I was having just a really shitty day and I saw for the first time that there was no way to escape how my life was going to play out, there was not going to be a last-minute divine intervention and then you guys show up with this car like the one he and I used to love so much, driving around with the top down in the summer, and it was all just, like, sensory overload." She held out her glass. Jamison picked up the bottle and steadied her glass with his hand and splashed it half full.

"This doesn't make any more sense to me than it probably does to you," she said. "Shit."

"No, it does, sort of," Jamison said, fumbling. "I mean, I think I understand your drift, if not necessarily the context. But I don't have to understand it all."

"No, you don't," Monna said. "I don't understand it all, either."

Ben had turned away from the bank of the river and was walking toward them, his jar held in the air, tapping the side of it and grinning, the small grasshoppers within rattling against the curved walls of their transparent prison like dried beans. He pointed over the top of the house and mouthed "chair." He would retrieve a lawn chair from the front of the house and join them.

Jamison leaned forward, resting his elbows on his bony knees, his long fingers interlaced. "Go for a ride with him," he said, startled by his own impetuous words. "Let him take you for a drive."

Monna locked her arms across her chest and looked away.

Ben appeared from around the corner of the house and flicked his lawn chair open as though cracking a whip. He tapped Jamison on the shoulder and Jamison scooted his chair to one side and Ben set his lawn chair between Jamison and Monna. "There was a yellow warbler out there across the river a minute ago," he said. "Very secretive birds. There's some of them around, but you never see them. That little sucker knew I was looking for him and he wouldn't move. He finally did and I spotted him. Monna's got this thing for yellow birds."

"I do," Monna said. "Yellow warblers, Yellow-headed blackbirds, meadowlarks, goldfinches, especially the goldfinches. You can't find an exact match of their color on a color wheel. They're not really yellow, it's more like honey or butterscotch, there's just a touch of red in it." She gave Jamison a knowing look. "Ben knows how much I like red." She touched her husband's hand.

"Red is the fastest color," Ben announced. "Fastest color for Monna, anyway." He had brought his jar of grasshoppers with him and now he held it up and examined it, frowning, selecting a specimen. "You," he said, tapping the side of the glass, "will be today's sacrifice." He unscrewed the top of the jar and fished out the hopper and then pinched off its head. He tossed it into the grass a few feet beyond where they sat, the beheaded insect kicking in feeble circles.

Monna had pointed out the house wrens a half hour earlier as they flitted from the willows along the river to the bird houses Ben had hung in the aspens outside their bedroom window. Now another darted by, an arrow-like flash of stiletto beak and stub tail, like a tiny brown missile shot from a sling.

"There he is," Ben said, lowering the pitch of his voice. "That was the recon run. He'll be back for that hopper when he works up his courage." Sure enough, as they waited, speaking in hushed tones, the little bird flew back, landed beside the still kicking hopper, and peered up at them, as if gauging the distance from where they sat to the hopper at its feet. Then it snatched the insect in its beak and darted around the corner of the house. "Ha!" Ben said quietly. He plucked another hopper from the jar, killed it, and tossed it into the grass, but this time half the distance away. A few minutes later, the wren returned, studied them cautiously for a moment, and then, as before, snatched the hopper and flew away. He'd plucked the hopper from the grass no more than three feet from the end of Jamison's outstretched legs. Jamison turned slowly toward Ben and beamed with delight.

"Now comes the hard part," Ben whispered, fishing out the last hopper from the jar. He pinched off the bug's head and held the kicking body in the open palm of his hand, the hopper's green blood on one finger, his forearm resting on the arm of his lawn chair. The three of them barely breathed.

The wren returned. It landed in the grass where the first hopper had been and peered up at them, then with a skip and a hop sprang to where the second hopper had been. It tilted its head to look at the grass and then peered at Jamison's feet and finally sized up the three of them in turn, each of whom gazed back in spellbound fascination. Then it darted to the eave directly above their heads and vanished. Jamison began to speak but Ben shook his head. Ever so slowly, he held up his free hand, palm out: *No. Wait.*

It wasn't long. Suddenly, the wren was on Ben's arm. Jamison couldn't have described how the tiny creature had appeared, only that it had seemed to plummet from somewhere above as if loosed unseen from the clouds. It was close enough that Jamison could marvel at the subtle colors on its back, the gradients of tan to chocolate brown, as if it had suffused the unlovely colors of bare earth and made them grand and fine to those who cared to *see*. The wren hopped cautiously a few inches down Ben's arm toward the dead hopper in his palm, desperately wanting what its innate caution would not allow it to have. It tilted its head toward Ben's face and Jamison saw Ben's eyes widen with excitement. And then with a flick of its stub tail it was gone.

Ben let the hopper drop to the grass. "God *damn*," he said. "I thought he was gonna go for it that time. I really did."

Monna exhaled as if she'd been holding her breath and bent over her knees, her face buried in her arms." Oh *god*," she moaned.

Jamison lay back in his chair, his legs splayed out before him, his hands clasped over his face. He felt as though he'd just stepped off a carnival ride, the ones that spun you around and around and then stopped just in time.

"That's the closest I ever got," Ben said. "I really thought he was gonna go for it."

Monna smiled at the wonderment of it all and shook her head. "What are you ever going to do, Ben, if you get one of your little wrens to eat out of your hand?" She smiled at him, her withered fingers resting lightly on his forearm, teasing. Jamison marveled at the transformation the bird had wrought. Monna seemed almost buoyant, as if this tiniest of creatures, a being no larger than a heart-beat and wings, had taken on its small shoulders the weight that had been dragging at the heels of her soul. He remembered her childhood in that very way: a slip of a girl so in love with her art that she seemed to glow when she talked about it. If feeding a wren was what it took to bring back the child in her, then he'd be happy to help Ben find bugs for every house wren in the Shields Valley.

Ben stood and slapped his hands on his thighs and said, "I'm thinking I need another beer. Anyone else?"

Monna wondered what they would do for dinner. She didn't feel like cooking tonight. Maybe the Infirmary? She'd heard they had beer at the Infirmary.

"I like the way you think," Ben said.

"It's a lovely night," Monna said. "Why don't we put the top down on the MG and drive down in style? Jamison can take his Honda and meet us there."

Ben turned to look at her, silence for that moment between them, and then he said he supposed that was fine, that was a pretty good idea he could get behind, and he mumbled something else Jamison couldn't hear and then he looked out across the river where the yellow warbler had been.

"It's a shame to keep it locked up in the garage," Monna said. "Let's show it off tonight. I've been wanting to get out." She touched Ben's hand.

"I'm on board with that," Ben said. He put his hands in his pockets, awkwardly, as if there were nothing left to do with them. "It's Friday; there'll be some guys down there might like to take a look at it, assuming that's okay with you."

"Of course."

"I've been wanting to take it out for a spin," Ben said.

"Me too," Monna said.

* * *

Ben returned to the table and slid onto the stool across from them. The man he'd been talking to clapped him on the shoulder and pointed at Monna and said nice car and then joined his friends at the bar.

"That's the third one tonight," Ben said. "This keeps up, I'll have to start charging admission. I took Barney there for a run up to the house and back. He was so goddamn excited I thought he was gonna pee in his pants. Said he hadn't been in a rag top since high school. Most of these old boys ain't ever been in anything but a truck. Or a horse."

Jamison had ordered a burrito in green sauce, remembering the last time and knowing full well he'd taken on more than he could handle. Sure enough, when Jessica brought their orders she could barely balance the three heaping plates of food on her arms. She reached across the table to set Ben's plate down and her breasts lightly brushed Jamison's shoulder and Jamison felt his heart flutter.

"I see you drove down in Monna's new toy," she said. "It's about time. Everybody here's been wanting to see it for days."

Ben displayed an exaggerated frown. "I thought you could keep a secret, Jessica. I buy a new car that's 'sposed to be a secret and the next thing I know everyone in Aden's talking about it. How do you suppose they figured that out?"

Jessica rolled her eyes and shrugged. "I'm just a bar wench," she said. "You want me to keep secrets, you gotta pony up a bigger tip." She cocked her hip, and the three of them roared with laughter.

Monna had put on a bright red blouse. "To match the car," she said. She ordered something in a martini glass that Ben labelled a "girl drink." Jamison and Ben sipped the beers Jessica had unilaterally decided they would order. There wasn't a band tonight but someone had turned on the juke box. Jamison thought it might be Lynyrd Skynyrd. When Ben started tapping his fingers to the music, he knew he'd guessed right.

Grant was behind the bar. Jessica walked behind the bar and spoke to him and he touched her hip and she smiled up at him. Then she glanced over her shoulder at Jamison. But Jamison was talking to Ben.

"That little bird was super cool," Jamison said. "Do they live in those houses you built for them all winter?"

"I can see you need an education on songbirds," Ben said. "No, to answer your question, they do not. They migrate all the way down to Mexico, sit on the beach and drink margaritas through their itsy bitsy little beaks. Some of them play through and keep going all the way to Central America. You gotta think about that: a bird the size of my finger"—he held up his index finger—"that flies a couple thousand miles down and back every year of its life. But they do."

Ben put his napkin in his lap and plucked his fork off the table. "So anyway, I used to think if I put up a bunch of houses I'd get a bunch of wrens. But they're like a high school kid with a new girl-friend: they won't let nobody else get near. You got to space them out. So usually there's one pair nesting in one of the houses by the bedroom window and another pair out in the house I put up on the stable. And then I put one in a tree down by the river and sometimes I get a pair in there, too. Just depends on how domestic they're feeling. This year it looks like we might get full occupancy."

"That would be really cool," Jamison said.

"It's as cool as can be," Monna said, jumping in. "Have you heard them singing? If there's a pair nesting in the house on the stable you might be able to hear those."

Jamison shook his head. "I don't think so. About all I can hear is the river. What do they sound like?"

"It's this beautiful warble, like a flute," Monna said. "Almost otherworldly. So much sound from such a tiny little thing. Some mornings, I wake up listening to them outside my window. It's the best thing about mornings for me. *Now* it is, anyway."

Ben wiped his mouth with his napkin and stared at his plate. Jamison waited, as if Monna had just handed them an unopened envelope. What had come before *now*? But she said nothing more, innocently glancing from one to the other as if she hadn't just left them with a statement she declined to elaborate on, and Jamison was left wondering if he'd read too much into it. He watched her sip her drink, the martini glass trembling in her unsteady hand, her eyes darting around the dim confines of the bar, watching the slowly circulating menagerie of locals. Jamison wondered how many locals had lived in Aden as long as Monna and Ben. Forty years. Forty years ago he'd been just a few years out of his rookie year in Minneapolis Special School District Number 1. The decades since had passed exactly like the older teachers he worked with had told him they would, as if he were watching his life on a highlights reel displayed on the grainy screen of a black and white TV. He hadn't believed them then, but he could not deny their prescience now. In a few months he'd be 73.

He'd followed Ben and Monna down to the Infirmary in his Honda. They'd taken their white cowboy hats off and put them in their laps to keep them from blowing away in the wash above the windshield. Jamison heard Ben run through the gears smoothly and expertly. He'd watched Monna put one hand on the top of the windshield to brace herself and extend the other straight out the side of the tiny car, the tremors in her arm unnoticeable in the buffeting wind, her small, fluttering hand diving and rising into the slipstream as though she were flying.

* * *

Ben pulled up a few feet away from the garage door and put the MG in neutral while the door opened. It rose slowly, in fits and starts, groaning in protest. Jamison had left the bar an hour before Ben and Monna, but light shone from the windows of the studio. Jamison had told them he wanted to get back to a book. He had waited until he had said goodbye to Jessica and then left, half his uneaten burrito on his plate.

"What did he say he was reading?" Ben asked. The moon was out, and it had grown chilly. But the air from the heater wrapped their legs in a cocoon of warmth.

"He told me, let me think." Monna frowned a little. "He said it was a classic, something he'd read before. Walt Whitman, I think that was it."

"Seems to me you read a book once, why go back and do it again? You already know how it's gonna end. It'd be like watching reruns."

"Yeah, but that's not the way Jamison sees it, Ben. He was always like that. He got a Masters of Arts in English so he could teach to support his reading and writing. He always knew that's what he wanted to do. Kind of like I did with painting. I think it's the Everett genetics."

Ben turned and rested his arm across the back of Monna's seat. "Your dad ever drive any heavy equipment? Because Jamison sure has the genetics for that."

"Really?" Monna said.

"Yeah. He's a fucking wizard on a Bobcat. I lined him out and two hours later he's a pro. You should see him out there. I expect him to pop a wheelie one of these days, just to prove he can do it. He's like a big kid in a sandbox, all hunched over in the cab so he can see out from under the roof, grinning like a Cheshire cat. I gotta tell you, it's entertaining."

"He really likes working for you, Ben. You know that, right? He told me."

"That's 'cause I'm paying his salary. He's *got* to like working for me."

"No. You know what I mean."

Ben tapped his fingers in a soft, rhythmic thrum on the steering wheel. "Well," he said, "I like working with him, too."

Above them, in a shroud of inky black that extended from the dark outline of the Crazies to the Bridgers unseen in the west, the stars shone like tiny, piercing lamps, the light from the moon brushing the mountains with a ghostly luminescence, as if they burned with a light from some unfathomable distance below the surface of the earth. Monna lay back in the passenger seat, ticking off the constellations she knew.

"I used to try to paint this, the light at night like this," she said. "It's really hard to paint colors that are this dark, there's such a narrow range of contrast. Everything gets sort of muddy. But Vincent Van Gogh did it when he painted *The Starry Night.* If you saw it you'd know which painting I'm talking about. They hammered that into me in the art history classes I took; it was like I had to try. But it never felt quite right. I just naturally seemed to gravitate to landscapes, that was always my métier. That's why I was so good at it."

"You *are* good at it," Ben said. "You *still* are." Frightened of where she was going with this, feeling the panic well up inside him like dark water rising.

Monna slid down in her seat, the back of her head resting on Ben's arm. The garage door had finally creaked all the way open, but Ben made no move to pull the MG inside. Looking into the garage was like looking into a black hole: no shapes that would delineate the yard tools and lawn chairs and unused bicycles she knew were in there, nothing but a void absent of light, as if they could drive into it and then keep driving forever into what would become of that which was left of her life, a future she took little pleasure in but no longer feared. There was great comfort in being free from the fear. She was done fighting.

"I'm *not* still good at it," she said, quietly, as if she were whispering to herself. She was looking at him now. "I can't do it anymore, Ben. I can't paint. My hands won't work. You saw the last one I did, the bridge and the river. Even on my good days they don't work. Not anymore."

"They got new drugs, Monna! They invent new stuff all the time. They got electrodes they can put in your brain."

"Ben, Parkinson's is incurable. I don't want anybody implanting electrodes in my head. It's not worth it."

"*What's* not worth it?"

"Ben, don't."

Chapter 13

Ben jumped out of the doorway of the bedroom with his six guns blazing, fingers slung from the hips, his thumbs tripping imaginary hammers. Monna clung seductively to the door frame and then slithered out into the living room like a femme fatale. Roy and Dale!

Both were dressed almost entirely in shades of white: cream satin shirts with intricate white piping, white cowboy hats and boots, a cream skirt with white fringe. Jamison applauded. "You look like the king and queen of the rodeo," he said.

Ben twirled his imaginary six guns and slid them back into their imaginary holsters. "Damn straight we do," he said. "You gotta be a real cowboy if you're gonna be in a real parade." He glanced at Monna. "Cow*girl*," he said. She drew her six gun and shot him in the chest.

Jamison grinned and folded his hands over his head, ankles crossed, legs extended on the sofa. Despite the warmth of the day, he was dressed in khaki pants, not shorts; he knew from a lifetime of painful experience that his fair skin, exposed to a relentless sun, would burn, peel and burn again. "Where are you guys going to be? I want to watch. I'll be cheering you on from the sidewalk."

"Good luck with that," Ben said. "Sidewalks are kind of hit or miss in Aden. I think there's one in front of the Infirmary, though. Monna and I been going there so long I forgot."

"There is, Ben," Monna said. She was digging through her purse. "Didn't you give me the keys to the MG? No, never mind. Here they are." She held up the keys and jangled them.

"Monna's gonna drive, so you might want to stand back a ways from the road, get behind somebody if you can. Her hands get to shakin' and she's liable to take out a row of bystanders. Couple guys I just may point out to her, you know, 'case it's unavoidable."

"Ben's worried about my *symptoms*," she said in a stage whisper. "But I'm feeling pretty good today. See?" She held out her hand, gyrating it wildly. She clutched it with the other hand and made it stop. Smirking at them. Jamison wasn't sure how much was supposed to be a joke.

The parade, Ben told him, was the world's shortest. Jamison didn't know if that were true but he really didn't care. The parade would precede the rodeo, and both Ben and Monna told him that everyone in town would turn out to watch.

"So we're gonna get in line on the edge of town and then go about 150 yards to the bar," Ben said. "Don't blink or you'll miss it. We'll be somewhere in the middle of the pack. Nobody ever drove a MG in the parade before. Monna's gonna be famous."

Jamison was excited about seeing the rodeo, which would begin shortly after the parade. He remembered watching them on TV with his parents as a child; Monna had not yet been born. He'd begged his parents to let him stay up late to watch the cowboys. But by the time Monna was old enough to be going through her own cowgirl phase, Jamison had outgrown his. What little he knew of cowboys and horses and ranch life came from an occasional television movie in which all the male actors wore pistols slung low on their hips. Jamison had never seen anyone wearing a pistol in Aden.

The parade was at noon sharp, and at 11:30 there was already a string of trucks stretching for several hundred yards out of town. There were stapled-together floats on flat-bed trailers and stock dogs barking and riders on horses, the riders somber and straight-backed in crisp, white, long-sleeved shirts. The sheriff's department had sent out extra deputies to monitor traffic; Jamison nodded at Gerald who answered with a distracted wave and then returned his attention to the throngs of people surging across the road.

Since the rodeo was the one day all year when it was impossible to find a place to park anywhere in Aden, Jamison had decided to walk to town. He found partial shade under a sparsely-leaved tree and took off his day pack and set it on the ground for a seat, the thin canopy above his head providing scant relief from the sun. Rain had been forecast, but as far as Jamison could see the sky was blue and relentlessly cloud free. He'd brought a raincoat just in case.

A few minutes after noon the parade began. Someone had put together a band, and the half dozen players, preceded by three somber veterans from the American Legion marching in lock step and carrying an American flag, played a booming rendition of the *Star Spangled Banner*, prompting all within earshot to cover their hearts with their hands. But the band passed quickly and in its wake came floats with queens of several varieties: the wheat queen, the cattle queen, and the North Dakota queen, a hugely overweight man in drag. People howled. Following them were riders on horses, men and women both, the youngest women dressed in Wranglers so tight that several of the men in the audience groaned. The women riders, who had been through this before, gazed resolutely forward.

There was a lull following the riders and then the MG wove into view. In a few seconds it was directly across from Jamison, Monna waving gayly from the driver's seat as though she were a newly elected mayor, Ben taking it all in from the passenger seat, grinning enormously. Jamison stood and waved and Monna spied him and pointed at the Infirmary.

When Jamison caught up with them Ben and Monna had joined a crowd of people milling around the bar waiting to get in. The three of them inched slowly toward the door until finally they were able to duck inside. There was a full contingent of bar staff working the crowd, taking orders for drinks, warning people that the kitchen was backed up and there might be a half hour wait for food; scurrying from one cluster of laughing, smiling patrons to the next. Jamison had never seen so many perfectly creased, spotlessly brushed cowboy hats. Several men nodded and grinned as he passed, none of whom he recognized. He towered above everyone else in the room.

Jessica scurried by with a full tray of drinks. She spied them and spun around. "You guys want these?" She said. "I can't find the

asshole that ordered them. On the house. Take them." Jamison noticed—it would have been almost impossible *not* to notice—that
she was wearing a skin-tight blouse with a deeply plunging neckline that revealed more of her tattoo than he'd ever seen, the fiery
oranges and yellows of the phoenix extending over the swell of her
breasts only to vanish seductively under the lacey black edge of her
bra.

Ben handed one beer to Monna and took the other for himself
and said thank you kindly. Jamison reached for the last and threw
a five on her tray and Jessica scurried away. He watched until she
vanished beneath the sea of expensive cowboy hats.

"Man," Ben said. "I was thinking we could get lunch, but this is
crazy. At least we got free drinks out of the deal. We'll be here for
three hours if we order lunch. I'll die of starvation by then. Maybe
we should just go back home and come back tonight for the dance."

"I can fix something up," Monna said. "How about you, Jamison?
Are you going to stick around and stare at Jessica's boobs or do you
want some lunch?"

Jamison felt his cheeks burn and knew that the flush would
extend to the top of his bald head. "It's that obvious?" he said.

Ben guffawed.

"Listen," Monna said. "All I'm saying is Jessica is really good at
what she does. That's why Grant hired her. You can use your imagination to figure out the rest."

Jamison lifted his beer. "Okay, I'll meet you guys back at the ha-
cienda. Maybe I can hitch a ride with someone." In the close heat of
the crowded bar his glass was wet with condensation and he wiped
his hand on his pants. "Got to be somebody here I know."

"Nah, we can fit you in between us in the MG," Ben said. "It's
only a mile. You can sit on the trunk. Make sure you wave to all the
nice people."

"You sure? I don't want to scratch the finish."

"Sure I'm sure. You ain't gonna sit in my lap, I'll tell you what.
It's only a mile. You can evaluate Monna's driving. She didn't get to
run over anybody in the parade."

Monna pouted. "Ben wouldn't let me," she said.

They'd got into the Infirmary just in time. It was now so packed there was barely room to turn around, and whenever the door opened to squeeze someone in or out, Jamison saw that the crowd outside had spilled across the street. Gerald was still attempting crowd control, pointlessly urging people with drinks to take them back inside the bar, which could not possibly admit another human body. Jessica flashed by, plowing through the crowd like a fullback while balancing a tray of glasses over her head.

After they'd finished their beers, they pushed through the crowd and walked to the MG. Monna slid into the driver's seat and after a couple of shaky attempts, stabbed the key into the ignition. Jamison slid in behind her, wedging his long legs to one side of the stick so Monna could shift gears. Ben squeezed into the passenger seat. Monna found reverse and tried to look over her shoulder, but in attempting to wrest her body around clumsily stomped on the gas and the car lurched backwards so abruptly Jamison's chin almost slammed into the windshield. "Whoa!" Ben cried. Monna scowled and ground into first and wove her way through the throngs of people on the street with grim determination, both hands gripping the wheel. Jamison perched between them on the trunk, one hand on his ball cap and the other braced on top of the windshield, looming above the car like a giant bespectacled bird, grinning into the wind.

* * *

They were talking about the rodeo.

"I can't figure out how they do that," Jamison said. He was still marveling at the team roping he'd seen that afternoon. "How on earth can you lasso a cow's legs running full tilt away from you?"

"Pretty cool, ain't it?" Ben said. "I used to feel the same way. My dad did a little team roping when he was younger and he showed me some stuff. We had a couple horses on the farm but you couldn't rope from them so he took me to his buddy's house one day, probably thought he was gonna turn me into a cowboy. Guy had this plastic calf he towed around behind a motorcycle. I could ride okay but I was a lot better at football than throwin' a rope, and I was nothing to write home about in football."

Jamison gazed around the bar. Knots of men and women in bright, embroidered shirts were clustered loosely around the perimeter of the neon-lit walls, laughing and gesturing, like luminous, darting fish above a coral reef. Ben had suggested returning early to beat the dance rush, and it had been a good call—after the zoo that had been the post-parade influx, the Infirmary was comparatively uncrowded.

Ben raised his beer. "But to answer your question," he said, "there's a trick to it. You time it so the rope bounces up off the ground when they got their legs in the air. It's like magic when you watch a really good team. Guy I went to high school with went pro and ended up roping at the NFR a couple years. He got his ass kicked, but he said he had a blast, partying with all those barrel racers after the show. And it's a steer, not a cow. They don't got cows in rodeo."

Ben and Monna had retired their Roy and Dale outfits in favor of Wranglers and pressed shirts. The dance would be starting early, timed to follow the conclusion of the rodeo by two hours so people could go home, eat, and then head to the bar at a civilized hour. The three of them found a table and had time to chat with Jessica and Grant, who were far less harried than they'd been earlier in the day, when it seemed like everyone in town had converged on the Infirmary, bought drinks, and wandered out into the street, only to be ushered back inside by a stern Deputy Metzger. Upon their arrival, Jessica gave Jamison a polite hug and Grant shook hands all around. Jessica, Jamison noticed, had switched into a less revealing blouse.

Monna caught Jamison staring at Jessica and her face twitched into a knowing smile. "When's the band start?" she said. Her voice was barely audible above the murmuring backdrop of laughter and conversation.

"I told them 8 sharp," Grant said. He was about Ben's size, but with straight black hair going to gray and a spray of fine lines creasing the corners of his eyes. "They're pretty good. I hired them out of Livingston last year and they pulled in a good crowd. When the band gets going it's gonna to be a zoo in here. I wouldn't give up my table if I were you."

"That's gonna make it hard to dance," Ben said.

"Don't say I didn't warn you," Grant said.

Ben bought them a pizza. Jamison thanked him and said he'd cover the tip. They watched a stream of couples, middle-aged and older, enter the bar. And then, shortly after the band took the stage, a younger crowd began filtering in, packs of grinning young men in their twenties in pressed shirts and expensive felt cowboy hats, their bright eyes darting around the room, appraising, predatory. The names hand-carved into their leather belts proclaimed who they were: Travis, Cody, Boone. Cody spied Monna and touched his hat. Politely flirting with the attractive older woman.

"Go ahead and look," Ben said. "They ain't nothing but babies still."

"Ben, I believe you're jealous," Monna said. "Are you jealous?"

"They ain't got nothin' I ain't got."

Jamison snickered and Ben glared at him.

Monna put her hand on Ben's arm, then cast a sideways glance at Jamison and pouted. Ben stuck out his chin.

The band began to play, jumping directly into a fast two step. "That's a pretty song," Monna said. "Will you dance with me?" Monna stood and extended her hand.

Ben made a show of frowning, but it quickly dissolved into a pleased grin. "What I gotta do to get laid," he said. Monna made a weak fist and punched him in the arm.

They walked toward the band, Monna's arm hooked in Ben's for support, then merged into the flow of dancers circling the floor. But the pace was too fast for Monna's blunt coordination. She stumbled through a turn, then stumbled again attempting to stay in time with Ben's easy cadence and finally Ben led her to a corner where the traffic was slower. They fell in behind an elderly couple and shuffled slowly through the remainder of the dance, Ben's hand resting on the swell of her hip, Monna's hand gripping his arm through his thick cotton shirt, gazing up at him and then past him at the other dancers. And then back again, into his face, his eyes. Jamison saw them talk, Ben smiling at something she'd said, turning his head away from her in a flicker of shyness or embarrassment, an unguarded moment. When the dance was over they waited for the other couples to clear the floor and then returned to the table. Monna was beaming, Ben's hand lingering on the small of her back.

"These guys are great," she said. "Same band they had in here last year, right Ben? I think that's what Grant said. The lead singer used to sing in Nashville. I think that's what he said."

Ben shaded his eyes and gazed at the band. "Yup, same guys, except the drummer may be different. I don't know about the Nashville thing. If you were good enough to play in Nashville, why would you move to Montana?" He folded his hands on the table.

"I did," Monna said.

"Yeah but, you're a painter. Music's different. Nashville's like the center of the universe for musicians."

"It's all art, Ben, it's all about how you feel. I've never played an instrument in my life, but I know how musicians *feel* when they get up there, when it's working the way it's supposed to work. Because it's the same for me. It isn't about money, not always." Monna tried to steeple her fingers, awkwardly touching the tip of each finger to the tips of the fingers on the opposite hand, as if each finger had to be willed separately into place. She gazed over the top of her hands at Ben, her words soft below the whine and yodel and thump of the band, as the murmur of a river is in quiet counterpoint to the tumult of all else around it. "It's about love. How much you love it. How much you fall out of love when you don't have it. It doesn't matter where you live. You used to feel that way, too. I remember you then," she said. "The woodworking."

Ben plinked his fingernail against his water glass. The ice clinked silently against the walls of the glass, drowned in the noise of the crowd around them. "I used to do some woodworking, back in the day," he told Jamison. He turned on his stool. "No money in it."

Monna glared, her soft voice suddenly abrupt and penetrating, edged with anger. "You were good, Ben!" she said. "You always say that! You saw those bird houses he built, right?"

"With the dovetailed corners, sure," Jamison said. "I gave one to Jessica."

"But that's all he builds anymore! Birdhouses. They're beautiful, but … that walnut dresser in our bedroom, that beautiful sleigh bed we sleep on. He built those. Have you seen them? He built those. Ben designed that dresser."

"There's just no money in it," Ben said. He spoke quietly, self effacingly, a man offering logical reasons. It was as though having found a passion of singular worth, he'd let it slip away before he knew what he had, before he'd had a chance to gauge the value of his life without it. "You can get stuff from China for half the price," he said. "You can." As if this were obvious. As if that were the point.

Monna's eyes rose to the ceiling. Grant was filling glass mugs from the beer taps behind the bar, his back toward them. Monna's gaze fell to the table and she reached for her margarita, the glass gripped awkwardly between her hands. "Sometimes we have these conversations," she said.

Ben drummed his fingers on the table, frowning. Jamison saw his gaze shift. "I think you got company, Monna," he said. Cody was walking toward them. He stopped behind Monna and touched her shoulder. "Dance?" he asked.

She swiveled around and peered up at him and smiled. "Sure," she said. She rose slowly to her feet and extended her hand, which Cody took.

"Hey, cowboy!" Ben said. He scooted forward on his stool. "You gotta take it easy with her, okay? Her coordination's a little off. So just take it easy."

The cowboy grinned back, displaying even white teeth below a sparse blond mustache. "Okay, grandpa," he said, then spun on his heel and walked Monna to the floor, who had to skip once to keep up. Ben stared at Jamison incredulously. "You hear what that little shit just called me?" he said.

Jamison certainly had. "You know that guy?"

"Fuck no. He's got his name on his belt. He's here for the rodeo. Probably from California."

Jamison watched them dance. The tempo of the music had picked up, and Cody began spinning Monna from one arm to the other, oblivious to the beat of the song. Monna gamely tried to follow the young man's frenetic moves, but her reactions, withered by her disease, lagged a half beat behind. Before she could register and follow one wild, arm-twisting lead she'd be yanked out of it and flung into another.

"God damn it!" Ben said. "I told him to take it easy on her!"

The song was nearly over. Monna spun halfway around and then stumbled and put her arms out to catch herself, but in the next instant the young cowboy had lifted her off her feet, flipped her end over end, and gently set her back down again. He grinned triumphantly.

Monna reeled backwards in astonishment. When the cowboy reached for her hand, she motioned violently that she'd had enough.

Ben bolted from his stool and charged across the dance floor, stopping inches from the startled young man, shaking his finger in his face, furious. "What'd I just tell you! What'd I just tell you, goddamn it!" he shouted. "I oughta … goddamn you!"

The cowboy's bewilderment burned away like paper in a flame and his face twisted into rage. He stepped forward and slapped Ben's hand away, his lips drawn in a violent sneer. "Ought to do what, old man? I'm right here so fuck you!"

Jamison launched himself from the table, his heart racing, trying to recall what he'd learned from the half dozen fights he'd broken up during his years as a teacher, reliving the sickening fear that clutched his breast even now. *Be calm. Raise your voice enough to show authority. Be direct and firm.* He stepped between Ben and the cowboy, arms dividing them like a referee at a boxing match, towering over them both. "Young man," he said. "Young man!"

Later, Monna told him he had turned to face the cowboy and had placed a restraining hand on the young man's shoulder and that's when the cowboy head butted him squarely in the chest, knocking him off balance and sending him reeling backwards. Jamison remembered seeing the blur of stunned faces around him as he collapsed to the floor and hit his head in a starburst of yellow light and then someone was kneeling beside him and talking to him and he was groping for his broken glasses and saw Ben and the cowboy grappling on the floor beside him while Grant straddled them both and punched the cowboy in the head and face, hard, his breath huffing out of him with the force of his blows. Jamison rolled away, his arms over his head to protect himself and then Gerald had lifted the cowboy completely off his feet and wrenched his arms behind his back, the young man's legs wind milling in fury, in impotence, in powerless rage. The crowd surged in around them and held him down while Gerald handcuffed him and dragged him out the door and into the bright hot sun on the street.

Now the bar was quiet.

Ben came back from the street and went first to Monna with his fists still clenched, snapping anger, the veins in his neck corded and red. He reached for her and spoke to her and then he saw Jamison on his knees trying to straighten the crumpled frame of his eye glasses. Ben extended his hand and two men standing nearby helped Ben lift Jamison to his feet. His glasses bent up off his nose at a crazy angle and after a couple attempts to get them to lie flat, he gave up and shoved them in his pocket. His head throbbed from where he had hit the floor but he could still see. He was ashamed of his failure, ashamed that he had been of so little help.

Ben's anger began to subside and he took Monna's arm and walked her back to the table, Jamison a step behind, his gaze on the back of Ben's boots, blurry and indistinct in his weak vision. By the time they had taken their seats Grant was back with three fresh glasses of beer.

When Ben reached for his billfold Grant quickly waved him away. "No way, Ben, no way." He winced and tried to spread the fingers on his right hand, which had already begun to swell. "You're on my tab for the rest of the night. Can you believe that asshole?

We threw him in the back of Gerald's truck and he radioed him in. The guy's in the back seat, starts trying to kick out the windows. He apparently has anger management issues. Gerald says he's gonna cool his heels in jail for a few days unless he can throw bail, which he probably can't. Fucking asshole."

"I'm trying to remember," Ben said, "but I don't think I've ever seen a fight in here before. That's forty-some years. First one I see, I'm in."

Grant pulled up a stool and leaned in toward them. "I hate fights. *Hate* them. People think bars like this place here, that stuff happens all the time, like it's part of the entertainment venue. But not *this* bar. I have zero tolerance for that shit. The minute I saw that asshole get in your face I told Jessica to call Gerald. The rodeo crowd's usually pretty good. Mostly it's guys that live in the valley. They get loud but that's as far as it goes." He examined his hand, frowning. A deep purple bruise had begun seeping down his swollen fingers. "Guess Jessica's gonna be pouring beer by herself tonight. I got to get this hand checked out. I sure hope it's not broke. Fucking asshole."

Jamison took a long drink from his glass. The cold beer was indescribably delicious. He drained the rest of the glass and set it down, his spirits ticking up. "I broke up some fights when I was teaching school," he said. "They put on classes in how to do that. But I'm not any good at that stuff, fighting. I never was."

"No," Ben said, breaking into a grin. "You looked real pretty out there, sort of like that Sugar Ray Leonard guy, black guy back in the eighties that was such a great boxer. Took a punch and got right back up. We're gonna call you Sugar Ray Jamison. What'd you think, Monna?"

"Oh my, well ..." Monna said.

Jamison looked around the table, trying hard not to grin too much, happy to be among these people, these friends. He imagined that this was what it felt like in a high-school locker room after a big game. It was a good feeling.

"Hey, I like it," Grant said. He waved Jessica over. She stopped beside him and put her hand on his shoulder. "Sugar Ray Jamison needs another beer. Get one for Ben, too, would you honey?"

Jessica seemed confused.

Grant reached across the table and made a fist with his good hand and lightly punched Jamison's arm. "This guy. Sugar Ray Jamison."

"Oh!" Jessica said. She put up her fists like a boxer, the way women show things that men do. "*That* Sugar Ray Jamison."

"You got it," Grant said.

Chapter 14

"We're gonna lift this wall up nice and easy," Ben said. "With two of us it won't be too bad. Normally we'd toenail it into the deck but you can't toenail into concrete. Obviously. That's why we sank those anchor bolts. So once we get it stood up, you got to kind of kick the bottom plate over a little so those holes we drilled drop over the bolts. Then you're gonna hold it there while I brace it. Think you can do that?"

Jamison nodded nervously. They'd poured the slab the previous week and then brought back the Bobcat to backfill it, which Ben had put him in charge of. Driving the Bobcat was just as much fun the second time around as it had been the first. But he wasn't so sure about the wall. It looked pretty heavy to him. He kicked it with the toe of his boot but it wouldn't budge.

"What if it falls over?"

"Ain't gonna fall over. But if it does, just get the hell out of the way. Don't try to stop it no matter what you do. I seen guys break their legs that way. Just let it hit the deck and we'll lift her up again."

Jamison tried to lift one corner of the wall. He pulled it up about six inches and let it drop, the dull crack of wood on concrete like a bat hitting a soft pitch. At least, he thought, he'd be able to lift it high enough to get his fingers under it. Ben was impressively strong, barrel chested and thick armed. At the lumberyard, Jamison had watched him toss fifty-pound boxes of nails into his truck as though he were selecting loaves of bread from a rack, spinning them around in his hands to check for freshness, and then dropping them into a shopping cart. Jamison was not nearly so sure of his own strength. He'd spent his life lifting books, not walls. "Should I take my tool belt off?"

"Why do you want to do that?"

"I don't know. In case it gets caught on something."

"It's not gonna get caught on something. Leave it on."

Ben walked around the wall for a final appraisal. With the nail gun, a tool Jamison had never seen, they'd hammered it together in less than half an hour. Ben had showed Jamison how to use the gun, another new toy Jamison found exotic and thrilling.

"Okay," Ben said. "Let's get after it. You stand down a little ways from that end, and when I say go, we lift it up. You ready?"

Jamison walked into place and nodded.

"Okay. Now."

As Ben had predicted, the wall went up without a hitch. Ben kicked his end of the bottom plate over the anchor bolts and told Jamison to do the same. When Jamison had kicked the last section of the wall over the anchor bolts, it fell into place with a satisfying *whump*. Holding it upright took little effort, and Ben used two by fours to brace it to the stakes they'd driven in the yard. He backed away and told Jamison he could do the same. Jamison took a step back and examined what they'd done. The wall was level and plumb, exactly how Ben had told him it was supposed to be.

"Congratulations," Ben said. "Your first wall. Two more to go. Then the trusses. Trusses are *really* fun, 'specially since we don't have a crane. You wait."

Jamison glanced at the sliding glass doors of the house. He hadn't seen the frenetic little dog for two days and Jamison wondered if the people who owned the house had locked it up in a bedroom. He'd been enjoying the quiet in the absence of the dog's hysterical barking. He worked side by side with Ben for the rest of the morning, building the two additional walls that would frame out the three sides of the addition, carefully matching them to the lines they'd snapped on the plywood sheathing they'd exposed on the house, then lag bolting the walls into the existing structure. All of this—construction work in the aggregate—was as foreign to

Jamison as deep sea diving. He'd spent one miserable summer in college working on an oil rig in Wyoming but most of the following summers in work/study positions around the Midwest: Omaha, St. Louis, Kansas City. Upon completing grad school he'd moved directly into a teaching position in the Minneapolis school system. In the same way that few wonder where food in the supermarket comes from, Jamison had never wondered how houses in subdivisions were built. He knew someone had to build them, of course; it just never occurred to him that he might someday be doing it himself. Yet here he was. It was interesting in the way that new experiences had always been interesting to Jamison: as an avenue to greater understanding.

When they'd raised the last wall and lag-bolted it in place, Ben hopped in his truck and sped off to buy them lunch. Jamison walked around the perimeter of the addition, pushing and shoving the walls, testing their rigidity. He was surprised that the walls, which, despite their weight, had seemed rickety and fragile lying on the slab, now, as an *edifice*, seemed possessed of a strength that defied any easy dictum of the whole being greater than the sum of its parts. Soon, these walls would support a strong, durable roof that would shelter a room, and hold within its walls the warmth of that room, and in turn comfort the family which lived within that warmth.

Ben had told him they'd set the trusses in a couple days and then sheath the roof and walls. He told Jamison he anticipated that would take less than a week; the entire job would be done by the end of the month. Jamison sat on the slab, his back to the wall he'd framed, his long arms wrapped loosely around his bent knees. Maybe the end of the month would be it. Maybe, at the end of the month, he would drive back to Minneapolis. Maybe it was, if nothing else, time for him to leave.

Yet he didn't miss the city, didn't miss his apartment. Certainly, he didn't miss the traffic. Aden seemed as though it were situated in a different galaxy, with constellations of people and shops and houses just like Minneapolis, but on such a reduced scale that any comparison seemed laughable. There couldn't possibly be a comparison, for a comparison missed the point. Aden, including the handful of people he had come to know who called the valley home, was exactly what it was regardless of any reference to anything or any place beyond it. It was, Jamison thought, exactly what it was *because* of that.

Jamison had come to Montana understanding that he would eventually leave, in the same way he understood that he would be exactly that many months older when he left—an article of faith of no more significance than the weight of an assumption. But now that it seemed time for him to go, he could no longer remember his reasons for wanting to do so, only that it seemed he should. He unbuckled his tool belt and placed it beside him on the floor of the slab.

Jamison heard Ben's Ford return and then Ben appeared, swinging white paper bags in each hand. He stepped onto the deck and dropped one of the bags beside Jamison. "McDonalds," he said. "Thought you might need a change."

Jamison peered inside his bag and discovered that it was stuffed with food, far more than he could possibly eat. "This is all mine?" he asked.

"Yup."

"Ben, I have to tell you something. I'm done growing. I can't eat this much. Save yourself some money. Really."

Ben shrugged. "It won't go to waste. I'll eat anything you don't want. Burn up a lot of calories in this line or work. And it's worse in the winter."

Jamison extended his legs and pulled a burger from his bag. There was another one beneath it. "I don't think I'll be here next winter," he said.

Ben pulled a hamburger out of his bag, slowly unwrapped it and then crumpled the wrapper in his hand. He glanced at Jamison and tossed the wrapper into the yard. They made a sweep through the job site at the end of every work day, picking up nails, collecting garbage and end cuts and anything else they might step on or trip over, and threw them in the dumpster Ben had rented. Jamison enjoyed that part of the job, the ritual of keeping their work space clean.

Ben took a bite of his hamburger and then balanced it on his leg. A tendril of thin red juice dribbled onto his pants, translucent and shiny. He wiped his mouth with a paper napkin. "I got work lined up through Christmas," he said. "I get calls every week I got to turn down. You got a job here if you want it."

"I don't know," Jamison said. "I've been here since March. I feel like I need to take care of things back home."

"Like what?"

Jamison placed his Coke on the slab, just so, so it wouldn't tip over. "I don't know. The stuff you don't do when you're not home. I've been here almost four months. Monna seems okay. I thought, you know …" A fly landed on his arm and he flicked it off. "I thought she would need a little more hands-on help, *you* and she would. I don't know what it was exactly I thought I was going to do, but it doesn't seem like I've been doing it. Monna was always independent, from what I remember. She lived in her own little bubble, her and her art, breathing that same air day after day. But why am I telling you? You already know all this."

Ben dropped his head back until it rested on the stud behind him. He crossed his legs at the ankles and gazed at the blue vaulted sky. Above the unroofed addition, far above the gently nodding trees that surrounded them, clouds furled and buffeted in violent white silence, a gathering together and a pulling apart, desperate and mute.

"You ever do this before, build anything like this?"

"You mean an *addition* like this? No, never. Dad had a few tools in the garage. I nailed a couple things together when I was a kid. And then that dog house I told you about. I never even took shop in high school. I was doing AP stuff, or whatever they called Advanced Placement back in the sixties. Some of those courses seem kind of silly now. But I thought I was pretty hot."

Ben grinned. "You may have already figured out I never took any AP classes."

Jamison shrugged self-consciously. "You didn't miss anything," he said.

"Maybe I did," Ben said. "You don't learn nothing if you always look at stuff the same way. So that's why I asked. So let's say you take this addition here. You got to be careful how it all goes up or you royally screw yourself down the road. Little stuff like being out of plumb half an inch, later on, you go to hanging the sheet rock and you find out you've just screwed yourself big time, because all of a sudden there's this big gap in the corner. You can slap mud in it but it'll eventually crack and fall out. Construction's all about preparation for the next step, and the next, and on like that until you're finished. It's why we snapped those lines on the wall, so we'd get the wall just right, so we don't got to go back and do it over again. I didn't know any of this stuff when I started. But I knew that I didn't know, so I learned from people who did."

"Well, I like it. Especially the Bobcat. I'm grateful for the work. The money helps."

"Shit, Jamison, I could hire any high school kid to do what you're doing," Ben said. He scooted away from the wall and folded his legs. "But I'd rather see you learn something for the long haul. You can take a trade like this anywhere. It's good money when the market's there."

"I've got a trade," Jamison said. "I'm an English teacher. I'm a *retired* English teacher. Teacher emeritus."

Ben pulled a cardboard carton of fries out of his bag and set them beside his leg. Jamison reached in his bag for his fries and took two and gave the rest to Ben.

"I just went to McDonalds because it was close," Ben said. "I can buy us lunch anywhere you want."

"McDonalds is okay with me," Jamison said.

"They got a Burger King, Taco Hell, Dairy Queen if you want ice cream, all the heavy hitters. They got everything in this town."

"Okay," Jamison said. He could hear the thrum of cars from the front of the house. The sound reminded him of the four-lane thoroughfare that fronted his downtown apartment in Minneapolis. Seven decades of life in an urban environment had numbed him to the perpetual sound of traffic. He had long ago stopped hearing it, a facility he wasn't sure he'd adopted so much as had forced upon him. The encompassing silence of the Shields Valley had been a revelation, an uneasiness, as if something unwanted but essential were missing. And then the unease had gone away. Now, even when the wind howled, driving stinging dust and grit into his eyes like fractured bits of glass, he heard the silence beneath the noise, silence delivered by a breathing land.

"Okay, well," Ben said. "So, I'll pay you $20 an hour. That's journeyman's wages. Pretty close."

"But Ben, I'm not worth that!" Jamison said. "I just started a couple weeks ago. I don't know how to do anything."

"You know how to drive a Bobcat," Ben said. "I taught you how to do that, I can teach you how to be a carpenter."

Jamison folded up the wrapper to his burger and put it inside the bag beside the other burger, then folded the bag closed and set it near Ben's bag. He finished his Coke and pushed the straw through the plastic lid. He would talk things over with Monna and see if there was anything she might still need. He didn't have a date in mind, no firm plans. He was just going to put it out there.

* * *

"You would miss the autumn," Monna said. "You haven't experienced autumn here yet. It makes all the other seasons worthwhile. The mountains are beautiful then."

"Ben told you already?"

"Yes. He said you were thinking about leaving because you weren't accomplishing anything by being here." She pushed the bottle of wine toward him and Jamison reached for it and topped off his glass. "This is that kangaroo wine from Costco you like," Monna said. "That *I* like. Ben's out in his shop."

Jamison rubbed the back of his neck and sighed. "It's not like what you think, Monna. It's not like I thought, that, you know, by my being here things would all of a sudden be hunky dory and you wouldn't still be sick, or anything remotely like that. I think I came out here with unrealistic expectations. That's my fault, not yours or Ben's."

"What did you think you were supposed to accomplish?" She put her glass on the table and put her hands on either side of it, palms down, as if she were a Tarot reader.

"I don't know. I didn't break it down into numerical bullet points. You sounded like you needed help so I came out. I never planned on being here forever. I never thought I'd even stay this long."

"Do you like it here? This valley? How about Aden?" Monna grinned. "You are kind of a city boy, aren't you?"

He *was* kind of a city boy, Jamison thought. But what else would he be? He liked hiking in the city parks. Once in a while he'd go tent camping with friends in the lake country to the north, but more often they stayed in a cabin that belonged to a fellow teacher. He enjoyed the woods but he was never in them for more than a long weekend: the Fourth of July, Memorial Day. His world beyond his spare and simply-furnished apartment was delineated by those activities he pursued in the city he had lived in all his life: solo plays and book readings, movies, the occasional morning coffee with an acquaintance, a restaurant.

Living in the valley had changed none of his affection for those things. But in moving to Aden he'd been presented with a choice, as if, walking on a known path, he had taken a fork for the first time and discovered a new route through long familiar terrain. There was more here than the absence of the city; more than that which could be defined by the lack of one. But in the same way that a deer hidden in tall grass vanishes maddingly when viewed with purpose and intent, he had been frustrated in his inability to see all that was here to be seen. He could feel what he was missing, those familiar ghosts which moved in the periphery. But this was not *living* as he had known life in any other context. It was life in anticipation.

"I wish you'd stay longer. Through the fall. Leave before winter, if you want. Ben and I have talked about this."

"*Ben* wants me to stay on? Is this the same Ben I work for?" Teasing her.

"He likes working with you, Jamison. He says you're a good hand. He says he wants to teach you to be a carpenter."

"He told me the same thing." Jamison peered over his sister's head and through the back window of the house, which gave on a view of the rust-pocked steel Quonset hut that was Ben's shop. The door was open in the summer heat and Jamison heard music, faint and recognizable. "He offered me twenty bucks an hour the other day. It's kind of embarrassing. I'm not worth that much. Sometimes I feel like I'm just in the way."

Monna steepled her fingers, as if in contemplation. On her bad days, her hands hung like useless claws at her side, hooked inward as if clutching invisible stones, rigid and unbending. He hated to see her that way. But today she seemed limber, flexible. She was smiling.

"I'll bet somewhere in Mom and Dad's genes you probably in-herited a talent for working with your hands," she said. "I did."

"I may have, at that. Turns out I'm pretty fair on a Bobcat."

"So you'll stay then? Stay until winter."

"Don't you want your studio back? I could find a place in Aden."

Monna put her chin in her hand. Looking at him.

"Where are you going to paint?" he said.

Monna said nothing. She held up the wine bottle and Jamison held out his glass. She topped off his glass and put a tiny splash in hers. One drop hung on the rim of her glass, gathering, then slid down the side.

"You still have that yellow cat down there in the woodpile?" she asked.

"Yes! Leviathan!" The mention of Leviathan made Jamison happy, as if he'd been personally complimented. It was silly. But he'd been moving the tins of cat food closer and closer to the door of the studio, and now had convinced the big cat that it was safe to eat on the studio's tiny front porch. He felt as though he'd tamed a wild mountain lion. He didn't imagine that his arm's-length relationship with Leviathan was remotely like the relationships other people had with their cats—content, purring kitties who butted their heads against their owner's shins and spent their days curled up on windowsills in the sun. He wasn't even sure he wanted a cat like that. What he did want was to see where his growing bond with the yellow, half-tamed creature would lead: that untraversed path, familiar and implicit.

Chapter 15

Ben had captured three grasshoppers in his mason jar. He held it up for Jamison's and Monna's appraisal.

"They're getting bigger," he said. "Maybe too big. But we'll try." He sat on the lawn chair he'd placed beside Monna's lawn chair and tossed a beheaded insect into the grass in front of his feet. But no wren came.

"Maybe they're down at the Infirmary having a beer," Jamison said. "It's pretty hot."

Ben slapped at a mosquito on his neck and peered at his hand. He wiped his hand on his pants. "Nope. They're here. We heard them when we got up this morning, right Monna?"

Monna nodded. They'd tucked their lawn chairs into the shade under the eve on the back of the house. The river had long since receded from the turbulent flows of late May and June, and now purled quietly in its bed twenty yards beyond where they sat, murmuring to itself like a contented child. The air above the water was cool and soothing, like the delicious rush of cold air from an opened freezer. Fluttering inches above the water was a loose, interlocking veil of cream-colored moths.

Monna had made iced tea. It was too hot for alcohol. Their glasses sweated and the cold drops of condensation wet their fingers in the still, afternoon heat.

"This little guy was sitting on the windowsill and looking into the bedroom this morning," Monna said. "Ben was still asleep. Sometimes they do that, just sit on the windowsill and look inside. It's like they want to come in. Which is funny, because I always have the exact opposite reaction. Every time I see a wren on the windowsill, I'm always wondering what it must be like to be a tiny little bird like that, knowing you have this great journey ahead of you, nowhere to escape to when it gets cold, nowhere to go to get warm like the inside of a house. You can't avoid the trip, every living part of you longs for the trip, even though you may never come back. All you can do is keep, you know, eating bugs."

"Here's to bugs," Ben said hoisting his glass. Jamison raised his glass and clinked Ben's.

"Bugs," Jamison said.

Ben pinched another hopper in half and tossed it on the grass, but no wren came. The severed hopper squirted green blood on his fingers and he wiped the blood on his pants and opened the mason jar and released the remaining hopper, which flew with a clacking sound for a dozen yards and then tumbled into the grass.

"Next weekend," Ben said, "is the Fourth." He gazed across the lawn at where the hopper had landed, his elbows on the arms of his chair, his hands folded casually in his lap. "We always go camping on the river. There's this nice little campground up on the north end of the Crazies, but it'll be packed over the weekend. Always is. So what I'm suggesting is we go a couple days early, beat the rush. We pull out by Saturday we'll miss the crowds. I got a real nice wall tent; it's one of those nylon Cabela's jobs, top half looks like a teepee with a center pole. I bought it off a guy used to guide pack hunts. There's plenty of room for three people. Shit, there's enough room for eight people. I got cots, too, the old-fashioned kind, army surplus, hell for stout. They're a bitch to put together but once you got them up they're tight as a trampoline. Probably not gonna be long enough for you, though." He nudged Jamison's foot with the toe of his sandals. "You want to go? You might have to sit around the fire with us and drink some whisky. You might even have to fish some in the crick. Couple paintings Monna did came from up there. Remember those, Monna?"

"I'm not ..." Monna said. "I don't think I'm going to make it this year."

Ben turned to face her.

"I just can't sleep on the ground anymore, Ben. Not like you and I used to. Or on a cot, either. I can barely get out of bed in the morning as it is. It takes me two hours just to get moving here at home. I guess I should have said something earlier. I knew you wanted to go."

"Yeah but, Monna …" Ben said. "We go every year. You got that thick foam pad I bought. You can use that."

"It's not enough, Ben," Monna said. "I tried that last year, remember? Of course, you remember."

"You were having a bad weekend last year, is what I remember," Ben said. "The symptoms were bad."

"The symptoms were bad because I was sleeping on a cot," Monna said quietly. "Not my bed."

"You never said that."

"I'm saying it now."

Ben stood and walked toward the river. He found the spot where the hopper had landed and shuffled his feet through the uncut green grass but the hopper was gone. He came back and sat in the lawn chair next to Monna and reached down beside his chair and picked up his glass of iced tea.

"You don't feel like going, that's okay. I understand," he said.

"It's not that I don't feel like going, Ben. How many years have we gone camping up there? I just can't anymore. I get too sore. It hurts." She peered at him over the edge of her glass. "Can we not do this?"

Ben shrugged. "Yeah, I guess so."

"Why don't you and Jamison go?" Monna said. "Just because I can't go doesn't mean you guys can't go. I'll cook up something for the first night you can put in the cooler. Maybe stroganoff. You like stroganoff."

"I guess that would be okay," Ben said.

"Ben." Monna rested her hand on Ben's arm. "Just go. You and Jamison will have a good time. Take him fishing."

Ben swiveled in his chair toward Jamison. "You still want to go, we can go. There's been an unscheduled vacancy. You want to go? Fine with me either way."

Jamison very much wanted to go camping. He had always enjoyed his sporadic camping trips in Minnesota; camping in the wilds of Montana would be an exciting adventure, something closer, he imagined, to a true wilderness experience. So why did he feel like the last man standing in a game of musical chairs?

"Sure," he said, straining for nonchalance. "That sounds like fun."

* * *

The tent was every bit as spacious as Ben had promised him it would be. It had taken them less than an hour to set up, but once the corners were anchored and the center pole fitted in place, the whole construction popped up off the ground like one of those fold-out cardboard displays in children's books. Jamison stood inside, his hands on his hips, gazing into the cathedral light filtering through the tent's green nylon walls. The interior was nearly as large as the living room in his studio, and the peak of the tent was still two inches above his head. Everything about the tent was cool.

Jamison walked back outside and helped Ben lift the folding wood stove from the truck and haul it into the tent.

"We may not need this, but boy, if we do, it's nice," Ben said. "It's a lot colder up here at night than down in the valley." They had stopped on the road on the drive up and picked up some firewood, but now that seemed like an unneeded precaution. A fire had swept over the mountainside above them several years earlier, and the limbs of dead pine trees were strewn on the ground like random clumps of giant gray matchsticks.

Jamison took in the campground around him. There was only one other camper in residence; he saw a fluorescent yellow dome tent winking through the trees on the opposite end of the campground. The owners did not appear to be around. Across the road was a brown concrete outhouse.

"Do they have showers in the outhouse?"

Ben snorted. He pointed at the creek that ran a few feet behind their tent. "That there is the hot and cold running water," he said. "Except you can forget about the hot part. Ice cold bath feels pretty good in the middle of the day if you're dirty enough and it's hot enough. Not that I could ever convince Monna of that."

At his mention of her name, Ben seemed to withdraw. He had dragged the two folding cots to the tailgate, and now hoisted one of the heavy cots under each arm. Jamison moved to help but Ben walked past him and disappeared into the tent. Jamison heard the cots clatter to the ground, and when Ben reemerged his momentary lapse into melancholia was gone.

"We can set those up later," he said. "Lot easier with two guys setting up a cot, they're tight as a drum. I used to be able to do one by myself when I was younger, but not anymore. I'll tell you what, it makes you appreciate those kids in the army."

Jamison walked over and examined the two spinning rods Ben had leaned against a tree. He picked one up and looked at the lure stuck to the cork handle.

"Hey, that's a Mepps," he said. "Right?"

"Yup. I thought you never done any fishing."

"I haven't done much. I went fishing for bass a couple times with a guy I knew and his sister. I was kind of dating his sister. Anyway, the guy was using Mepps spinners like these. We caught some, too. He did, anyway. I'm kind of like the black plague on fishing trips. But that was a long time ago. I was still in my fifties."

"That was the last time you got laid? Jesus."

"I didn't say that," Jamison said. A mosquito landed on his arm and he slapped at it in irritation, then buttoned down the sleeves on his long sleeved shirt. The sun was warm, and the thick flannel shirt would soon be too hot, but it was better than being eaten alive by mosquitos. Ben had told him he'd brought insect repellent, but they had not yet unpacked it. Jamison slid the cooler onto the tailgate and tried to lower it to the ground before quickly realizing that it was too heavy for him to lift by himself. He grunted and pushed it back. Ben rolled his eyes.

"You get one end and I'll get the other," Ben said. Between them, they slid the cooler off the tailgate and hauled it into the shade behind the tent. Even with two of them, the cooler was heavy. Inside the cooler, beneath a plastic tub with the frozen stroganoff Monna had made for them, Ben had brought enough beer for a week.

"Technically, we're not supposed to be doing this," Ben said, tapping the cooler with his foot. "Supposed to hang your food so it don't attract bears."

"They have bears up here?" Jamison said. They had bears in Minnesota but he'd never seen one. Seeing a bear would be cool, he thought. As long as it wasn't trying to steal their food.

"I only saw one in all the years we been coming up here," Ben said, "and it wasn't a grizzly, thank God. We yelled at it and it ran away. Been a grizzly, *we'd* of run away."

They moved everything from the truck into the tent within forty-five minutes. Ben flung the tent's nylon doors open and tied them back, filling the interior with sunlight. He began unpacking one of the cots. The old, wood-framed cot slid from its bag and thumped to the ground like the tightly bound, embalmed remains of an Egyptian mummy. Ben pried it apart and slid a crosspiece through the sleeve on one end. He picked up the final crosspiece and held it up, as if hefting a baseball bat.

"Now comes the fun part," he said. "We gotta hook this over both ends like I just did with that last crosspiece, except now it's gonna be tight. It's a mother. So you're gonna hold onto the frame and pull back and I'm gonna hold onto the crosspiece and pull back the other way and between the two of us we should be able to stretch it enough to get the crossbar to snap in place. You think you got that?"

Jamison had no idea what Ben was talking about. He nodded.

Ben studied him for a moment. "This is harder than it looks," he said.

"No, I'm ready."

"Okay, then." Ben slid the crosspiece through the canvas sleeve and dropped one end into place. "Okay. I got that end hooked up.

Pull back on the frame like I told you while I pull back on this end of the crosspiece. Ready? Go."

Jamison heaved on the frame. Opposite him, Ben put his back into it, grimacing with the effort, the wooden crosspiece slowly stretching the coarse, Vietnam-era canvas. He finally got an edge hooked over the anchoring pin and for an instant relaxed his grip.

It was an instant too soon. With a dull *snap* the crosspiece sprang back toward Jamison. Ben was catapulted toward him and into his face. Their foreheads met with the soft thump of two ripe cantaloupes. Ben rolled on his side, his arms cradling his head.

"Oh fuck *me*," he said.

Jamison bent over his knees and squeezed his face between his hands. He touched his forehead, feeling for a bump. Damn, it hurt. He closed his eyes. When he opened them tears blurred his vision. Ben had rolled into a squat and was watching him with a painful squint.

"I ain't sleeping on *that* cot," he said.

Jamison tentatively explored his forehead with the tips of his fingers. There was now a small bump. He looked at Ben. Ben's ball cap was askew, like a character on the Little Rascals, that ancient television show. He started laughing. He couldn't help himself.

Ben punched Jamison's leg hard enough to hurt and it made Jamison laugh even harder. Ben joined him. They howled. They laughed to the moon not yet risen. They laughed, their laughter twining around the dead matchstick pines, into the air, into the hot sun.

* * *

"You ever use a pole like that?"

Jamison inspected the spinning rod and reel in his hands dubiously. Aside from a handful of fishing trips he'd taken with friends, he'd seen reels like this only in sporting goods stores, and since he wasn't a real fishermen he'd never examined one up close. It seemed a petite marvel of stainless steel and powder-coated aluminum engineering. He had no idea how it worked. He shook his head.

"Nope," he said. "The ones I used had these push button thingies."

"Yeah. Well, we don't do push-button thingies in Montana," Ben said. "But that's okay. It's easy. Here, I'll show you how." He took Jamison's rod. A small pond had been impounded on the creek above their campsite, and Ben's cast easily arced his spinner halfway across it, trailing a gently settling coil of blue monofilament.

"Now you try." He handed the rod back to Jamison.

Jamison's first cast splatted into the water at his feet. Ben grinned.

"Let go the line a little quicker, at the top of your cast, you might stretch that out some," he said. "Just sayin'."

Sure enough, Jamison's second cast went almost as far as Ben's. Within a couple casts he felt like he had a rudimentary grasp of technique.

Ben seemed pleased. "Okay, you're getting the hang of it. Good news is you probably won't have to make a cast that long for the rest of the day. Let's go fish."

The creek chortled happily over a bed of smooth, multi-hued stones, slowing and becoming quiet as it increased its depth against the bank. That was where the trout were, Ben told him: in the bends against the bank, in deep water. The fish would be small and native: cutthroats mostly, with a few rainbows that swam up from the Shields River below. All were good eating. Jamison wanted to catch a fish and eat it. It would, he thought, be like living off the land.

He wandered the banks of the creek, plunking his Mepps into the deep pools where Ben told him to cast, but in half an hour had not had a hit. Occasionally, one of his still clumsy casts would snag on a limb. He was trying to untangle his Mepps from a willow behind him when Ben wandered up and asked how he'd done.

"Zip," Jamison said. "How about you?"

Ben had caught three. They'd been too small to eat so he'd turned them loose.

"Three? Really? I haven't even had a bite. I told you I was like the black plague. They heard I was coming and moved out."

Ben leaned his rod against a tree. "Okay," he said. "Let me watch." Jamison walked to the edge of the river and cast his Mepps into a deep pool on the opposite bank and reeled it back in. He did not get a hit.

"You do it like that every time? Just walk up and throw your spinner in the crick like that?"

Jamison sensed he was being set up. He gazed over Ben's head. Behind him he glimpsed their tent, and beyond that the fluorescent yellow tent of their unseen neighbors, a sliver of color half hidden by trees. Cream-colored moths fluttered over the creek, tumbling into the quiet, green water under the willows and then fluttering into the air again.

"Yeah," Jamison said. "That's what you told me to do. At least I *thought* that's what you told me to do."

Ben pursed his lips. "Okay, my bad. That *is* what I told you to do." He dropped into a squat. "So I'm gonna paint you a picture 'bout how all this works." He made six guns with both hands, thumbs up and index fingers out, tapping out his points as if he were shooting them out of the barrels. "Fish are, like, wild animals," he said. "You can't just walk up to the water and start casting, especially a guy as tall as you. It's like the deer in our pasture. They seem like you could just walk right up and pet them, right? But you go and walk up on them and they see you coming a mile away and vamoose. So you got to sort of sneak up on fish, 'specially on these little mountain cricks."

This had never occurred to Jamison. But why would it? He had never been trout fishing before today. He nodded. He liked the idea of sneaking up on a fish. He still wanted to catch a fish and eat it for supper.

Ben rose to his feet and reached for his rod.

"There are a couple more pools upstream, let's go give them a try," he said.

Ben took the lead and they walked upstream. They rounded the first bend and Ben stopped.

"Okay," he said. "You see up there? Where the river slows down? There's a pretty good hole under that bank. But if you just walk up to the river like you own the place the fish will be long gone before you ever get there. So you got to sneak up, like I told you. Closer you get to the water, the lower you got to get. So go on, I'll be right behind you."

Jamison felt silly but he did it anyway. He hadn't snuck up on anything since he'd played Cowboys and Indians in grade school. He bent over at the waist and took several cautious steps, until he was several feet back from the water, then got down on his hands and knees. When he was just a few feet back from the bank, he made his first cast.

The spinner hit the water with a tiny, hollow plop and Jamison began reeling it back in. The light resistance of the lure in the current tugged at his line and he expected a hit at any moment, but by the time he could see the Mepps flashing in the water, the lure was just a few feet from his rod tip. Disappointed, he lifted it out of the water and glanced behind him. Ben was sitting with his back against a tree.

"Try it again," he said.

Jamison cast again.

The spinner plunked quietly into the water as before and Jamison turned the handle to flip the bail and felt the lure tug against his rod in the current. He turned the handle twice more and the rod bucked and instinctively he set the hook.

"I got one!" he said. "I got one!" He stood up. And then remembering dropped back down. But now Ben was standing at his side. Jamison clambered back up.

"I think it's pretty big," Jamison said, excitedly. "It feels like it's pretty big."

"He's nice," Ben said. "I got a look at him when he hit."

"What if he breaks the line? He's pretty big, I can feel him," Jamison said. Jamison stared at the spot where the line was cutting sharp, quick arcs in the water. The fish had yet to show itself, but

Jamison's rod was bent in a deep, throbbing arc. The tip of the rod danced one way and then another as the fish shot from the safety of the pool and into the shallower water downstream.

"Lower your rod!" Ben said. "Lower your rod or he'll break you off!" Jamison dropped his rod to the water.

"No! Shit! Not that much! Just a little. You got to keep some pressure on him but not too much."

The fish was plowing downstream. Below them was a spruce tree that had fallen in the water and lay halfway across the current. Water boiled around the bare black limbs and the black limbs waved in the water like the bony, clutching fingers of a witch.

Ben spied the spruce tree and immediately recognized the danger. If the trout made it that far he'd wrap the line around a limb and break off. Ben plunged into the creek and churned halfway across, the water up to his knees and instantly filling his rubber work boots. When the trout shot across his feet he lunged for the line and grabbed it, jerking the fish out of the water. He gave the line a wild swing and the fish landed on the bank. It beat the wet bank with its tail until Jamison pounced on it.

"*Oh, God*," Jamison said, his voice rapturous. "It's *beautiful*." Streaks of luminous red orange slashed the lower edges on both sides of the fish's hooked jaw. Its gill plates glowed with the same sunburst of luminous red orange and its coppery, iridescent sides were spotted with large black dots, as though an underwater artist, a mermaid, had flung ebony paint against them with her brush.

Ben waded back to shore. It would take him the rest of the trip to dry out his boots. He didn't care.

"That's just a damn nice fish," he said. "It's a cutthroat. See those orange slashes on its jaw? I'll bet it goes 16 inches. That's enough fish for both of us." He picked up a rock and held the fish down and thumped it sharply on the head. It quivered and the life went out of its eyes and it lay still in Ben's hand. He handed the fish to the beaming Jamison.

"That's your fish," he said. "You oughta be proud of that one. That's a damn nice trout for a crick this size. Let's clean it and then go back to camp. I brought a fry pan and corn meal. We'll save Monna's stroganoff for tomorrow."

* * *

Ben had assembled a camp table and placed his ingredients upon it: canned pineapples, brown sugar, yellow cake mix and a mixing bowl. On the ground, in a space he'd meticulously cleared of debris, was a cast iron Dutch Oven, blackened and greasy from use.

Ben explained the process, commanding Jamison's attention with flourishes of his hands. He'd grease the inside of the Dutch Oven and then pour in the ingredients in sequence: canned pineapples, brown sugar, and finally the yellow cake mix. They would bake in the oven and be golden brown and ready to eat after dinner. Ben assured Jamison that he would love pineapple upside down cake. *Everybody* loved pineapple upside down cake. Ben moved around the perimeter of the table, opening the canned pineapples with a can opener and mixing the yellow cake mix with a plastic spoon. His boots squished when he walked.

"How did you get your boots wet?" Jamison asked.

Ben knocked the spoon on the rim of the mixing bowl. "What do you mean, 'how did I get my boots wet?' I was standing in the goddamn river retrieving your trout. You don't remember?"

Jamison pinched his ear lobe self-consciously and tried to remember, but all he could recall was the fish hitting the spinner and the adrenaline rush of the wild, sinuous creature on the end of his line, the rod bucking in his hands and the surge of panic he felt when he thought he might lose it, and then the beautiful and desperately flopping fish on the bank in those last, electrifying moments before Ben had killed it and he had owned it at last. There was no memory of Ben's urgent instructions, or of his plunge into the river to head off the trout from the downed spruce. For Jamison there had been only the fish, in the same way there is only the beloved in the eyes of lovers.

Jamison shook his head. "I *think* I remember," he said. But he didn't.

"Wow," Ben said. He paused for a moment, the spoon resting on the rim of the bowl. "All right. Okay." He put the mixing bowl on the table and licked off the spoon. "So, like, you need to do something useful. There's a coffee can and lighter fluid in that box in the truck. Fill up the can with charcoal and light it. We're gonna need it for the Dutch Oven."

Jamison found the coffee can and charcoal and placed the coffee can beside the Dutch Oven and filled it with charcoal and doused the charcoal with lighter fluid. The charcoal ignited on the first match and quickly grew into leaping yellow flames. Jamison bent over the coffee can. Although it was still two hours before dark, the air was cool and the warmth from the flames felt good. He cupped his hands over the flames to warm them. He was surprised at how much colder it was in the mountains. When they'd left the valley that morning the temperature had already risen into the low eighties. Jamison walked back to the table and watched Ben prepare their dinner. His trout, gutted and headless, lay on a paper plate beside the mixing bowl, its pink body cavity dusted with yellow cornmeal.

Jamison walked behind the tent and dug through the cooler.

"There's beer in there, you want some," Ben said. "I'll take one."

Jamison grabbed beers for both of them and fished through the melting ice for the spinach salad Monna had told them she'd packed. He found the plastic container of salad under the stroganoff and pulled it free, then shook the ice water off it. He set it on the table beside the trout.

"Monna is taking good care of us," Jamison said. "She thought of everything."

"She usually does," Ben said.

"You guys come up here every year?"

"Until this year," Ben said. He walked over to the coffee can and peered inside. "These are just about right." He used tongs to arrange a dozen charcoal briquets in a circle, then set the Dutch Oven on top of them. He wiped the inside of the oven with oil and then dumped the contents of the canned pineapple, brown sugar, and yellow cake mix inside. Then he replaced the lid and put the remaining charcoal briquets on the lid, evenly spaced. The briquets glowed red beneath a frosting of gray ash. He squatted on his heels, his palm held open over the oven, testing the heat. Then he pushed off his knees and rose to his feet.

"It seems kind of weird not having her here," Ben said. "She used to love camping. She'd bring a lawn chair and sit and sketch all day long while I fished, put on that big straw hat she's got. That pole you got, I bought it for her so she'd go fishing with me. And she did, she even caught a few. But it wasn't her thing. She never once got like you got when you caught that trout today. She just wanted to do her art. Sometimes we'd go for a hike. She liked that better'n fishing. Me, hiking's what I do to *go* fishing. But not her. I'm still trying to figure out why the hell I married her in the first place."

Jamison sat on the ground with his back against a tree, his long legs crossed at the ankles. His pants had rucked up above his hiking boots, exposing an inch of pale white shin. This was an odd thing to hear about your sister, but Ben was an odd man. Or a different *kind* of man; at the moment, the semantic differences escaped him. He sipped his beer and then stuck it between his legs and hugged his arms across his chest. It was almost, but not quite, cool enough to retrieve his pile vest from the duffle bag he'd thrown in the tent. A few more minutes.

He gazed around their campsite. He'd heard the people in the yellow tent return, and now and then caught snippets of their conversation. But he had yet to see them, and it was as though their faint voices, disembodied, originated from the yellow tent alone. He couldn't see the mountains; the dense trees in the campground blocked his view of the ascending hillsides he knew surrounded them. Just visible through the green pines in the campground, like bones bleaching in the sun, were the white and gray skeletons of trees that had burned in a long-ago fire; the ground below them rank with the almost surreal beauty of hot-pink fireweed, as if, in losing a half century of life to the flames, a riot of color had been offered as compensation. But Jamison wanted to see the mountains.

He thought maybe he'd climb up there tomorrow, on the hillside where the dead trees were, so he could see the mountains.

He had thought he had no innate love for rock and snow. He had not known, until he'd moved to Aden, that it was the mountains that would become the center of his life there; not in adoration but rather, as an entity that ordered the lives of all those who walked and rode and hunted and fished and farmed and ranched and drove in and around them, their contours hated and loved and dismissed and remarked upon with reverence, or equally, cursed; their spires gazed upon and painted. This is what had drawn his sister here so many decades ago. Her sense of that, her intuitive understanding. She was a painter of mountains.

"Maybe you married her because she knew what she wanted," Jamison said.

Ben walked to the Dutch oven and squatted on his heels, his palm hovering just above the lid, gauging the heat. He seemed satisfied and rotated the lid with the tongs, then rose to his feet. He dropped the tongs beside the oven.

"There was never any doubt about that," he said. "I mean, she told me that before we got married. Wanted to know what it was I wanted to do. So we bought the place in Aden and moved in. I thought that's what I wanted to do."

"You don't want to live in Aden anymore?"

"That's not it," Ben said. "It's not like that at all. There's no place else in the state I want to live more'n Aden. I love the Shields Valley. Always have. Monna loves it. But that wasn't what she meant. She meant, what was I gonna do with my life? What was I gonna do that really matters? She already had that figured out. I think it took her a long time to realize that most other people had to think about it, that it doesn't come natural. It didn't come natural to me."

The beer between Jamison's legs was cold. He put it on the ground beside him, plucking at the tab on the top of the can with his thumb. The tab made a clicking sound. He took a sip and put it back down, aware now of his awkwardness, the small, tight knot of fear within. "I thought I wanted to write books," he said quietly.

Telling this to Ben, of all people. "Novels. I was into my forties before I started being honest with myself."

"Monna said. About the writing."

"What she probably didn't say is that I didn't ever do it. I've been working on a novel for the last fifteen years and it's still not finished. It'll never be finished."

Jamison saw that Ben was facing him, listening.

"So I've had to think," Jamison said. "And lately I've had to think about whether that was ever what I really wanted to do, or whether it was just what I thought I was *supposed* to do. And if that wasn't it, than what was it? And the thing about it is that I realize I still don't know. I'm almost 73 and I still don't know."

Ben sat on the ground facing Jamison and put his arms around his knees and rocked back and forth, slowly, as if settling into the earth. He had left his can of beer on the table. His legs below his canvas shorts were deeply tanned and laced with ancient white scars. There was a fresh scrape on one knee, crusted over and blood black.

"I never thought it was fair," Ben said. "Some people just know what they want from the day they're born. Some people like me and you don't know shit. You live your entire life and it's like in the back of your head is this little voice telling you you better get off your ass and get after it but you don't and pretty soon it's just like the water in the river, background noise you don't pay any attention to."

Jamison listened. He could no longer hear the people in the yellow tent. He drew up his legs and put his arms around his knees.

"What was it Monna said when we were talking a while back? She said you used to make furniture and you don't any more. What was that all about?"

Ben looked to either side and then up at the table. He pushed off the ground and rose to his feet and retrieved his beer and then sat back down, facing Jamison as before.

"In high school I took shop classes and learned to weld and do a bunch of other stuff but I liked woodworking the best," he said. "All those different kinds of hardwoods, some of it's so pretty you just want to pick it up and feel it, you know? I made this roll-top desk out of red oak and mahogany veneer and sold it to one of my mom's friends and I thought, 'I can do this.' I loved it. I did. So I went off to college and we all know how that went but I was always thinking if range science didn't pan out maybe I'd be a woodworker. Set up a shop someplace and make beautiful furniture, but practical. You had to be able to use it, not just look at it. That was important.

"Well, range science didn't work out. And woodworking didn't either. I bought all those tools in my shop, and then I got busy doing remodeling jobs, and the money was good so I didn't think about building furniture any more. Except I did, you know? Like part of me knew I was missing something, even if I didn't know exactly what it was. Like there was this little voice I could only hear when it was real quiet, after maybe a couple beers, driving home by myself after a job."

"You still could," Jamison said.

"So could you," Ben said.

Jamison heard a truck on the dirt road below the campground and turned toward the sound but the sound faded. It was quiet again.

"You want to eat that fish, you got to build a fire so we can fry it up," Ben said. He rose to his feet and slapped the dust off his shorts. Jamison followed. He'd gathered some dead limbs that had fallen around the campground, and with the wood they'd collected on the drive up, they would have plenty of coals for a cooking fire. Jamison made a teepee with dry twigs in the iron fire ring and touched a match to it. The flame caught and licked up the sides of the teepee and smoke rose and then bent toward him and he backed away from it. The smoke curled into the air and braided into tendrils before dissipating into nothing, as ephemeral as abandoned dreams, the scent of wood smoke like the taste of an almost forgotten memory.

* * *

"I was going to say something," Jamison said. Ben had cooked and then offered Jamison the entire trout and Jamison, too thrilled to share, had selfishly agreed. Now he was finished, the skeleton of the trout on his paper plate picked clean.

"What we were talking about before," Jamison said. "Monna did that, the things you and I didn't do. Your wife. My sister." He lifted the skeleton on his plate by the tail and dropped it and the plate into the fire. Flames surged around the plate and the skeleton twisted black in the fire and turned to ash.

"That makes it worse," Ben said. "Because she did it like that all her life and now she won't."

"She *can't*," Jamison said.

Ben dropped his paper plate into the fire. He sat back and laced his hands behind his head and watched the fire burn the paper plate. It was cold now that the sun was down and the warmth from the small fire felt good to both men, a rough warmth like a course woolen blanket thrown around both that drew them closer to the fire and each other.

Ben sat close to the fire and folded his legs. "Dish soap's in the box in the truck," he said. "I cook, you clean."

Chapter 16

Monna set the bottle of wine beside her lawn chair, halfway between her chair and Jamison's. On a whim, Ben had driven the MG to Livingston to buy what fireworks could still be had on this, the afternoon of the Fourth of July, the vanishing rumble of the small red convertible reverberating off the baking gray asphalt of the highway like distant and barely audible thunder. Monna had invited Jamison up to the house to relax and await her husband's return. Relaxing with his sister, Jamison had learned, usually involved drinking wine.

Now he watched her creep across the lawn, far too unsteady for her 64 years, hesitant and cautious. She moved slowly in the uncut grass between their house and the river, shuffling her feet in clumsy, pigeon-toed half steps, the Mason jar clutched in one hand, the other raised and poised, as Ben's had been, to capture a grasshopper. But Ben's speed, Ben's dexterity, were missing. Trapping a grasshopper involved Monna easing into a painful crouch, then extending her hand and grasping the insect so slowly that it apparently didn't realize what was happening until it was too late. Jamison's thoughts settled on a Zen truism: *beginner's mind.* Had he not watched her do it, he would not have believed it possible for her to get within five feet of one of the hair-triggered insects. He had offered to catch them for her, but she had refused. She dropped the last insect into the Mason jar and screwed down the lid, then held it up triumphantly. She handed the jar to Jamison and used both arms to lower herself into her lawn chair. Jamison saw a fleeting grimace, but it was gone in the next instant, as if she'd smoothed the pain from her face with the bent and crooked fingers of her hands.

She fumbled for the bottle of wine, partially filled her glass, then set the bottle back down between them. The grasshoppers pinged angrily against the walls of the jar.

"Ben says you're going to stay," she said.

"For a while," Jamison said. "He says he has another project lined up next month. I feel like I'm doing something productive, finally. He said he'd put me in charge of Bobcats on all future projects. I can add that to my curriculum vitae: BFA, MFA, Master of Excavation."

Monna grinned. "You love driving that machine, don't you? I never knew that about you. I'm kind of surprised he lets you do it. He's hired guys before, but you're the first one he let drive the Bobcat. He likes driving those things as much as you do. I'm half amazed he hasn't bought one for himself. Like we need more vehicles around this place."

Jamison picked up the jar of hoppers and jiggled it. The bugs went crazy, pinging like hot kernels of popcorn against the underside of the tin lid, spreading their wings and launching into flight, only to dash themselves against the invisible glass walls in the space of a wingbeat. Jamison felt a pang of regret, knowing they'd be sacrificed to the wrens soon.

"Yeah, but a Bobcat isn't like an MG, Monna," Jamison said. "Not exactly the same class of transportation."

Monna turned toward him in herky jerky movements. "Don't think I don't love that MG," she said. "When you two brought it home that day, I thought, well … it was a bad day, like I said. But then we drove it to town, and all these old feelings came flooding back. All the things I remembered from the first one he and I had. Everything except this." She slowly extended her trembling hand. "I didn't have this stupid disease then. You never think about things like that happening when you're young, or maybe you do but you don't really think it's going to happen to you. That kind of stuff always happens to somebody else. And then it happens to you and you're in denial and you can stay in denial for a long, long time, if it hurts too much to face what you know you have to face. The MG had nothing to do with any of that. It wasn't about that."

Jamison sat facing the river but there was a strong breeze today and he couldn't hear the current, that familiar solace lost in the wind, in the swish of the grass and the soft rustle of leaves in the willows. Ben had told him that tonight, shortly after the sun went down, those who lived on the river would send up fireworks and it would be quite a show and when he got back with the fireworks he'd gone to town to buy they'd send some up, too, and they would enjoy the show because they always had.

"What is it you had to face?" Jamison asked, struck in that moment by Monna's quiet surrender to Ben's hopeless, desperate faith, understanding that she was telling him these things because she was not yet able to tell Ben.

"That I'm going to die, Jamison. Parkinson's is always fatal. I may live another fifteen years but it will still get me. It's already killed the part of me that's *me*. But I still have choices."

"So what are you saying?"

She clumsily patted his arm. "We all go sooner or later, Jamison. I'm going sooner. That's all." Monna set her glass in the grass beside her, steadying it so it wouldn't tip over, then reached for the Mason jar. She handed the jar to Jamison.

"Would you get one out for me? Unscrewing the lid is too hard."

Jamison opened the jar and got a hopper and handed it to her but she wouldn't take it.

"Kill it," she said.

Jamison killed the grasshopper and handed it to Monna. She put the hopper in her palm and rested her arm on the arm of the chair, her palm up, her ruined fingers crooked and trembling, the dead hopper's legs twitching convulsively.

"Aren't you going to throw it out in the grass?" Jamison whispered, as if he were in a cathedral, this curious devotion to a small bird.

"Shhhh."

The wren flew by as before, as Jamison remembered: a headlong dart of purpose and movement left to right, the nervous flick of its tail, then retreating to the eave somewhere above them. The breathless waiting. The wren plummeting down from above to alight on her arm, cocking its head at her and then him. At the dead grasshopper in her palm. At her, again. Wary of the prize that could be for no other creature than him alone. And then, while Jamison watched, spellbound, the wren hopped down her wrist and in a twinkling snatched up the hopper and was gone. Monna slowly turned and faced him, the painful lines in her face gone for this moment and replaced with peace, with something like radiance.

"We need to tell Ben," Jamison said.

She picked up her wine glass and cradled it between her trembling hands, as if in prayer. She did not raise the glass.

"Ben's been trying to do that for years," Jamison said. Excitement and disbelief coursed through his blood; it was as though he'd witnessed a miracle. "He'll be thrilled! I still can't believe I saw what I just saw." Jamison leaned forward and sought confirmation from his sister but she offered only a weak smile and lifted her eyes to the cottonwoods along the river, their green leaves moving in the wind and the dissipating evening heat.

Jamison straightened up in his lawn chair and picked up his glass and swirled the wine around. "What?"

"He doesn't know," Monna said. "This isn't the first time."

"But Ben's been trying to do that for years! That's what he said. We were both here the last time he tried, remember? We were here." Jamison leaned forward again, tucking his feet under the aluminum rungs of the chair. But his long legs wouldn't quite fold; instead, his knees were thrust toward his chin, as if he'd been crammed into the front seat of the MG. He wondered where the wren had gone after it had snatched the hopper from Monna's hand; it had darted around the corner of the house with the decapitated insect in its stiletto beak and disappeared. Maybe, Jamison thought, one grasshopper was enough.

Monna swiveled in her chair and faced him. "Ben's been trying to get his wrens to eat out of his hands for years, Jamison. He's been trying since we moved here. But he tries too hard. When I got …" She shook her head in resignation. "The first couple of years after I got sick I was raging inside, like I was locked in a cage and there was no way out. It was terrible for our marriage. Absolutely the worst. I finally told Ben I wanted a divorce. I couldn't take what was going on with me and him at the same time. He kept going on and on about, you know, all that positive thinking shit they teach you on TV, with the doctors or psychologists or whatever they are. But all the positive thinking in the world wasn't going to make my Parkinson's go away." She gazed into her glass and then set it beside her. "I'll bet you didn't know any of this, did you? Ben never told you anything."

"He never said anything," Jamison said. "Not to me."

Monna nodded. "No. Well." She folded her arms, as if she were chilly, as if she were trying to contain the memory of her thoughts within her own frail grasp.

"So we didn't do that. And it was because I finally gave up. I wasn't going to fight him or me anymore. If I was going to spend the rest of my life in a cage, then that's just the way it was going to be. And that changed things, I can't explain it. It wasn't long after that—Ben was at work someplace, I think—I was just sitting out here one afternoon like you and I are now and it was hot like it is now and I thought I'd see if I could feed one of the wrens myself. Ben had always done it before; it was like a mission with him. I caught a hopper and a bird landed on my arm like they always do and then it flew away. But I just kept my hand out with the hopper in it and it came back a few minutes later and took it. That was three or four years ago."

"But you haven't told Ben?"

"Ben wouldn't understand *why*. He doesn't understand letting go. He doesn't know how. His reaction to everything is just to lower his head and ram through it. Trying to feed a wren means letting the wren be in charge. But he can't do that. He won't let himself."

"You told him that? Maybe if you told him like you just told me."

Monna clasped her hands together in a gentle, gnarled fist. "We've been married a long time, Jamison."

Jamison looked at the river. He still couldn't hear the current. "I would imagine that's difficult. Difficult for you."

Monna extended her clasped hands before her and rotated them slowly in a half circle, as if she were holding a dousing stick and divining for water in the silent, subterranean world beneath their feet.

"So we almost split up," she said. "But I was the one who changed my mind. He has never stood in my way, and he wouldn't have stood in my way then. I decided to stay."

* * *

After Jamison and Monna had finished half the bottle, Ben returned. It was nearly dark, the butterscotch sweet light of dusk behind them. Jamison heard the muffled crunch of gravel in the driveway and then the door of the MG quietly click closed, as if Ben had eased it shut to lessen the noise. Already, fireworks were going off up and down the river, starbursts of blue and red and green splashed like paint against the purple canvas of sky, the staccato reports like distant gunfire. Jamison waited for Ben to appear from around the corner of the house. He glanced at Monna, and sensed from the cant of her head that she too had heard his return.

In the next instant, a shrill, piercing whistle directly above their heads ended in a thundering white explosion that made Jamison bolt six inches out of his chair. Beside him, Monna had slumped forward, her hand pressed against her chest, her eyes closed. She spat silent curses under her breath.

"Jesus Christ," Jamison said. His heart slammed against his ribs.

Ben strode around the corner of the house grinning. "You hear that one?" he said, smirking. He held a cardboard box in his arms. It was packed with fireworks, colored cardboard tubes with fuses and silvery pointed rockets attached to dyed, spindly sticks. In one hand he held the still smoking cylinder from the rocket he had fired over their heads.

"Turns out you get a killer deal on this stuff if you wait until the last minute," Ben said. "Look what I got: Roman Candles, ground spinners, Black Cats, fountains. Guy told me what it all does. I don't even remember all the stuff he said it would do. He just threw everything in a box and gave me a great price so I bought it. What do you want to blow up next?"

An hour later, his ears ringing from the explosions, whistles, whirrs and pops he had lost count of, Jamison excused himself and retreated to the studio. Ben was still sorting through the box, mesmerized, plucking Roman Candles and M80's and bottle rockets from his slowly diminishing collection and briefly admiring them— look at this one!—before scurrying across the lawn to the bank of the river and sending another arcing contrail of colored sparks into the starry sky above. Monna seemed to be enjoying Ben's child-like delight, pleased that her husband was so thoroughly in his element.

When Jamison was ten feet from the studio, the serial thunder-claps of Ben's fireworks only slightly less thunderous, Jamison saw the hunched, shivering form crouched before his door, his matted yellow fur silvery in the moonlight. *Leviathan.*

He stopped, certain that another step would send the cat dashing for the woodpile, but instead, Leviathan watched him warily, as though anxious for his arrival. Jamison eased closer, until he was beside the cat and able to crack open the door. When he'd opened it enough to squeeze inside, Leviathan bolted past his legs and ran into the studio and in two bounds dashed to the farthest corner of the room, where he crouched once again, his green and unblinking eyes on Jamison, wary and distrustful.

Slowly, Jamison switched on the lamp and carefully pulled out a chair from the kitchen table. In the gentle light, the studio's log walls muting the piercing explosions outside, he saw that Leviathan was terrified. The realization struck him in a wash of pity for the creature who sat trembling and miserable across the short breadth of room between them.

Jamison didn't move, not knowing what best to do, wanting more than anything for Leviathan to stay.

Leviathan's tail twitched and he rocked nervously from side to side, lifting and then replacing his tightly curled paws beneath him. He squinted as if sleepy but behind the half closed lids his eyes shone with feral suspicion.

"I have kitty food," Jamison whispered, as if the quiet tenor of his voice, after the ear-splitting detonations outside, might send the big cat bolting for the door. "Do you want some kitty food?" Jamison slowly rose from his chair and opened the cupboard above the sink and retrieved a can of cat food and pulled open the tab. When the lid snapped open Jamison glanced behind him, but Leviathan hadn't moved. Jamison held the can before him and stepped forward, then again. When he had halved the distance between them, he saw the cat's shoulder muscles bunch. It was as clear a warning as if Jamison had tripped a flashing red light: he could approach no further. Slowly, easing onto his knee, he set the can at his feet, then rose and backed to his chair.

Jamison watched. Leviathan raised his pink nose and flared his nostrils as the pungent odor of the cat food permeated the room, but made no move to approach the can or even to rise above his defensive crouch. Instead, he studied Jamison with a calculated indifference belied by an immediate flaring of his eyes whenever Jamison moved, no matter how measured and slow the movement.

Jamison watched. He saw again the lattice of scars on the big cat's face, testimony to a violent and brutal life. He saw that Leviathan's compulsively twitching tail had been broken; a crook two inches back from the tip wasn't right and now jutted down and to one side like the disfigured finger on an arthritic hand. He saw that a toe on Leviathan's right front foot was pure white, and that the same toe opposite the white one, on the opposing foot, was misshapen; it extended loosely from the tightly curled paw, the claw turned under and black with necrosis.

Beyond the thick log walls of the studio, Ben's fireworks popped and whistled and roared, and with each report Leviathan seemed to crouch nearer the floor, his eyes scanning the room as if there might be relief from the terrifying explosions somewhere else; but finding none would then resume his unwavering gaze on Jamison, who returned his gaze with fascination and wonder and a quiet, joyful stirring within that was very much like tenderness.

The explosions ended. At midnight Jamison heard the whistle and clap of the last rocket and Ben's faint whoop and then it was silent. He heard Ben and Monna enter their house and heard the door close behind them. In the silence Jamison became aware of small sounds: the faint creak of the plywood floor when he shifted his weight, the whisper of the river beyond the open window.

Jamison sat at the kitchen table and watched Leviathan and for many minutes the cat crouched opposite him, in the corner where he had huddled unmoving for two hours. Then, suddenly, Leviathan arose and walked to the open can of cat food and sniffed it without interest and walked to the door. He stood by the door with his tail upright, the broken tip twitching, waiting.

Jamison rose from his chair and walked cautiously to the door until he was standing directly above the cat. The cat's wariness seemed nearly gone; instead, Leviathan peered up at him expectantly. Jamison pushed open the door and the cat glanced outside, then up at Jamison. He made a noise—Jamison saw Leviathan's mouth open and heard something between a croaking purr and a meow—and then the big cat closed its eyes and butted Jamison's shin. Then he dashed outside and was gone, lost in the night rushing in, Jamison's gaze following the vanishing image of the yellow creature as if he were following an arc of colored sparks illuminating his heart.

Chapter 17

Ben jabbed his finger at the bug splats on the windshield as if they were imperfections in the sheet rock they had spent the day installing. Grasshoppers rose in mechanical, clacking swarms from the shoulder of the interstate and hurled themselves at the truck's pitted windshield with suicidal abandon. Ben cradled a beer between his legs, and periodically he lifted the bottle to his lips, took a sip, and then reinserted it between his legs. Jamison mentioned the Highway Patrol. Ben handed him a beer.

Hanging the sheetrock had been challenging. They'd rented a hoist, so lifting the rock into place wasn't the hard part. But screwing in the screws without tearing the paper had given Jamison fits. He'd ruined several sheets before he got the hang of it, and he still wasn't sure he was doing it correctly.

Now Ben was fine-tuning his technique. "If I wasn't such a cheap bastard I'd buy drills with a clutch, and then you don't have that problem," he said. "Clutch stops it before you go too far. But it's not that hard to do with the drills I got. You just need a little practice, is all. Besides, I got these drills back in college. Back in the day, they were top shelf, Sears Craftsman, back when Sears still made quality tools in the U.S. They're like old friends, you know? I'm kind of reluctant to shit-can them." He strummed his fingers on the neck of his beer bottle. "Those cordless drills they got these days are pretty nice, though. Milwaukee's and Makita's and like that. Maybe one of these days."

"I think I was getting the hang of it toward the end, there," Jamison said. He knew he was giving Ben an opening to continue his one-sided discourse on power drills, but over the summer he had begun to look forward to their conversations on the hour-long drive back to Aden. Most, like this one, involved the evaluation and fine tuning of Jamison's plodding evolution as a carpenter. Far from finding them pedantic, Jamison valued the advice. Ben's enthusiasm for seemingly everything job related made even hanging sheetrock enjoyable.

Ben continued the discussion, wanting Jamison to get this, pleased that his brother-in-law seemed eager to learn. He made a pistol with his right hand. "So you hit the trigger"—he waggled his index finger—"and when the screw just starts to crease the paper, you back off the trigger real quick. They'll be just enough momentum left in one of these old drills to drive that screw in perfect, no tearing. You were getting it toward the end there. I was watching."

Jamison felt a surge of pride. At no point in his career as a teacher, or perhaps even across the breadth of his lifetime, had it ever occurred to him that he might enjoy hands-on construction work. But the surprising complexity of it, the deliberative process of excavating, framing and finishing an addition or a barn or a house, was uncharted and new, a terrain with its own vernacular and customs, as foreign to Jamison as another language. Each day presented new problems the two of them had to solve, and Jamison looked forward to Ben patiently walking him through them, his hand on Jamison's shoulder, explaining what they were going to do and why it mattered. He thought of the family who would soon be living in the addition they were building: a young architect and his young, pretty wife whom he had met only once. His own clumsy hands were building an addition to their home they would learn to love, and their children would learn to love in the way grown children always love those places in which they recall their early years, and after all were gone and Ben and Jamison were gone the addition that he and Ben had built would still stand.

Jamison knew that, were he to be in the construction business another fifty years, it might indeed become tedious. But in fifty years he would long be dead. He grinned and pulled off his cap and scratched the pink, unprotected skin on his scalp. For some reason, the thought of his own death struck him as funny.

They were approaching the Infirmary. Ben flicked on the turn signal and suggested they stop in the bar because by God a man needed to have another drink and Jamison reckoned that was true. He said "reckoned" again, out loud, and wondered where *that* particular verb had come from. He hadn't seen Jessica in several weeks.

There was no one parked outside the bar, and when they opened the door it took Jamison a moment to become accustomed to the dim light. When he regained his focus he saw Jessica sitting at a table with Grant.

Grant waved them over and kicked out a stool. "Might as well join us," he said. "It's been a slow day. Too hot. Everybody's home drinking margaritas." Jessica pointed at her drink, a margarita. She slurped her margarita loudly and said "ahh" and tossed her hair.

Ben grinned. "You let the help drink on the job?" He propped his feet on the rungs of his stool, flexing the short, muscular legs below his canvas shorts.

"The help gets to do whatever she wants," Grant said. "Or the proprietor doesn't get any."

Jessica slugged Grant in the arm, who winced in mock pain. She turned grinning toward Jamison and Ben and then saw Jamison's painful confusion and stopped grinning and reached for her margarita, her fingers circling the glass as if cradling a figurine.

Ben glanced at Jamison and settled uneasily into his stool.

Grant sprang to his feet. "What can I get you guys?" he asked. "Beer?" He put both hands on the table, poised, as if their answer, any answer, would propel him to spring into duty.

"You want a beer, Jamison?" Ben said. "I'm buying."

Jamison said he'd have a beer. Smiling broadly. He caught Jessica's eyes and smiled at her and said that beer was always good on a hot day like today. Jessica said he sure had that right and slid off her stool and touched Jamison's arm and said she had prep work in the kitchen. Grant went behind the bar and poured them two beers and brought them back and then went into the kitchen and

Jamison thought he heard Grant and Jessica talking, their murmurs lost in the chop of the ceiling fan above his head.

Jamison and Ben sat at the table and Ben stared at his beer. Ben made a joke and Jamison laughed. The joke was about women but it wasn't very funny.

"I should of said something," Ben said. "But it was none of my business. I could see what you were thinking. I should of told you."

"Maybe I just didn't want to be told," Jamison said. "It's like …" He wrapped his arms around his bony chest. "You know at a subconscious level but you don't want to let yourself know what it is you actually know. You don't want to see stuff, the things that remind you of who you've become. You get old … you get *older* and your mind plays tricks. You don't see yourself as other people see you. You see yourself like you used to be. When I was her age."

Jessica was much younger than him, too young, and of course he had not thought that through. Opposite them, on one side of the heavy plank doors, was a stained glass window of a cowboy riding a white horse, a lost calf cradled in his arms. The stained glass window hung from hooks within the casing of the bar's only east-facing window. Late in the morning, while Jessica and Grant were in the kitchen prepping for the lunch crowd, sun struck the stained glass window and the cowboy and his horse shone with the otherworldly light of transcendent angels, the calf in the cowboy's arms lulled to sleep, its eyes closed. Then the first customers of the noon rush barged in and glancing at the radiant image before them and put up their hands to shield their eyes from the sun and saw nothing.

Jamison had not seen his age steal upon him. Instead, youth had crept out of his life like light stolen from a room at the end of the day, so stealthy in its diminishment that his awareness of the change had been only beginning as it was nearly complete. And what had he gained?

He now had the busy years of his life behind him. In less than a month he would be 73. He had not married and he had not had children; instead, he had devoted his life to teaching the children of others. It had seemed then like a worthy cause. Perhaps it still was. There had been special students, students who moved his heart when they remembered him, who sent him Christmas cards and glittery new novels at Christmas, but there had been no son of his own and no daughter. He read most of the novels and the rest he gave away. He gazed at the stained glass window but the sun was on the wrong side of the valley and there was no light and the cowboy and the white horse were hidden in shadow, their colors without luminance, as if drained of blood. He stared at the back of his hands and saw in them how he must have appeared to Jessica: a silly old man with a hopeless crush, the thin, sun-spotted skin on the back of his hands wrinkled and pale, the uncalloused hands of a reader of books.

Ben gently punched his shoulder. "Drink up," he said. "It'll make me feel better." Jamison reached for his glass and took a drink and made a weak smile and put the glass back on the table. The cold beer was a salve and he reached for it again.

"Hey!" Ben said, grinning. "You're back! Sugar Ray Jamison is back."

* * *

On Saturday morning, Jamison borrowed a spinning rod from Ben and drove his Honda back to the campsite he and Jamison had camped in six weeks before. He hadn't been fishing since then and wanted to try again before fall.

He sensed the season nearly upon them: an imperceptible fading in the color of leaves, the brown of cured grass, as if it had bequeathed what remained of its green life to the summer, then retreated into its dark, protected roots for the cold that lay ahead. He left shortly after daylight, tasting the air, tendrils of gauzy mist rising phantom-like from the Shields River, the robins in the cottonwoods announcing the light. In the studio, at night, he slept with the windows open, for the sound of the river soothed his restlessness and eased his sleep, and at daylight the robins sang him into morning, and both were an escape from the tiny prick of sorrow that remained stubbornly lodged in his heart.

He drove along the Shields for several miles, following it upstream into the mountains, and the mountains, too, were different now. He flicked on the radio and soon was singing along to a song. When he arrived at the campsite, he noted with pleasure that he was the only one there. He tried to remember what he'd learned about approaching fish and keeping a low profile. He dug through the plastic box of lures Ben had given him and found the Mepps that had caught his big fish and tied it to the line. Then he walked to the first pool he saw and crawled to the edge of the stream on his knees and chucked his Mepps into the current.

His cast was poor and it fell well below the pool he had been aiming for, but he felt a tick through the line and when he set the hook discovered he had a fish on the end of it. It was small—no more than six inches—and he quickly pulled it to shore. Despite its size, he felt his heart skip. He lifted the trout onto the bank, where the fish gaped up at him with round, unblinking eyes.

Jamison didn't want to kill it. Not such a little fellow. He wet his hands as Ben had shown him and gently grasped the fish and tried to work the barbed hooks back out of its jaw. The tiny fish had struck the lure in blind, carnivorous fury, and he worked carefully not to tear the soft, white cartilage in the fish's open mouth that two of the hooks had deeply penetrated. But he got them out and gently released the fish back into the stream. It hovered for a moment, as if in disbelief that it had been given its freedom. Then it shot into the current and disappeared.

Jamison sat down and crossed his legs and laid the rod beside him. He raised his eyes to the mountains, which he glimpsed through the alders and willows along the river, the rocky, barren ridgeline above rising like a continent of stone and sagebrush above the gray, skeletal remains of the trees in the burned-over forest below. He felt a startling and disconcerting urge to go there, to climb above the superficial parameters of his life, to abandon that which he knew and ascend into the thin air of uncertain terrain. He bent his head and pinched the bridge of his nose and then picked up his spinning rod and walked upstream.

He caught two more fish, both as small as the first. He released them both and then pulled apart the rod and put the Mepps in Ben's plastic tackle box and drove back to Aden.

As he pulled into the road to Ben and Monna's home, he saw that a truck and horse trailer was blocking the driveway. Ben and Monna were behind it and peering inside. When they saw Jamison, Ben motioned him to pull to one side of the driveway. Jamison killed the engine and walked over to see if he could help.

Monna turned toward him and smiled. "We've got another horse we're boarding," she said. "We didn't know until last night or I would have said something." She reached out to him, her hand unsteady, and patted his arm. "It's Jessica's horse. It's a gorgeous animal. A paint."

Jamison heard the trailer thump and Jessica's voice and then the horse backed out, its brown eyes wide set and intelligent. Jessica followed gripping a rope lead clipped to the paint's thick nylon halter. It was indeed a beautiful animal; mostly white with a solid chestnut head and a large chestnut patch that covered half its back. It gazed at them with friendly curiosity. When it spied the horses in the pasture it tossed its head and nickered. Jessica caught Jamison's eye and grinned. Jamison nodded self consciously.

"How do you like her?" Jessica said. Ben put his hands in his pockets.

"She's real pretty," Jamison said. "I don't know much about horses but she looks like a good one to me."

Ben stepped forward and ran his hand roughly along the animal's neck. "This here is a damn good horse. Give all the other horses we got an inferiority complex."

Jessica beamed. "She's officially half Grant's," she said. "I've been nagging him about a horse for, like, *years*. I finally wore him out and he agreed to go in on her, but I had to find a place to put her up. So of course I called Monna soon as I knew and here I am." She held the lead in one hand and fiddled with a strand of her hair with the other. Jessica's face was flushed; it was as though she were in love.

"It's a real pretty horse," Jamison said. He blushed with embarrassment and hated how ignorant he must have seemed to Jessica, to all of them. He knew nothing about horses. He took off his glasses and squinted through them, then cleaned them on his tee shirt.

"You can ride her sometime, if you want," Jessica said. She stroked the mare's face, whose eyes were sleepy and half closed with pleasure. "Whenever you want. I'll show you how. She's really sweet."

Jamison hadn't ridden a horse since the pony ride he'd been on as a child at the Minnesota state fair. Horses were for cowboys and he wasn't a cowboy. Neither was Ben, for that matter. But Ben had ridden plenty of horses. So had Monna, before she got sick. But not him.

"I don't know how," Jamison said. "I'm afraid I might break something."

Ben, Monna and Jessica laughed out loud. "You ain't gonna break a horse, not a horse like this," Ben said. "What do you think, Monna? You think he'll break it?" Monna's expression didn't change, but her eyes sparkled. She slowly shook her head.

"Well, I didn't mean ..." Jamison returned his hands to his pockets, flustered. He hadn't meant "break" as if one of the horse's components might snap off, he of course had meant something else, something that he realized he couldn't explain, because he'd meant to imply that he didn't want to do anything *wrong*. Now they were humoring him.

"Well," he said, taking a step back. "I've got to go." He extended his hand to Jessica and Jessica took it and they shook hands. "It is very good to see you again," he said.

"Why don't you come up to the house for lunch, Jamison?" Monna said. "I'll fix something for all of us."

But Jamison was already walking away. He turned but could think of nothing to say so he waved self consciously and smiled and kept walking and when he got to the studio he watched them through the window, settling at last into his disappointment, as Jessica and Ben led the paint, prancing and high-headed, to the pasture. Jessica removed the animal's halter and with a shake of her fine head she trotted out to meet the other horses, who approached tentatively, a step at a time. They stopped when they were a few feet from her, their necks extended, bridging the distance between them. Then the paint took a cautious step toward them and they began milling around her like the slowly turning blades of pinwheel, pink nostrils flaring and pricked ears swiveling in curiosity and guarded interest, Jessica, rapt, pressing the heavy nylon halter to her breast. Ben spoke to her and reluctantly she turned and the two of them walked out of the pasture and returned to the house.

Jamison went into the bedroom and retrieved a book from beside his bed, John William's *Stoner*. He removed the bookmark, a cottonwood leaf he had plucked from a tree along the river, and laid the open book page down upon the kitchen table. Then he pulled out a chair and sat down and folded his hands in his lap. He had thought to read, but he was not moved to do so.

He could no longer hear the horses. He stood and walked to the window and looked across the river toward the pasture, drumming his fingers nervously on the sill. The horses—there were five now—were calmly grazing side by side on the late-summer bunch grass, gone to red in this, the final week of August. In a brief moment—the time it had taken him to retrieve the book—a new horse had been received into the tightly knit herd as though they had taken the measure of her in a complete but unremarkable way and extended their acceptance.

Jessica, Ben would tell him, had been living with Grant for nearly a dozen years. She had never had any real interest in Jamison, other than casual flirting, an adjunct to her trade. He had misread her interest and been wrong from the start, and it embarrassed him to think of the discomfort his silly crush must have caused her. He walked back to the kitchen and picked up his book, and mercifully, as reading had always done, he was able to forget his failure for a while, the pain soothed by the words on the pages, as the heat from a hot stone dissolves in cool water. An hour later he heard her voice again and put the book down and walked to the window. Jessica was in the pasture talking to her horse, a treat in her extended hand. Jamison took a breath and closed his eyes. Then he put on his ball cap and walked out of the studio and across the bridge and into the pasture.

She saw him coming and greeted him.

Jamison said, "You never told me her name. Your horse's name."

"It's Kisomma," Jessica said. "It's Blackfeet for sun, like the *sun* sun." She pointed at the sky. "The people I got her from bred her up on the Hi Line by the Blackfeet rez. I call her Kiso for short."

"It's a pretty name," Jamison said. "She's a pretty horse."

"I'm glad you like her." Kiso stood between them, nuzzling Jessica's hand. "I just gave her an apple," she said. "Kiso loves apples, don't you sweetheart?" Kiso gently tugged at the hem of Jessica's blouse. Jessica scooted around so that she was on Jamison's side of the horse. He caught the faint, lavender scent of her perfume.

"Do you want to ride her? I can get her bridle. All her stuff's in the shed."

"Oh, I don't know, Jessica. I don't know anything about horses. I haven't been on a horse since I was a kid. It's probably not a good idea."

But Jessica was growing animated. "Don't be ridiculous. Of course it's a good idea. Kiso is as gentle as they come, that's why I bought her. She likes being ridden. She's great with kids. She's great with everyone."

"I don't know, Jessica …"

"Hold on, I'll be right back." And she was gone, striding briskly to the shed. She returned swinging a bridle, her blue eyes sparkling.

"What about a saddle?" Jamison said.

"You don't need no *stinking* saddle," Jessica said, grinning. "I'll help you up if you can't jump on her back. She's not a very big horse and you're really tall. You can do it."

Jessica slipped the bridle over Kiso's head, who eagerly took the bit in her mouth, then tossed her head from side to side as if displaying an expensive pair of earrings.

"See?" Jessica said. "She likes going for rides."

Jamison gazed over Kiso's back. He put one hand on her withers and one hand on her back, then flexed his knees a couple times. He wasn't at all sure he could spring all the way onto her back, not in the way he saw cowboys and Indians in the movies do it.

"I'm not exactly sure how to do this," he said. "What if, you know, I kick her or something and she bucks?"

Jamison sensed that perhaps Jessica had begun to lose a teensy little bit of patience.

"Jamison," she said evenly. "She's not going to buck. And you're not going to kick her, either, okay? Just get up there any way you can and then rearrange yourself. Just flop across her back and sit up. That's the way everyone else does it. I'm gonna count to three. One, two …"

Jamison jumped. He hung with his long legs dangling from one side of the horse, his arms grasping for a handhold on the other. He found her mane and pulled himself into a semblance of balance. Tentatively, he slid one leg up and over and then he was sitting up. Kiso turned her head to look at him.

"I'm going to give you the reins," Jessica said. "Just lay them against her neck if you want her to turn. She doesn't need a lot of power steering. She'll go anywhere you want her to go. When you want her to stop, just pull back a little on the reins, don't yank. You okay with all that?"

"I haven't done this ever before," Jamison said. "This is the first time."

"I know. Let's take her around the pasture. First time I'll go with you. Then you're on your own. Sound like a plan?" Jamison nodded and Jessica whispered to Kiso and then they were walking. He clutched her mane and tried to grip her wide back between his legs, nervously adjusting his precarious balance with each rolling step. But eventually he began to relax, and as he relaxed his apprehension, incrementally, began to fade. Jessica walked ahead, Kiso's head over her shoulder, her hand stroking Kiso's proud neck.

Jamison found the mare's broad, warm, back comforting in a way that begged an easy comparison to anything else he had ever done. Riding Kiso wasn't like sitting in a recliner; it wasn't like riding in a slow-moving car. He couldn't remember when he had last been on a horse; his childhood ride at the state fair was the only one he could think of and that had been so long ago that the sensation he must have had then, of sitting astride and controlling, with a flick of the reins, an animal vastly more powerful than he, had long vanished. He released the anxious tension in his legs, and found that with the release his balance improved.

He looked around. The reins hung in a loose belly from his hands to Kiso's bridle. He turned the mare and saw his studio, the hand-hewn logs Ben had laid up those decades ago honey colored in the sunlight, the glint of the tin roof and the dandelion-choked yard and Leviathan's woodpile delineating his new place in the world, as familiar and as welcome now as the song of a wren. On Kiso's back he was only a few feet higher than he had been standing on level ground, but the difference in perspective was remarkable. He could see over the willows and gaze into the green, quiet water of the Shields; he could see the highway beyond Ben and Monna's quarter section of land; and beyond the highway, looming above the ancient rolling sagebrush hills, he could see the barren spine of the Bridger Mountains, the distant parameter of this new life. He turned the horse again and Jessica stepped away to watch and he and Kiso were walking. Jamison rode on alone, around the pasture walking, and around the pasture again.

Chapter 18

At the end of the day, in that last hour of light before darkness, the two of them went to the mountains. Ben folded back the top of the MG and backed out of the garage and onto the highway, Monna silently watching the country they passed, the road swinging west and rising through rangeland as familiar to both as the fear lodged like embers in their souls. Neither spoke.

Ben accelerated and hit a level spot and shifted up and the noise from the engine settled into a throaty purr. Metal fenceposts leaned away from the road and beyond the fenceposts the sagebrush grew cottony and gray green, and on the slope falling away from the road the sage surrendered to willows green and lush along a narrow, purling creek hidden from their view. A line of plodding red Angus followed the twisting contours of the willows. Ben glanced at Monna's rigid face and she turned toward him and smiled. She had once told him she loved painting cattle.

"This is where you want to go?" Ben asked. He thrust his chin at the turnoff just ahead. He knew where Monna wanted to go.

"Yes. We used to come up here all the time, don't you remember? I used to paint here."

Ben turned onto the gravel road that cut due west from the highway. Monna pointed to the wide spot in the road and Ben pulled over and killed the engine. He felt the motor vibrating through the wooden steering wheel and then it stopped. Ahead, in palisades of stone etched with the white veins left from the previous winter's snows, the north end of the Bridgers rose above an immense forest of fir and pine, gone from dark green to black at this late hour. The road before them, like an undulating roller coaster, would take them to Flathead Pass. But this was far enough.

Ben sat behind the wheel of the MG, his hands restless in his lap, waiting for Monna to speak, desperate and stricken, not wanting to hear what he knew she was going to say. He gazed through the windshield at the road, as if deliverance lay at the end of it. The road, after a long and tortuous ascent, paused at the top of the pass and then fell away in a precipitous decline, but he had never driven the road down the other side, into the valley beyond the one in which they had spent all their married lives. It was a very difficult road, and he had not wanted to risk the trip alone. Driving to the top had been sufficient.

"Do you know why I wanted us to come here?" she asked. "You know, don't you? You've known this was coming." She reached unsteadily for his hand and he began to cry.

"You have to go?"

"I can't do this any longer," she said. "I can't, Ben. I just can't. I can't paint any more. Do you understand what I'm telling you?"

Ben turned away from her and gazed across the road. A quarter mile distant was an old, log-sided ranch house encircled by out buildings with mismatched red and brown roofs. Weak light, like the flame from a candle, shone from one window of the house. A dog barked.

"Are you afraid?" He put his face in his hands.

"Yes."

* * *

Jamison walked down the center of the highway straddling the dotted yellow line. Traffic was light and the walking was easier on the pavement than on the rocky, weed-choked shoulders on either side. He assumed he'd be able to hear, or see, approaching cars from either direction and so far he had.

The summer-long, intermittent stream of fishermen and hikers that buzzed through Aden enroute to the rivers and mountains to the north was nearly gone. Bowhunters in military camouflage, their faces streaked with black and brown grease paint like Indian warriors, nursed beers in the Infirmary and prowled the two narrow aisles in the General Store across the street. Jamison's galumphing gait moved him quickly, if inelegantly, toward town. Midday traffic at the Infirmary was typically light, and he hoped to spend some time talking to Jessica.

He had set out wanting to apologize, but the exertion of his brisk walk had jarred loose his convictions, and he was now unsure of what, among his many awkward missteps, he should apologize for. For having had a hopeless crush on a woman nearly thirty years his junior? For having been so willfully blind to her relationship with Grant? She had to have been mortified at his clumsy infatuation. He strode to the shoulder of the highway and paused for a rest. He loosened the straps on his daypack, then held up his hand to block the sun's glare. The cottonwoods along the river, lustrous and green and lazy in the September heat, were offset with solitary yellow boughs, the bursts of color presaging the coming of fall. Soon, Ben had told him, there would again be snow in the mountains.

He had driven to Montana in March and had seen all the snow then that he had ever hoped to see. Seven months on he remained. He had thought to stay only through spring.

He continued walking. He heard a truck approaching and he walked to the shoulder and waved at the driver and when it had passed he began walking again down the center of the highway. Nothing had materialized, nothing had come together, in the way he had imagined it would. What he had imagined then he could scarcely remember now. But the failure of his imagination had forced a reassessment; and in movement, in the lumbering cadence of his feet on pavement, it had risen to the top of his thoughts like a bubble rising from the bottom of a pond: *friendship*.

He rounded the last bend and when Aden was in view he saw that there was no one parked in front of the Infirmary. Gerald Metzger's patrol truck drove toward him and slowed, and when it passed Jamison saluted. Metzger draped an elbow out the open window and nodded.

He found Jessica behind the bar, her back to him and her elbows propped up behind her on the counter, idly watching a football game on the wide screen tv above her head. She saw his reflection in the mirror and waved, then reached for a glass.

"You missed the rush," she said. "Four people. Thought I might have to call in reinforcements. How's my girl?"

"Kiso's fine. She seems to be getting along with the other horses real well. But, I mean, I'm not exactly an expert at this equestrian stuff. You should come out. She probably misses you."

Unasked, Jessica filled the glass with beer and set it before him. Like all the others.

"I miss *her*," she said. "But right now it's tough to get away. Most of the time it's just me and Grant running this place. If one of us leaves, the other's got to come in. Even when it's like this." She spread her arms as if accepting an encore in a vacant auditorium. "Hard to believe we're not swamped, I know, but there you go. I feel bad because she loves being ridden."

Jamison sipped his beer. The sound was off on the TV, and without sound, he had no idea who was playing.

Jessica leaned over the bar, the open neckline of her tee shirt revealing the red and orange Phoenix tattooed across the swell of her breasts. "You okay?" she said.

Jamison nodded self consciously. "Sure. I'm fine. Why wouldn't I be?"

"I don't know," Jessica said. "Just asking."

"No, I'm good," Jamison said.

"Okay. Gotta keep our customers happy, you know?"

Jamison nodded.

Jessica turned toward the TV and Jamison drank his beer. He slid off his stool and caught Jessica's eyes and smiled and then strode across the bar to Monna's painting. The painting was still there. He strode back to his stool and sat down.

"Actually, I was kind of thinking about something," he said. "I thought, you know, I could help you exercise Kiso, if you want. It's not like I've got a lot of other pressing responsibilities. If that were something you'd be interested in."

Jessica spun to face him. "You mean, like, ride her when I'm working? She'd love that! She loves people, you've seen her. That would be wonderful!"

Startled, Jamison sat upright on his stool. He hadn't thought about *riding* Kiso. He just assumed he might trot her around the pasture once a day, like he'd seen horse trainers do on television. Or every other day, something. In fact, he wasn't exactly sure what he'd been thinking about, or what Jessica might have envisioned. He'd just put it out there.

"Well, I don't know about the riding part, but ..."

"Oh no, that would be fun!" Jessica said. "I can show you how to put on her bridle. It's easy, you saw me do it. Her saddle's in the shed if you want it. But she's so gentle you can just ride her bareback. Like we did before. I asked Monna if she'd ride her sometimes, but Monna says she can't anymore. She doesn't have the balance. I'd have asked you first if I'd had any idea you were interested. This is just wonderful! Thank you so much!"

Jamison put his hands on the edge of the bar and straightened his arms, pushing himself back an inch. Jessica's tide of gratitude threatened to wash away the barricade he'd painstakingly erected around himself.

"Yeah, okay," he said. He hadn't expected to be pulled in this direction, but he felt virtuous, as though he were being genuinely helpful, as though Jessica, of all people, might actually want his help. "I mean, you'll have to show me how to put the bridle on, like you said. I don't want to put it on backwards or anything."

"You can't put a bridle on backwards," Jessica said. "Their head only goes one way." She grinned and reached across the bar and squeezed his arm and Jamison felt his pale skin flush behind his glasses. "I just so much appreciate this. When you get some practice, maybe we can go for a ride. There's lots of cool trails up in the mountains. You can do twenty miles easy. I can't wait to tell Grant. He said I shouldn't get her because he said I wouldn't have time to ride. But now I do!"

Jamison finished his beer and ordered another and finished that beer and walked back to the studio. He peered in Ben and Monna's home as he passed, slowing in expectation; but although the lights were on, he saw no one within, no one who might pass an open window and upon seeing him, invite him inside; and he could summon no pretext for an unannounced visit. He had hoped to share the exciting news: he was going to be a cowboy! He snorted at the thought of it. The whole idea was of course preposterous, he was no more a cowboy now, nor would riding Jessica's horse make him one, than his months in Aden had made him a farmer. But his talk with Jessica, her delight at his offer to ride her beloved Kiso, had left him feeling good about their conversation, about his trip to town, about himself. Visiting her, after all the silly turmoil he had put himself through on her account, had been exactly the right thing to do, a hand offered in friendship, not desire; an unspoken hunger, abandoned.

He strode into the small, spare living room of the studio and peered out the window toward the river and watched a churning web of fluttering, moth-like bugs career in headlong flight from the willows to the surface of the water, then ascend in crazy spirals toward the sun. Ben had told him they were caddisflies, he remembered that now. A taut, sudden movement arrested his gaze, and Leviathan appeared on top of the woodpile. Upon spying Jamison the big cat arched his back in delight, the broken tip of his tail proud and erect.

And then, in an instant, Leviathan's demeanor changed, and in the brief, wrenching discussion that followed the cat's departure Jamison would know. He saw Leviathan crouch and flatten against the logs and then leap over the side and vanish in the willows along the river; Jamison stepped back and turned away from the window and knew who it was even as he heard the heavy knock on the studio door. He opened the door and Ben stood before him, the sun behind him like the halo of an angel, ravaged.

"I have something to tell you," Ben said.

Chapter 19

Jamison sat across from Ben at the small kitchen table in the studio, his hands folded rigidly in his lap, and listened to Ben's outpouring of grief. Ben was so inconsolable that Jamison longed for something stronger than the two glasses of wine he had poured for them and which neither man touched.

Jamison wanted certainty, as if certainty, that imposter, might be found in something as meaningless as words. So he had pressed Ben to repeat the decision his sister had made, asking in a hollow, emotionless voice that did not seem to belong to him, and then again. Ben told him there had been no mistake. Monna would take her life before the first snow; she loved autumn and would remain long enough to see the leaves change one more time. She had implored Ben's help; she needed his strength. She could no longer stay in a world riven by pain and begged his understanding. Ben, his fists pressed against his ruined eyes, did not understand. Maybe Jamison would, maybe he could explain it in a way that made sense.

But Jamison could not.

Ben told Jamison that Monna wanted to escape the imprisonment of her own wasted body. Ben choked and coughed into a paper napkin and began sobbing and Jamison, frantic and despairing of his utter helplessness, reached across the table and held the clutched fist holding the napkin. Ashamed, Ben pulled his hand away and gazed across the room and made a joke and Jamison laughed. Then Ben laughed too and said he was okay, he was fine.

For all that day, and then another, Jamison could not find the courage to talk to Monna. He did not know when, or from where, that courage would come. Finally, he walked up to see her, his heart pounding in his chest. Ben was away. The day was warm and the door was open and through the screen door he saw his sister sitting on the sofa. She turned around awkwardly and smiled at him over her shoulder. He let himself in and sat in the recliner opposite her.

"Ben talked to you," she said.

"Yes."

"So now you know." She was wearing a pleated skirt, made from fabric that looked as though it had been hand quilted. She ran her hand down one of the pleats as if to smooth it, but her strokes were uncertain and fitful, as though her fingers had been momentarily arrested, and then released, by the folds in her dress. "I've been thinking about it for a long time, Jamison. I was thinking about it when I called you this spring and asked you to come out. But I didn't know for sure then."

"When did you know for sure?" Plucking at the recliner, his eyes burning.

"When I knew once and for all I wasn't going to get any better. You go through this long phase where you think this can't be happening to me, and then you get over that but then you think that you're going to have a spontaneous remission if only you can keep positive thoughts in your head long enough, like having happy thoughts makes everything go away." She shook her head. "Which no one has ever done of course but that's what you think. But none of it's true. You don't want the truth, you want a miracle, because miracles are easier to believe in."

"But they have things they can do, Monna, don't they? Implant electrodes, drugs, stuff like that. I know they do."

"That's what Ben says." She looked at him. "But it's not a question of what they can *do*, Jamison. They can keep me alive in a facility somewhere for another twenty years. It's a question of *how* I want to live. Sometime you should go into our bedroom and open the drawer of that beautiful walnut dresser Ben made, the big drawer on the bottom. I've got piles of research on Parkinson's Disease in there. I quit reading it when I couldn't fit any more in. Ben's read it all."

Jamison rose and excused himself and went to the bathroom. His image in the mirror reflected his confusion and pain, his features grotesque in the single overhead light: his eyes bloodshot behind the thick, black-rimmed glasses, the thin tufts of white hair ringing his bald head twisted in uncombed whorls, his ashen skin tracked with faint blue veins. Books, the wonderful novels he loved that he had read throughout his life, had taught him all about the endless configurations of death. But now, faced with his sister's calm surrender to a relentless disease, he discovered he had learned nothing about the fear of confronting death head on, of the certitude of mortality in thrall to the whims of a God he did not believe in.

He took off his glasses and turned on the faucet and let cold water run over his hands. Then he splashed water on his face and wiped his face with a towel. He returned to the living room.

"Tell me how I can help," he said.

Monna pulled her knees onto the sofa one at a time and tucked them beneath her, in that way of women. "Help Ben," she said. "He going to need someone … after. He needs someone now."

"I don't know how to do that with Ben," Jamison said. "I'm not sure he wants my help."

"He wants your help," Monna said. "He's just not going to ask you for it."

Jamison clasped his palms together, as if in prayer. Behind Monna was the window that overlooked the front yard, and the unmowed grass in the yard grew in tall, tangled stems around the barbed wire fence that bordered the ditch that bordered the highway, and the trucks and cars on the highway slowed as they reached Aden and then sped up again as they passed, as if in a hurry to leave this country that was home to so very few; as if, on this warm October day, the cold he sensed in his bones had already begun chasing them away. As if, Jamison thought, warmth lay elsewhere, in the solace of knowing where you would be when the snow came.

"Ben never told me that," Jamison said.

"He does."

* * *

They sat at a table in the Infirmary, but none spoke of what they had spoken of the week before.

Ben seemed resolutely happy. He bought Jamison and Monna glasses of beer, and while they drank and waited for their food, Jamison watched the ebb and flow of the people around them, coming together and then decoupling and then coming together again, as if drawn like drops of mercury to a human nucleus. It was Friday night, and although there was no band scheduled for the evening, the bar was full. It had been a warm day, but the night was chilly, and each time someone entered the bar, they let cold air into the room, which eddied around Jamison's legs like the current of a river. Then it would dissipate, absorbed by the moist, encompassing warmth of bodies.

Monna tugged off her jacket and draped it over the seat of her stool.

"I'm hot," she said.

Ben grinned. "I'll be the judge of that," he said.

Monna gaped at him, then burst into laughter. Then, seeing Jamison's confusion, she tried to apologize. But she sputtered over her own speech, her rigid face unable to make the words, which made the two of them laugh all the harder. Perplexed, and unsure if he should join in, Jamison looked from one to the other. He would never understand Ben's back-handed humor.

When Jessica came with their orders, they were still chuckling. It was as though a dam had burst, releasing a pent-up torrent of dark water. Jessica caught Jamison's eye and arched her eyebrows.

"What?"

"Ask them," Jamison said, shrugging. "They're both crazy. My family." But even he had begun laughing now.

Monna had wanted to drive down in the MG but Ben had said it was too cold, that with the top down *she* would be too cold, and Monna had reluctantly agreed. They made the brief drive to the bar in Ben's truck, Jamison wedged in the back seat, his long legs folded, as always, against the back of the passenger seat, his knees pressed awkwardly against his chest. He hoped Jessica would ask about Kiso, because Jamison wanted to tell her that he'd ridden her as he'd promised.

Several days earlier, Jamison had walked into the pasture and called to the beautiful mare, and she'd trotted over to greet him, unlike the rest of the horses in the small herd, who watched him indifferently, holding out for a bribe of a coffee can full of grain. He'd found the mare's bridle in the shed and tried to remember, exactly, how Jessica had put it on. There was a loop on the top which went over one ear (he remembered that much) so he slipped the loop over her ear and then discovered there was no room left to insert the bit into her mouth. Instead, the bit straddled the end of Kiso's chestnut nose, giving her the look of a bemused spinster peering over reading glasses. Patiently, Kiso waited while he removed the bridle and tried again, this time nudging the bit against her teeth. To his surprise, she opened her mouth and took it in. He patted her neck and then flopped onto her back and spun around until he was sitting upright. Then he walked her in circles around the pasture, his apprehension fading with each rolling step. When he touched her sides with his heels her gait became clipped and staccato, faster than before.

Jessica set his plate before him. "I rode your horse," he said.

Jessica was thrilled. "That's wonderful! I've been trying to get out to see her, but it's been like this all week." She nodded at the people milling around the bar. "I don't know what this is all about, but the money's good. How was she? She try to buck you off?"

"No, no," Jamison said. "She's really nice. One time I got going kind of fast. She was running, I think. I started to slide off a little and she stopped until I could regain my balance."

"That's my Kiso," Jessica said. She leaned forward and braced her arms against the table. "How fast was she going? Was she, like, loping along? Like this?" Jessica held her hands before her as if she were holding reins and bounced rhythmically up and down. Ben and Monna cracked up.

"Could you do that while I get my phone?" Ben said. He wiped the tears from his eyes.

Jessica slugged him in the arm. "We were talking about my *horse*, you moron," she said. "You try to have a serious conversation with these guys …"

Jamison too was grinning. "No. It wasn't like that. It was kind of bouncy. It was hard to stay on."

"Ah," Jessica said. "That's what I thought. That horse you were bouncing around on wasn't running, she was *trotting*. She's from jackpot barrel racing stock. Her mother won a ton of money. If she'd been running, you'd have known about it."

"Well, it seemed pretty fast to me," Jamison said.

"*Jessica* seems pretty fast to me," Ben said.

Monna buried her face in her hands. "Can we kill you now or later?"

Ben held up his hands. "See what I got to put up with?" he said.

* * *

They drove home and Monna invited Jamison to the house for a drink. It was dark. They had spent the summer sitting by the river but now the nights were cold, and the cottonwoods and the willows along the river were yellow and blood red as if summer had bled into the color of the season upon them. They sat in Ben and Monna's small living room. Monna retrieved a bottle of wine from the kitchen and Ben laid up a fire in the woodstove and the scent of burning pine and the heat from the stove eased their souls.

They spoke little, for the growing warmth softened and dissipated the sharp edges of their thoughts and turned them inward, in the way a blanket slowly warms the person it is thrown over.

Monna had spread a bright woolen afghan over her legs. "It won't be so bad," she said, "if it's like this." She sat beside Ben on the sofa and touched his hand. "I'm not afraid of this. I'm not afraid of the dark." She turned a little to face him but Ben would not look at her. He rested his hands on this thighs, as if bracing himself. Then he pushed himself to his feet and walked to the stove and opened the door. Heat surged out, and he took a step back. He shoved in another log and returned to the sofa.

Ben folded his hands over his thick torso as if he were relaxing, as if they were still at the Infirmary. "Jamison here ain't had work since that remodel job we did this summer," he said. "Been a long time. I don't know what he does down there in the studio all day long, do you?"

Monna glanced at Ben and then shook her head. She put her hand back in her lap. Ben did not seem to notice.

"Now that Jessica's out of the picture, maybe he's got himself a new girlfriend down there. Or maybe he's …" he took a swig from his glass, "or maybe he's talking to the animals or something."

Jamison sat up and then forced himself to ease back into his chair. He looked at Monna, his heart rate ticking up.

"Ben," Jamison said, "I *read*. You know that. I always read. You should try it sometime."

Monna gave a curt nod and glanced from Ben to Jamison and then back again. Ben was facing her now.

"I think he talks to the animals," Ben said. "Like that Dr. Dolittle guy. The horses and the deer, whatever. They had a song about that in the movie."

Monna pulled the afghan off her legs and rose unsteadily to her feet. "Ben," she said, "what on earth are you talking about? Did you hear what I just said? Does that mean anything to you?"

Ben stared at the floor. "What do you want me to say?"

"Maybe that you heard what I just said. Maybe that you understand."

Ben went white and looked at Jamison and Jamison saw at once Ben's terror and his anger and his shame.

The logs in the stove crackled and something skittered across the roof, a windblown twig, a mouse. Jamison and Monna's eyes arose in unison, drawn to the sound as to a tap on a window. Ben did not move.

The afghan had slid to the floor and Monna slowly reached

down and picked it up, then folded it in half and laid it across the back of the sofa. "I'm going to get us something to eat," she said. "I think I have some cheese in the fridge." She returned a minute later and offered Jamison a small plate of cheese and Jamison took a slice and when Monna insisted, he took another. She offered the plate to Ben but he refused. She set the plate on the coffee table and slowly and elaborately, as if in pantomime, cut two small slices with a paring knife. She balanced one slice on her knee and raised the other to her mouth. She did not look at Ben. Jamison watched with intense unease.

Suddenly, Ben plucked the slice of cheese from Monna's knee and popped it into his mouth, his eyes locked on Monna's.

Monna coolly returned his gaze. Again, she offered him the plate.

"Do you want more? We have plenty, Ben. Just ask."

"*You didn't ask me!*" Ben scooted across the sofa, forcing Monna to lean away from him. "You never asked *me!*" He jabbed himself in the chest, hard. "I thought *I'd* have some kind of say in this, in a decision like that! I thought you'd ask *me* before you decided to run off and fucking kill yourself! But instead it's like, 'Okay Ben, here's what we're gonna do.' Like you're the one who's in charge of calling the big play on game day! Like it's my job to just sit on my goddamn thumb and suck it up, like I'm some kind of stupid kid who doesn't understand what's going on, like it's not *my* life too!"

Monna pushed herself away from him, horrified and shaking. Robotically, she reached for the cheese plate but her palsied hands fumbled and it clattered to the floor, and before she could pick it up, Ben kicked it away. The plate skittered across the room and smashed against the wall, breaking into halves.

Jamison said, "Monna. Ben." But neither saw him, neither heard. Both sat in painful silence, Monna as if on the verge of flight, Ben staring angrily at his feet. Jamison sat woodenly with his hands in his lap, his blood pounding.

And outside the weather changed. A breeze picked up, and the rustle of leaves spoke of rain. When it came, the rain would melt the dusting of snow that now lay on the high, barren peaks of the Crazies, granting a brief reprieve before the coming winter. But the snow would be back; the cold snows of November would be given their due.

Ben sagged forward and squeezed his eyes shut and lowered his forehead to his hands.

"I'll clean that up," he said.

Monna rose and walked to the kitchen, and in her hesitant footsteps Jamison saw the welling doubt, the uncontrolled hands twitching at her sides as if grasping for an apology, as if all about her lay steeped in remorse.

Chapter 20

Monna braced her herself against the back of the kitchen chair, but the chair writhed beneath her fingers and the linoleum swam beneath her feet in sickening waves of feeble blue light. She had hoped she would not have to endure this again. She hadn't had hallucinations in months—the doctors had prescribed new meds which for a time seemed to put an end to them—but now they were back. Gripping the chair with both hands, she shuffled around to the front and slowly lowered herself into the seat.

Ben's help during previous bouts had been to park her someplace—the living room sofa or, against her mild protests, their bed—and then hover over her until the hallucinations passed. Despite her intense feeling of corporeal displacement, as if her senses extended beyond the confines of her physical body, she had found his solicitousness almost oppressive, as if she were too helpless to care for herself, as if, unattended, she might disappear someplace he could not follow. But Monna said nothing; Ben's earnestness was as deeply touching as it was clumsy. Now she was alone in the kitchen. Ben had gone to the shop early that morning; she could hear the music he always played while he was working, and she knew he wouldn't be back until lunch. By then, she hoped, the symptoms would pass. Today she would suffer them alone.

Her first bout of hallucinations, many years ago now, had been terrifying. She'd fled the suddenly claustrophobic confines of their home and stumbled into the yard—it had been a warm summer afternoon—in the thin hope she might escape her afflictions in flight.

Ben had stayed by her side, clutching her arm, his eyes wide with confusion and fear. But Monna could not tell him what was wrong. Apart from the undulating landscape, apart from the dim, pulsing blue light that illumined everything she saw, panic surged in her breast, her heart pounding as if trying to break free of the rigid shell in which it was confined.

By the time they got to the specialist in Bozeman the hallucinations had passed, and her doctor explained to her what had happened. There would be more, he told her, but certain medications should lessen their frequency. And they had. Now she greeted their infrequent return with a grim resolve. But a hard, small kernel of panic remained, a sharp-edged pebble lodged in her bones.

She gazed at the half-finished cup of coffee she'd set down when the hallucinations began. The cup shimmered as if submerged in water. She pushed herself out of her chair and put the cup in the microwave and punched the start button. When the microwave pinged she retrieved the cup and shut the door. The cup was hot and she was forced to steady it with both trembling hands, but the heat against her numb hands felt good.

She walked unsteadily to the back window and gazed out at the yard and across the river at the mountains. Most of the aspens were barren; at this distance, the trees that had been brilliant yellow just two weeks earlier were now subdued, more gray and white than brown, a color she'd spent half her life trying to put on paper. It was not the color of death, but rather withdrawal, and the challenge had always been to render the dormant trees in a way that revealed the life still in them, the richness that had burst forth just a few short months earlier merely resting, gone to somewhere as familiar as it was unknown.

Along the river, a handful of cottonwoods still clutched solitary leaves, survivors twisting restlessly on barren limbs, anxious to join the carpet of speckled, fading leaves on the brown grass below. Monna thought, *soon*.

She returned to the kitchen and put her cup back in the microwave, and when the microwave pinged she removed the cup and then spied the cat sitting on the sill outside the window. She stared. This was Jamison's yellow cat, the one she'd caught a glimpse of only once that summer, but of whom he often spoke when the two of them were safely out of Ben's earshot. The cat peered through the window and mewed—although she could hear nothing through the glass—then lifted a big paw and meticulously groomed its face, its eyes never leaving hers. The creature shone with a faint, pulsing light, which lent it a ghostly presence, as if the light came from the animal itself.

Then it arched its back and flicked the crooked tip of its tail and with each flick the cat seemed to grow until in Monna's delirium there was hardly room on the narrow sill to contain it. It opened its mouth in a silent lion roar and she saw its teeth, yellowed and cracked with age. Its vast eyes shone pale green and luminous, and she felt as though she were swimming through them in bottomless, translucent water. It opened its mouth again and the silence moved her to open the back door, where she might hear the cat's voice calling out. But when she crept outside it had vanished. She took another step, her eyes scanning the yard, and spied it disappearing behind Jamison's studio, not looking back, its crooked tail flicking once, then gone.

* * *

"I saw your kitty," Monna said.

Jamison pulled out his chair and sat across from her at the studio's cramped kitchen table, his back pressed against the slats. "Did Ben see him? I remember what you said about him and cats."

"Ben was in the shop. Your cat was in the window. He was outside on the sill. It's like he wanted to come inside, like he was talking to me or something. But when I opened the door he ran down here to your place." She said nothing about her hallucinations. "It was weird. I really thought he was trying to talk to me."

"Well, maybe he was," Jamison said. He wondered how much he should tell her. Certainly, Leviathan talked to *him*. He'd been feeding the big cat on the front porch for weeks, trying gently to coax it inside, but the closest Leviathan would come was the threshold, where he would sit, his big paws gathered daintily beneath him, purring contentedly while he licked clean his can of Delicious Salmon in Alfredo Sauce. He thought that with the colder weather the cat could surely be enticed back into the warmth of the studio—where he had, in fact, already been once before—but as soon as the sun set he vanished outside, a captive of the moon. Jamison wouldn't see him again until the following morning, waiting on the top of the woodpile until Jamison tapped on the window and Leviathan trotted around to the front porch to be fed. He finally relented and bought a red fabric cat bed in Livingston. He hid it under the porch, out of sight of Ben and his rifle. Periodically he hauled it out to check for hair, and the fur stuck to the fabric proved Leviathan was using it. Jamison hoped he enjoyed the respite from his spartan home in the log pile.

"I forgot you called him that, Leviathan. That's a cool name."

"Yeah," Jamison said. "It's funny, I read all these writers and you wonder how they come up with names for characters, because the names always seem to be a perfect fit. I never understood how they made that work. So that day I named him Leviathan; the name just jumped into my head. It wasn't exactly like it rolled off my tongue. I thought it was too long. Cats are usually named Boots or Whiskers, something like that, one or two syllables. But now it seems to fit him perfectly. Like there's nothing else he *could* be named."

"Well," Monna said, "I like it. It does fit him. I mean, he's pretty big." She folded her hands in her lap. The hallucinations had faded and then stopped, and for now, at least, some of the trembling in her hands was gone, as if the psychic energy spent on her hallucinations had temporarily exhausted her physical symptoms, as well. "I know it's kind of early, but do you have any wine?" It was close to noon, and she wanted to talk before Ben returned from the shop.

"I think so," Jamison said. "I still have most of the bottle we opened the last time you guys were down here." Jamison found the bottle and two glasses in the cabinet and held the glasses to the light and then set them on the table. Clean enough. His pour lapped over the top of Monna's glass and trickled down the side and made a tiny puddle on the table. He wiped it off with his thumb.

"Boy," Monna said, examining the brimming glass. "I guess this means you're ready for a drink, too." She raised her glass. "Here's to getting shitfaced with your brother." Jamison grinned and they clinked glasses.

"Where's your cat?" Monna asked. "Don't you let him come inside?"

"He won't come in," Jamison said. "He lets me feed him in the doorway, but if I put his food in the kitchen, he won't come in for it. He sits on the threshold and howls at me. It's like there's this invisible barrier between what he really wants and what he won't allow himself to have. You would think …"—Jamison ran his finger around the rim of his glass—"… you would think he'd *want* to come inside. It's a lot warmer and a lot safer. There's no owls, no coyotes, none of the animals that kill cats. He could sleep by the fireplace at night and run around outside during the day. But that's evidently not his plan. Actually, I don't know what his plan is. I wish I could figure it out."

"We all have plans," Monna said.

Jamison stared at his glass and nodded. He didn't look up.

"Not Leviathan," he said quietly.

"No, not Leviathan."

Jamison cradled his glass in his lap. He no longer felt like drinking. He glanced at Monna's glass and saw it was down by a third. She smiled.

"The good thing about having plans is that I know I'm not going to die from alcoholism," she said. "Hey!" She slapped her hand on the table, giving Jamison a start. "I've got a question for you."

Jamison raised his eyes.

"Do you think I'll see mom and dad?"

Jamison set his glass on the table and pushed it away from him and his gaze rose to the water-stained plywood that Ben had used all those years before to sheath the ceiling. They were nearly halfway through the first week of November. This late in the year the sun hung low in the southern sky, as though a closer proximity to earth might melt away the glassy shelf ice clinging to the banks of the river.

Jamison had allowed the fire in the stove to die down and the studio was chilly. He scooted his chair back and excused himself and put a log in the stove, then returned. He said, "I don't see why not. They have to be up there someplace."

"Good," Monna said. "Good. That's what I think, too."

* * *

When Jessica's truck pulled into the driveway, Jamison's heart fluttered in spite of himself. *Still.* They'd spoken a dozen times over the course of that fall, and always it was the same. It was frustrating that he still harbored a trace of the feelings he hoped would have disappeared by now. He recalled Blaise Pascal: "*The heart has its reasons, which reason knows nothing of.*" How very true.

Yet he was excited by what was becoming, in fits and starts, a tentative camaraderie between the two of them, as though both were survivors of an embarrassing skirmish neither had had any real desire to engage. Now that what had never been was over, the murky clouds of ambiguity had parted, and Jamison's initial disappointment had been replaced with relief. He'd committed to riding the mare at least once a week, and now, tingling like a child at show and tell, he wanted to show off his new skills, his growing abilities as an equestrian. He strode into the pasture, and when Jessica saw him coming, she grinned and waved.

She was speaking to Kiso under her breath, quietly, one hand stroking the horse's chestnut neck, the other holding an apple in her open palm. The mare finished the apple and nudged the bulging pocket in Jessica's coat.

"Oh! So you think there's another one in there, do you, sweetie?" She held out the second apple, and Kiso nickered and happily tossed her head. "Kiso *loves* apples," Jessica said. The sun was shining, but on this November day it offered little warmth, and her face was flushed from the cold.

Jamison thrust his hands into the pockets of his down coat. "I've been riding her some, since the last time I talked to you," he said, nodding somberly. "I know the difference between a trot and a canter now. I've been using her saddle, like you suggested. It helps a lot."

Jessica beamed. She was so enraptured with her horse it made Jamison happy just to be around her, as though the beautiful mare threw off an aura of joy that encompassed them both. Jamison was suddenly struck with a thought: *Leviathan, too.* When no one else was around, Leviathan would show up on the studio porch, and Jamison would ease outside and sit in the wooden rocker Monna had retrieved from Ben's shop and the big cat would curl around Jamison's legs and purr with contentment. Sometimes he'd let Jamison pet him, and the surge of affection Jamison felt surprised and thrilled him. He had not grown up with animals and had never understood that about them, that joy in their presence was an unspoken pact of friendship, the hand stroking their fur a gesture of love.

"It's been a while," Jamison said. "I thought you forgot about us out here." He moved closer to Kiso and clumsily rubbed her neck. The bulging muscles beneath the chestnut coat warmed his cold fingers.

"It's been crazy at work," Jessica said. "Halloween was a zoo, like always. I thought I'd see you guys, but no Monna, no Ben." She let Kiso finish the apple and then wiped her hands on her jeans. "And no Jamison." She raised an eyebrow as though expecting an explanation, but Jamison had none to offer. He hadn't celebrated Halloween since he'd retired from teaching. This year's Halloween, in particular, had not seemed celebratory.

"So it's like, I couldn't get away until today," Jessica said. "But I wanted to get in a ride while I still could. Before she forgets me. Before the weather they're talking about moves in."

Jamison stepped around Kiso until he faced Jessica. "What weather?"

"Snow next week," Jessica said. "Lots. Wednesday's what they say. Makes me wish I was still in California."

"They said snow? *Next* Wednesday?" Jamison felt as though he were bound to a blinding arc of cold light hurtling him out of the pasture and into the thin, scudding clouds above.

"Yeah," Jessica said. She gave him a look. "This is *Montana*, Jamison. It snows. That white stuff that falls out of the sky? Like that." She took a step toward the stable. "You want to ride her first? I can critique your technique." She grinned, then saw his stricken demeanor.

Jamison backed away from the mare and thrust his palms out as if to distance himself, as if she must be mistaken; surely the weather forecast was wrong, certainly they couldn't be predicting a storm so soon. Wednesday was less than a week away.

"How much did they say?" he asked.

"Six to eight inches. That's a lot for this valley. That's why I want to get in a ride while I still can. It'll gum things up for a while, that's for sure." She was staring at him.

"Jessica," Jamison said, "I can't ride today. I've got ... Ben wants me to help him in the shop. I just came out to say hello."

Jessica gave him a look. Then shrugged. "Okay," she said.

"It was good to see you," Jamison said. "It was."

Jessica was already halfway to the stable. She waved over her shoulder. Jamison turned and walked numbly back to the studio, to the warmth he craved on this bitter early November afternoon, to the solace he sought within its hewn log walls. He took off his coat and hung it on the nail beside the door and sat on the sofa and removed his boots. He had banked the fire in the stove that morning and the sofa was warm from the stove. He placed his boots side by side at one end of the sofa, the laces coiled and dropped inside. Then he stepped to the window and saw Leviathan on the woodpile, and when the big cat saw him he arched his scarred, yellow back and squinted with pleasure. Jamison put his face in his hands and wept.

Chapter 21

Jamison strode down the graveled shoulder of the highway and when he hit long stretches where he could see oncoming traffic he moved a little further onto the pavement, where the footing was better. It was cold, and the bitter wind sweeping the valley floor scent icy fingers down the collar of his down coat and stung his cheeks, forcing him to burrow into the woolen scarf wrapped around his neck. He wished now he'd taken his Honda, which he'd parked outside Ben and Monna's garage and hadn't driven for weeks. Jamison always rode with Ben when the two worked together, but Ben had informed him they would be taking an indefinite break from remodel work. Jamison said take as long as you like and Ben grinned and said he would, because by god he was still the top dog in this outfit. Squaring up a little as if daring Jamison to disagree.

Jamison no longer timed his walks to town; he knew exactly how long it would take him. He'd pick up cat food at the general store and be back well in time for dinner with Monna and Ben.

She'd slipped an expensive envelope under his door the previous evening with a formal invitation printed on embossed stationary: *Your presence is requested for a family celebration tomorrow at 6, cocktails shortly thereafter. No RSVP, no gifts, no long faces!* And in an uneven, tiny scrawl below, she'd hand written, *I've got wine! The good stuff!*

Jamison bought a dozen cans of cat food at the general store and put them in his daypack and walked back to the studio. By the time he arrived he was chilled through, and he stood before the stove for several minutes warming himself, his hands held before him to capture the heat. Then he walked to the window and gazed at the river, the banks now rimmed with shelf ice, the trees barren of leaves, the cheerful, brimming flows of summer diminished and cold. Then he put on his coat and made his way up the slight incline to Ben and Monna's home.

Monna greeted Jamison at the door and as soon as he closed the door behind him she handed him a glass of wine. She urged him to try it and Jamison tucked the small beige book he'd brought under his arm and took a tentative sip, then thoughtfully swirled the wine around the glass. It was very good.

"You like it?"

"Geez yes, Monna. This is great! Not exactly what I'm used to drinking, though."

"Me neither. This was the best stuff I could find in Livingston without paying an arm and a leg. Even Ben likes it. I bought two bottles so have all you want. I should have dinner ready in half an hour."

Jamison took another sip while Monna watched, her dark eyes sparkling. Then she spun unsteadily on her heel and returned to the kitchen, the pleats in her long skirt flaring out as though she were dancing.

Jamison took a seat at the kitchen table. Across from him, Ben raised his glass and nodded. Jamison did the same.

"It's cold," Jamison said. "You never told me it got like this in November." He thrust his chin toward the living room window, darkly reflective in the fading light. "I thought I was moving out here into the banana belt, what with the winters in Minnesota."

"It'll get better." Ben glanced at Monna, but she had bent over the oven checking the turkey roast and turned away. "It gets, you know … you get bad weather but then it warms up again. Not, you know, *warm* warm, not like September or anything. But you get hit with bad weather, you ride it out." He looked at his wife again. "You ride it out. You ain't gonna change the weather."

Jamison set his book beside him on the kitchen table. Ben glanced at it and then at Jamison and then excused himself and went to the bathroom. When he came back his eyes were red and he made a joke and sat down. He seemed shrunken, as if his thick shoulders had collapsed under an incalculable weight. He stared at his half-finished glass.

Monna turned with the wine bottle in her hands and topped off Ben's glass. "C'mon, Ben, drink," she said quietly. "I never thought I'd have to urge this guy to drink," she said, grinning. Jamison smiled. She topped off Jamison's glass as well, although he'd barely touched it. She cocked an eyebrow at her husband. "This stuff's thirty-eight bucks a bottle. You two better start drinking or I'm taking it with me."

Ben wouldn't look at her.

Monna set the bottle on the counter and touched his cheek. "I'm sorry, Ben. I'm so sorry I said that."

"It's all right. You can say anything you want." He turned his glass slowly in his hands, as if he were examining a precious ornament. "You always did."

"You never liked that much, did you?" Surrendering.

"I always listened, Monna. Every time, I listened."

Monna set the bottle of wine on the counter. She gazed past their reflections in the living room window, as if she could see beyond them into the night to the sagebrush and the wheat stubble and rising still to the boundaries of the life she'd painted, the terrible beauty of the rocky escarpments far above. And she would rise into them. And the river would collect snow from the mountains and the following spring the river, too, would rise, and she had painted it all, down to a solitary blade of grass, the exquisite, living color of a single blade of grass, green to red and finally to a soft, faded tan the color of rest, the color or peace.

* * *

Monna heaped their plates with turkey and buttered green beans and mashed potatoes. Neither Ben nor Jamison were hungry and both men picked at their food. Monna offered wine and clucked when Jamison politely declined. Ben had begun to drink from his glass, a little. Monna set the bottle on the table and announced that she needed to ask a favor: she wanted to go to town over the weekend and see her friends—Jessica and Grant, the people at the general store who had always been so kind to her. There were others. Ben said he'd drive; he could still do that. If she wanted him along.

"Of course," Monna said. "Of course, you'll go with me." She reached under the table and squeezed his hand, and again, Ben rose from his seat and lurched to the bathroom. Jamison heard the fan flick on.

Monna sagged into her chair. She closed her eyes for a moment and then opened them. "This is just wrenching for him," she said. "It's worse for him than it is for me."

"He doesn't understand," Jamison said. The fan whirred, the sound muted and staccato, as if a moth were tapping at the window. "I don't either. Still."

Monna tucked her long hair behind her ear. She'd put on earrings, and the golden hoops glittered under the soft glow of the lamp suspended above the table. "I don't understand anything anymore," she said. "I just know it's time. I'd rather go while I can still move a little and walk a little and appreciate what I still have. I want to be remembered that way, the way I used to be, not what I'll become if …" She closed her eyes, then opened them and reached for her glass. "It's not like I have all these great options."

Monna rose from her chair and stepped to the kitchen counter and began forking sliced turkey into a Tupperware container, one palm flat on the countertop to steady herself.

Jamison stared at his hands. "I don't know what I'm supposed to do," he said. "I don't know how."

"You have to help him do this. He's not strong that way, not like everyone thinks. He needs somebody. When we were young …" She laughed a little under her breath. "Ben was very handsome. Men don't notice that like women do, they just don't. You never got married so you don't know what's it's like. He was handsome in a way that went beyond good looks. He had this vulnerability inside.

That's what I saw in him. That's not common knowledge about our Benjamin." She dabbed at her eyes, then smiled. "I don't know what that has to do with anything. It's just that he was so damn … *hot.*"

"*That* Benjamin?" Jamison jerked his thumb toward the bathroom. He was teasing now.

Monna picked up the serving fork and waved it in his face. "Don't make me come over there and slap the shit out of you, Jamison."

Jamison chuckled and held out his glass. Monna tried to top it off, but he stopped her before the glass was full.

"Remember when you called last March?" Jamison said. "You knew about this then, right? You knew."

Monna emphatically shook her head. "I *didn't.* I did *not.* I would have told you if I had. I never would have misled you about that. But of course I had a sense of where things were going. You can call it woman's intuition." She smiled impishly and took a long sip from her glass. "C'mon, Jamison. This bottle was thirty-eight bucks. The least you can do is drink with me."

Jamison reached for his glass.

Ben returned from the bathroom wiping his face with a towel. His eyes were ruined and his skin was damp from the cold water he'd splashed on his face and he hung the towel on the back of his chair and tried not to look at Jamison and sat down.

Monna watched her husband, leaning toward him even as she spoke to Jamison. She put her hand on Ben's arm but Ben didn't move, as if he had not noticed. "You brought a book, Jamison," she said. "What is it?"

"It's Kahlil Gibran, *The Prophet.* It's a famous book. Ever hear of it?" Jamison opened the book to a page he'd bookmarked and then closed it around his finger.

Ben had not. Monna had heard of *The Prophet* but had not read it.

"He was a Lebanese poet and philosopher who lived around the turn of the last century," Jamison said. "He was also an artist, a polymath like Michelangelo. There are a couple pages I was going to read, but I didn't know how well they'd go over. It's poetry, but it's the best poetry." He pulled the closed book into his lap. "He was a young man when he died."

Monna leaned forward. "I want to hear it," she said. "I want to hear a poem."

Jamison slipped his glasses over his nose and opened the book. "He wrote two pages on friendship," he said. He read silently to himself for a few seconds, then once again closed the book and removed his glasses.

"I was going to read them to you, but I can't. That's what I was going to do tonight, put on my little show, but now I just can't. It wouldn't be right to let someone else speak *for* me. I have to put things in my own words, or what kind of English teacher would I be? I have to run Gibran's words *through* me, the way I would say them, or it doesn't mean anything."

He touched his fingers to the book, reverently, in the way he might lay a hand on sacramental cloth.

"Gibran talks about the value of friendship. He says that in friendship expectations are shared and joys are unacclaimed." Jamison paused and touched his nose. "So to me that means that there's an inherent beauty in friendship, beauty in the sense of sharing unspoken communication. It's a communication you can feel but you can't hear or see or touch." He paused again, his voice barely audible. "And finally he speaks to grief: that when you lose a friend, the loss of that beauty is greater than the singular event of the loss."

Jamison laid his hand on the book and the parchment skin on his hand was softened by the lamplight. He pushed the book across the table to Ben. "I wanted to say, I wanted to tell both of you, that I don't know any longer if that's true. I don't want to lose this friendship."

Monna sat with her hands in her lap and then rose from the table and reached for the wine bottle and put it on the counter behind her. Ben sat as if struck, his eyes tightly closed, as if his voice and his breath had been drawn from his soul. But when Jamison's eyes met his sister's, he saw in them not sorrow, but something inarguably like serenity; not loss, but joy.

Chapter 22

Ben came to the studio early Tuesday evening. Jamison opened the door. It was dark, the night encroaching on the remaining sliver of pewter grey above the horizon. Jamison peered into the night but did not see Monna.

"I didn't bring nothing to drink," Ben said.

"I got us covered," Jamison said. Ben shrugged.

"I can pour us a couple glasses," Jamison said.

"I'm okay," Ben said. He stood in the doorway.

"Do you want to come in?"

"Well, I thought … it's a little chilly out, but I thought, if you wanted, we could go sit by the river some. Like this summer. It's not too bad out, you got some warm clothes you can put on. River's nice this time of day. Water's low and real quiet, it's like…" Ben shrugged again. "I don't know what. It's just nice."

"It's restful, maybe?" Jamison said.

"Yeah," Ben said.

Jamison put on his down coat and his fleece stocking cap and followed Ben to the river. Ben had set out two lawn chairs. At their feet the bank fell away to the water, obsidian under a thin moon. Behind them, inside the house, lights shone. Jamison heard a horse nicker from the pasture, as if to welcome them.

They sat without speaking and then Ben said tomorrow is the big day. He caught Jamison's eyes but in the dark Jamison could not see his face.

"Monna's inside?"

Ben nodded. "She says she's ready. She's waiting, is all."

Jamison put his hands between his knees. He hadn't brought his gloves, and his hands were cold. He pulled his hands back into the sleeves of his coat. He watched the river, then stared at the moon, which hung like a silver crescent over the ghostly palisades of the Crazy Mountains. The scant early snow that had fallen in the valley was gone. He had thought the snow on the high peaks would have melted away as well, but it hadn't. It was much colder up there, higher than he'd ever been, than it was down here.

"I should ask what you want me to do tomorrow," Jamison said. "I have a tie. I can put that on." A little joke.

"Monna wouldn't recognize you," Ben said. Jamison thought he heard Ben chuckle under his breath. "No, you can just wear the same ratty-ass stuff you always wear." Ben moved in his chair. "It's Monna's show."

Jamison's gaze rose again, but there was no comfort in the moon, no epiphany writ in the tableau of stars. They were as they had always been, forever. "What are you going to do, Ben?"

"I'll be damned if I know how to answer that."

"I mean …" Jamison clenched his hands into tight, white fists and then opened them again.

"I'm just along for the ride," Ben said. Jamison felt Ben's hand grip his arm. "It's gonna be okay. I got this."

Jamison felt Ben's hand slide into his hand. Ben squeezed Jamison's hand with rough, calloused fingers and the two men watched the river. Then Ben pulled his hand away and rose from his chair and walked into the house, into the light from within.

* * *

Jamison left his bed the following morning and dressed and went to the house. He had not slept.

He opened the front door and Monna and Ben rose from the kitchen table to greet him. She made an elaborate curtsy. "Guess who?" she said. She was wearing a white satin blouse with white pinstriping, and the same white hat and white skirt Jamison had first seen her wear at the dance that spring. A pair of embroidered stallions, facing off across the pearl snap buttons on her blouse, reared and pawed their hooves in a satiny white landscape. Ben had put on a matching embroidered shirt and white pants. Both wore the polished black cowboy boots they had worn to the dance.

"Roy and Dale," Jamison said quietly. He touched his hand to his eyes. "You're going in style."

"I wanted to dress up," Monna said. "So Ben said he would, too." She slipped her arm through Ben's and clutched his hand. Ben, as if he had suddenly lost the strength in his legs, sagged against her side.

"You want some coffee?" Monna said. "I can make us some."

"Coffee? No, I don't want any coffee."

"I have a Danish in the refrigerator. It's from this weekend. They had a special at the general store. Ben likes them."

Jamison shook his head. "I'm just not hungry, Monna. Ben can have the Danish."

Monna looked from one to the other and smiled. She, or Ben, had turned on all the lights in the house, eliminating the shadows. Monna stood in the warm, bright light beneath the lamp over the kitchen table, and the light brought color to her face, smoothing the fine wrinkles at the corner of her eyes, as though youth had reclaimed her in a final, hopeless gesture. She touched Ben's hand. "Well. Okay, then. I guess I'm ready whenever you guys are," she said.

"No!" Jamison said. He felt his eyes burning and knew he was crying. He rubbed his forearm roughly across his face. "I'm *not* ready. I'm *never* going to be ready. *I don't know what to do.*"

"Just go to town and wait," Ben said. "Jessica and Grant are opening up early. I'll call …" He took a breath, then spoke evenly, as if explaining the operation of a Bobcat, the levers that moved the gears that got the job done. "They know you're coming. I'll call."

Monna stepped forward to embrace Jamison. Then she pushed herself away, dabbing her eyes. "Oh jeez," she said, smiling through her tears. "I'm going to ruin my makeup." She took Ben's hand and

Jamison followed them to the front door. They stepped outside into the cold air and Jamison saw that the garage door was open. The MG had been backed inside, the polished chrome grill facing out, the engine idling. The back of the garage was already carpeted with exhaust, some of it spilling out from beneath the access door.

Ben took Jamison's hand and said thank you. *Thank you.*

Monna drew Ben close. "Can we dance?" she said. And she seemed a girl.

Ben held out his arms, and they spun down the sidewalk to the garage in time to their boots tapping on the concrete, Monna's silver hair flaring from beneath her hat, dancing to the cadence of memory. When they reached the garage Ben took Monna's hand and led her inside and put his arms around her waist and buried his face in her hair. Jamison stood in the driveway as the garage door howled and lurched closed. Then he turned and walked to Aden.

Chapter 23

Jamison walked with his hands thrust into the pockets of his down coat and his fleece hat pulled down over his ears. He'd left his scarf in the studio and the wind chilled his neck despite having pulled the zipper up as far as it would go. But the bitter wind that stung his face and eyes kept him from crying. He walked with his head into the wind.

The deer were where they usually were, clustered nervously in the ditch just before the last bend of the highway north of town, crowding the shoulder. Ben heard the truck accelerating from behind him at nearly the same time he spied the deer and watched them lift their heads in alarm and swivel their ears toward the sound. He was close enough to see the confusion in their eyes.

The truck was still a hundred yards away. Jamison stepped out onto the asphalt and waved his arms. The deer spun away from the shoulder and up the far side of the ditch and disappeared into the sagebrush. The truck slowed, then stopped, and a window rolled down. Jamison bent over to see the driver.

"You okay?" The driver said.

"Deer," Jamison said. He jerked his thumb over his shoulder. "I didn't know if you saw them or not. I didn't want you to hit one of them."

"Oh, okay. I didn't see them, but thanks." He waved and drove off. Jamison heard the truck accelerate and then slow on the outskirts of Aden.

In a few more minutes Jamison was inside the Infirmary.

Jessica and Grant were sitting at a table. Jessica met him at the door and threw her arms around him. Then, clutching his arm, she led him back to the table. Grant shook his hand, gripping his arm. "What do you want, Jamison? The bar's open. Anything you want, really."

"I don't know, Grant. I don't normally drink this early in the morning."

"Neither do we," Jessica said. "She pointed to a glass of Scotch on the table. There was one in front of Grant, as well. "But today isn't normal."

Jamison said *that* was the truth. But no, he was okay.

Jessica sat close to Grant, her arms folded across her chest, hugging herself. She had been crying, and her eyes were streaked and bloodshot. She hadn't put on makeup, and she seemed older and graying, as if grief had stolen the color from her cheeks. Grant was wearing a fleece vest, open at the collar. Even in the bar, it was chilly. Jamison took of his hat but kept his coat on.

"We called Gerald," Jessica said. She stared at her glass.

"We had to," Grant said. "He said he'll be here in an hour. You have to report things."

"What did he say?"

"He said we have to report stuff like that." He slid his glass slowly between his fingers, back and forth. "He said they would have to talk to Ben. There are laws, apparently."

"Okay," Jamison said. "I thought that might happen."

His eyes rose to the bar, then to the wide-screen TV above the mirrors and the racks of liquor bottles. The TV had been turned off.

"He told me to wait here until he called," Jamison said. "That's what Ben said."

Jessica had begun sobbing, and Grant tried to comfort her. But she would not be comforted.

"How was she?" Jessica asked. "Did she say anything?"

Jamison was at a loss for words. What good were words now? What could he say? He smiled.

"She asked me if I wanted a Danish," he said. "My sister." He reached across the table and touched Jessica's hand. "She was happy, I really believe that. She was ready. She and Ben danced."

Jamison wiped his eyes with a paper napkin. Then he walked to the window and braced his arms against the sill and gazed outside at the low, scudding clouds. The snow had begun, small, hard flakes drifting down, melting as they touched the pavement.

Jamison's phone rang at 10:45. He closed his eyes and on the third ring reached into his coat pocket for his phone and saw *Ben Van Hollen* on the screen. He hit "reply," but instead of Ben's gruff voice, he heard music.

For a moment he was confused. He put the phone on the table and a tinny melody wafted into the empty bar. Then he understood. "Do you know who that is?" he asked. "I know who that is."

Grant and Jessica waited.

"It's Lynyrd Skynyrd."

Jamison turned off his phone and put it back in his coat. He squeezed Jessica's hand and then his eyes were burning and Grant stood in the doorway behind him as the door closed, the snow flecking Jamison's thick glasses and melting on his nose and cheeks. He spied Gerald's patrol truck parked across the street and, when he approached, Gerald rolled down the window. They spoke. Gerald listened, his jaw working, a hand on the wheel. Then he unlocked the passenger door and Jamison got inside and Gerald pulled onto the highway and drove him home.

They parked a few yards back from the garage door. Jamison saw tendrils of exhaust curling up from under the door and when he stepped outside the smell of exhaust was faint but pungent, like the scent of burning tires. The acrid odor and his wrenching sorrow almost made him sick to his stomach and for a moment he thought he might retch, but he didn't and he straightened up and walked into the house to comfort Ben. Gerald had opened the access door on the garage and was searching for the button for the garage door opener, one hand inside the garage, the other holding a handkerchief over his mouth and nose.

Ben was not in the house. Jamison stared out the window at the shop, but there were no tracks leading to the shop door in the light skiff of snow covering the graveled walkway and no lights from within. In a growing panic, he strode through both bedrooms again. But Ben was not there.

He flung open the front door and ran outside. Gerald had opened the garage door and switched on the overhead lights, then strode to the MG and switched off the key. A low, billowing carpet of fumes surged into the bitter air. Jamison saw Ben and Monna sitting side by side in the little red car, their faces waxy and colorless under the harsh fluorescent lights, each turned toward the other, their hands twisted unnaturally in their laps from where they had fallen from a final embrace. Ben's cowboy hat was cocked at a rakish angle, as if snapped down with the tip of his finger, the hero in a cowboy movie.

Jamison rushed to the car but Gerald caught him in his strong arms and pushed him away, out of the garage, into the cold falling snow, into clean air.

"Jamison, you can't," he said. "They have to stay there for the investigators. For a few more hours."

"He was supposed to call me!" Jamison said. His voice broke. *"He was supposed to call!"*

"He couldn't," Gerald said. He held Jamison at arm's length, gently. "He wouldn't leave *her*."

Chapter 24

Less than an inch of snow fell, hard, tight flakes in that early and unseasonably bitter air, but soon the sun returned and the days grew warm again, and the snow retreated to the sparse shade under the tall brown grass bordering the driveway and to the shadows behind the house and studio, the places hidden from the light.

Jamison awoke and stared at the ceiling, his sleeping bag pulled to his chin. Then he tossed it aside and swung his legs into the morning chill and dressed in the clothes he'd flung over the chair in the corner.

He walked into the living room and stood with his hands on his hips and stared through the window at the woodpile, then at the river, which he could just see through the barren willows. The mountains wore a gleaming coat of new snow. He nudged open the door of the stove with his boot and placed a log on the glowing ashes and then heard Leviathan outside the front door.

Leviathan was waiting patiently on the porch, crouching and peering up at him. When he saw Jamison he stood and arched his back and happily butted his head against the corner post. Jamison said hold on pardner and walked to the kitchen and opened a can of cat food. But when he returned to the porch Leviathan was gone. Jamison looked to his right, from where he usually came, then to his left, toward the house, the pungent scent of salmon wafting up from the opened can he held in his hand. He spied Leviathan fifty yards away, at the corner of Ben and Monna's house, peering over his shoulder at him, nearly hidden in the grass. Then he turned the corner and vanished. Jamison set the can of food on the porch and went into the studio for his coat and boots. Then he walked to the house, his hands in the pockets and his head up, searching.

He rounded the corner where he'd last seen Leviathan, hoping the cat would be waiting for him. But Leviathan was not there. He took a few more steps and looked around. The paint on the south side of the house was flaked and peeling, exposing the raw Masonite siding beneath it. The siding was broken by an ancient double hung window that Jamison knew opened into Ben and Monna's bedroom. The tree-shaded south side of their home, an airy, leafy redoubt protecting their bedroom, had seemed sacrosanct to Jamison, and he'd been here only once before, when Ben had proudly shown him the wren houses he'd built and hung from the aspens opposite the window. Jamison turned toward the trees and there they were, three small dovetailed wren houses suspended with baling wire, their bare, untreated sides graying and weathered, but the gay scenes Monna had painted still proud and bright even from a dozen feet away. One house, the only one Ben had hung at head height, had something white protruding from the entry. He stepped forward for a closer look. It was a sheet of expensive drawing paper, tightly rolled and pushed inside, where all but one exposed edge would be hidden and protected from the weather. Jamison pulled it out and held it open and stared at the opening salutation: *Dear Jamison …*

He walked back to the studio, clutching the letter in his hand. Leviathan had returned to the porch and was crouched before his cat food, growling as he thrust his head into the can. He didn't look up when Jamison opened the door and stepped inside. Jamison threw his coat on the sofa and then sat at the kitchen table and opened the letter.

Dear Jamison,

I figured you would find this sooner or later. Monna said to give it to you but I said you be snooping around the house sooner or later, knowing you. Haha!

I am very sorry about the way things turned out. You probably think I planned it this way but I didn't. Monna said to stay and help you but I said you could take care of yourself because you already have for 73 years. I already lived long enough.

Everything is yours. We never had kids. I taught you enough about carpentering this summer you can take care of the place. You know where my tools are. There is some stuff in the kitchen cabinet you might want. Monna said to tell you she is going to take the sheets off the bed and put them in the washer, so they're clean. That is the way she is. She said goodbye.

We were good friends, weren't we. You are my best friend.

Love,
Ben and Monna.

At the bottom of the letter, drawn in coarse, hesitant lines, was a pencil sketch of a wren, a grasshopper clutched in its beak.

* * *

Jamison spent that night in the studio, and the next. Then he began moving the few possessions he'd brought from Minneapolis into the house. He would have time the following spring, when the weather was better and the drive across North Dakota less perilous, to return to Minneapolis and retrieve his books and the few remaining things he owned.

He'd never been in Ben and Monna's bedroom. It was small, like all the rooms in the Van Hollen home, although not as cramped as his bedroom in the studio. Besides the wooden sleigh bed Monna had loved, there was the chest of drawers Ben had also built, and an exquisitely crafted Windsor chair in the corner. Hung on the wall above the dresser was one of Monna's paintings. Jamison recognized her brush strokes immediately. Ben put on his glasses and stepped closer.

But it was not a landscape. It was a watercolor portrait of a much younger Ben, his thick hair long and raven black and brushing the tops of his shoulders. He had one foot propped on a stump and a heavy splitting maul resting across his shoulders, the sleeves of his dirt-caked Henley loosely rolled up his muscular forearms, his elbows draped over either side of the maul. Nearly hidden in the background, watching him with her arms crossed, was Monna. Monna had signed and dated it: October 6, 1980. They would have been married less than a year. Ben was grinning.

Jamison looked at the painting. Then he took off his glasses and slowly cleaned them on his shirt and walked into the bathroom and put the damp bed sheets from the clothes washer into the dryer.

* * *

He had driven the MG out of the garage and now it sat idling in the sun, airing out the remaining scent of exhaust. He slid into the driver's seat and tried to push the seat back as far as it would go but his legs were still uncomfortably bent, his knees almost touching the steering wheel. Well. It would be a short trip. Ten minutes later he was parked outside the Infirmary.

He'd brought a small manilla envelope and a handkerchief he'd found in the bedroom dresser and after he shut off the engine he wrapped the keys in the handkerchief and put them in the envelope. He licked the flap and stuck it closed, then felt the bulge of the handkerchief inside. It softened the outline of the keys just enough. He walked into the bar.

Jessica saw him and grinned and began pouring him a beer.

"Where's Grant?" he said.

"It's his day off. You get days off when you own the place." Jessica rolled her eyes. A man and two middle-aged women sat at the end of the bar, and Jamison caught one of the women staring at him. She smiled self-consciously, then, embarrassed, turned back to her friends. Jamison and Jessica talked, and then Jessica touched his hand.

"I miss them," she said.

"I do too."

"Shit, I'm going to start crying again." Jessica squeezed her eyes shut and fiercely clenched her fists. When she opened them she said, "Okay, I'm better. A little."

Jamison rested his hand on the envelope.

"What's that?" Jessica said. "You win the lottery?"

"Nope. Actually, it's for you. A little something of Monna's I thought she'd want you to have. I sure don't have any use for it."

"What is it?"

"It's a surprise. Nice try, though."

Jessica reached for the envelope but Jamison snatched it away. "Not so fast. You have to wait until I finish my beer."

They spoke of the weather. Grant had taken the day off to fish; there wouldn't be many more days this warm before winter hit. Jamison finished his beer and pushed the envelope across the bar and told Jessica goodbye and walked home. He was nearly at his driveway when his phone rang. He looked at the screen, smiled, and put it back in his pocket.

* * *

Jamison pulled a chair away from the kitchen table in Ben and Monna's kitchen and spun it around facing the front door, which he'd thrown open to the sun, to the last sweet warmth of autumn. Leviathan crouched on the threshold, his pale green eyes intently watching Jamison. Jamison had placed an open can of cat food at the foot of the chair.

"Kitty, kitty," he said.

Leviathan lifted one paw, carefully extended it inside the house, then yanked it back, shaking it as if it had been dipped in scalding water. He raised his head and yowled.

"My, my," Jamison said. "Such a big voice from a such big kitty. But you know where the cat food is, buddy."

Leviathan yowled again. Jamison nudged the can with his toe.

"There's more where this came from," he said. In the cabinets above the kitchen sink, in a green plastic grocery bag from the Aden General Store, Jamison had found two dozen cans of Delicious Salmon In Creamy Alfredo Sauce. Jamison had counted them out and then stacked them one by one on the counter, his vision blurring without the glasses he suddenly couldn't find, tears running unashamedly down his cheeks.

Now he waited. He gazed at the big cat, who rocked anxiously from side to side, desperately wanting the food that was nearly within his reach, but terrified by the brief foray into uncharted territory, by the commitment he did not understand he was being asked to make.

Jamison waited. He said, "Do you know how Bobcats work? Not the feline kind, the earth-moving kind. Machines."

Leviathan did not appear to know.

"So it's like this: if you let off on the levers, it stops. When you take the pressure off, everything swings back into balance, and you get a chance to catch your breath. Then you can try again."

Jamison nudged the cat food with his toe once more, and Leviathan rose, leaned in agonizing desire over the threshold, and then slowly sank back into a crouch. He stared at Jamison, his piercing gaze flitting from Jamison's face to the cat food at his feet. But still he would not move. Not yet.

Jamison laced his long fingers together and placed them in his lap. And waited.

Acknowledgements

Although writing a novel is a solitary, challenging, and for me an immensely enjoyable undertaking, writing is only the half of it. The second half is finding a publisher who will shepherd it through publication.

In that, I got lucky. After uncounted rejections from publishers and agents, nearly all of whom wouldn't even look at my manuscript, much less read it, Guernica Editions editor Michael Mirolla not only looked at it my first book, *Leaves On Frozen Ground*, he liked what he saw and agreed to publish it. It was virtually the same story for my second book, *Red Is The Fastest Color.* To Mirolla and his very capable staff I owe a sincere debt of gratitude.

I would also like to thank in particular my editor Margo LaPierre, a woman wise in the ways of literature far beyond her tender years. Her insight, superb editing, and encouragement have been, without exaggeration, indispensable.